HOMECOMING

Visit us at www.boldstrokesbooks.com

Books for Today from Bold Strokes Books

Such a Pretty Face by Gabrielle Goldsby

"...Goldsby, skillfully mixing sharp humor and incisive insight, sorts out...emotional issues with solid plotting—and plenty of hot sex on the side." – *Q Syndicate*

Not Single Enough by Grace Lennox

"In *Not Single Enough*, Grace Lennox has once again given readers an enormously engaging modern romance that takes many twists and turns before its satisfying conclusion. Her characters are complex and real. They are also extremely likeable, quirky, funny, and they keep the reader turning pages to see how they will solve their problems." – *JustAboutWrite*

Learning Curve by Rachel Spangler

"Spangler has given her readers two intriguing characters whose lives are the antithesis of each other's. ...The ... title, Learning Curve, refers to the growth both of these women make, as they deal with attraction and avoidance. They share a mutual lust, but can lust alone surpass their differences? The answer to that question is told with humor, adventure, and heat." –*JustAboutWrite*

Running with the Wind by Nell Stark

"A fun read with engaging characters..." – *Books to Watch Out For*

"*Running with the Wind* is a wonderful debut novel ... Stark's characters are richly drawn and interesting. ...the discussions of the nature of sex, love, power, and sexuality are insightful and represent a welcome voice from the view of late-20-something characters today." – *Midwest Book Review*

By the Author

Running With the Wind

Homecoming

HOMECOMING

by
Nell Stark

2008

HOMECOMING

ISBN 10: 1-60282-024-4
ISBN 13: 978-1-60282-024-1

This Trade Paperback Original Is Published By
Bold Strokes Books, Inc.
New York, USA

First Edition: August 2008

CREDITS
EDITORS: CINDY CRESAP AND STACIA SEAMAN
PRODUCTION DESIGN: STACIA SEAMAN
COVER DESIGN BY SHERI (GRAPHICARTIST2020@HOTMAIL.COM)

Acknowledgments

E.L. Doctorow once famously said that "[w]riting is like driving a car at night. You never see further than your headlights, but you can make the whole trip that way." To extend his metaphor—I may have been this particular car's driver, but without the support and encouragement of many "passengers," I would never have made it to the end of my journey. In particular, Lisa's comforting presence in the "front seat" has helped me to stay the course.

I am indebted to Radclyffe for the seed of this story, for the opportunity to publish it, and for her shining professional example. Jennifer Knight's past advice about matters of both style and content were indispensable as I began this project. Cindy Cresap was instrumental in helping me to transition from a rough draft to a honed and polished final product, and Stacia Seaman's careful fine-tuning of the manuscript is very much appreciated. I owe my beta readers— Lisa, Jane, and Ruta—a debt of thanks for being willing to serve as both sounding boards and cheerleaders throughout my process. And last but certainly not least, I am grateful for my family of choice, whose unconditional love and pride in my accomplishments are the greatest gifts I have ever received.

Dedication

For Lisa—my anchor in the storms.

For Jane—my gift is my song.

And for all of the men and women who have contributed to the efforts of Fair Wisconsin and other likeminded organizations—your courage, persistence, and hard work are inspirational.

Chapter One

Late July

S arah Storm drove around the block twice before parking a few yards away from Corrie's driveway. The windows of the ocean-side bungalow winked cheerfully at her as they reflected the light of the setting sun. Next to the mailbox, a yard sign encouraged passersby to "Vote No" on the upcoming referendum to define marriage in Rhode Island as between one man and one woman.

She wanted to find the sight comforting, but pride refused to let her. Had it been a mistake to come here? Corrie Marsten had been her sailing instructor for a few weeks during the summer, two years ago. *And then there was the time in the bathroom when I...* Sarah shook her head in an effort to dispel that particular memory. The point was, she and Corrie were barely even acquaintances. And yet here she was on Corrie's doorstep, begging for shelter like a stray cat. *She's the only person older than me who's also a lesbian that I know. She's all I've got.*

"Dammit," she muttered when she was still clutching the steering wheel five minutes later. "Just do this. Get it over with." For about the billionth time that day, Sarah wished that she could hear Dar's voice. Of course, she was probably busy having dinner right now with her family—all four of them sitting around the table, eating their mashed potatoes and making small talk like the Cleavers.

Sarah slammed the car door harder than she needed to and winced. *It's not her fault. You're the one who was stupid enough to get caught.* She marched up the path to Corrie's porch and rang the doorbell without any more hesitation. Feet planted widely on the welcome mat, she threw back her shoulders and waited.

When the door opened, a large gray dog immediately lunged forward to push its nose against Sarah's hip, its whiplike tail wagging furiously.

"Frog!" Corrie said, reaching for the dog's collar to drag him back. "Jeez. Take a chill pill." She smiled apologetically. "Hey, Storm. Sorry about that."

"Oh, it's all right," Sarah said, smiling at Frog's antics. "He's fine." It felt good to have someone be unequivocally excited to see her—even if that someone was a dog.

"Come on in."

Sarah followed Corrie down the short hallway, suppressing a sigh of relief. Corrie was still ridiculously attractive, of course—tall and blond, lithe and tan. In fact, she looked much the same as she had on that fateful night at the yacht club when she had seduced Sarah out of the closet. But Sarah no longer felt the same sense of compulsion as she had then, and she was glad.

"Have a seat," Corrie said as they emerged into a small living room. "Want something to drink?"

"A glass of water would be great. Thanks."

But before Corrie could make a move toward the kitchen, a woman stepped through the sliding door leading out to the deck. She was a few inches shorter than Corrie, with shoulder-length brown hair and a gentle smile. *She has a good face.*

"You must be Sarah. I'm Quinn."

"My girlfriend," Corrie said. The note of pride in her voice was unmistakable. Sarah couldn't help but think of Dar, and felt her stomach flip-flop. How nice would it be to share a house with her? All by themselves, where no one could interfere.

"Nice to meet you," she said, shaking hands. "Thanks for putting me up for the night."

"You're welcome to stay as long as you'd like," Quinn said.

For one awful second, Sarah thought she might cry. Instead, she managed to blink, swallow, and attempt a smile. Fortunately,

Corrie held out a glass of water to her in that moment, and she took a long sip.

"So," Corrie said as she sat down on the love seat, Quinn beside her, and looked at Sarah. "We'll have plenty of time for pleasantries over dinner. Why don't you tell us what happened, Storm?"

Sarah nodded, putting the glass down and resting her hands on her knees. Unconsciously, she hunched her shoulders.

"It all started yesterday morning, I guess, while I was out for a jog and my mom came into my room to drop off some laundry. I had left a chat window open on my computer—I'd been talking to my girlfriend, Darla, the night before." Sarah flushed and reached for the glass. "It was pretty…um, obvious from the chat that Dar and I are together. Mom waited until Dad got home and I guess they talked things over. I was out to dinner with friends, but when I got home, all hell broke loose."

She sat back against the soft fabric of the couch and took several long gulps from the glass. The memory of what had come next made her hands tremble.

"Just take your time," Quinn said softly.

Sarah tried to smile at her, but she wasn't sure her face muscles were working properly. "They sat me down at the kitchen table, and I think I sort of knew right away, you know? That they had found out. Mom was furious. She didn't even ask any questions, just started in on the accusations. And then the threats…"

"We've already called a counselor. You have an appointment for tomorrow morning."

"A counselor?" Sarah could feel her heart pounding against her rib cage, as though it were trying to escape. Just like she wanted to, from this moment, this room, this house in which she'd grown up. "But there's nothing wrong with me!"

"And you will not be returning to Yale this fall. Your father and I will not be paying for you to learn how to disgrace us."

"Disgrace you?" Sarah felt the fear temporarily melt away as a white-hot tide of anger rose inside her. "How exactly am I disgracing you?"

"You are shaming this family!"

"So that's what this is all about? You're worrying about what other people will think of the fact that I'm a lesbian?" It felt so good to finally say the word out loud—to finally come out, metaphorical guns blazing. *"This is the twenty-first century, Mom! Lesbians are everywhere."*

Her mother stood up so quickly that her chair fell backward, clattering against the kitchen tile. "Not in my house, they're not."

When Sarah paused to drain the rest of her glass, Corrie got up abruptly and headed for the kitchen. She returned a moment later with an open beer, which she put down on the table. Sarah wanted to crack a joke about serving to minors, but she was too tired to make the effort.

"I couldn't stay there," she said quietly. "I couldn't make myself. So late last night, I packed up a bunch of clothes and stuff, and just…drove away." She rolled the beer bottle between her palms and watched the golden liquid foam up into the neck. "Got on the highway and just drove for a few exits, until I felt…safer. And then I pulled over into a rest stop and called Dar."

"Hey, sweetheart. Been missing you—what's up?"

Sarah closed her eyes and took a deep breath, willing herself to keep it together. Dar's voice sounded so damn good. A lifeline. She remembered how incredible it felt to hold Dar as they fell asleep in her narrow dorm bed—how right it felt to kiss her, touch her, be inside her. Sarah's breath stuttered in her throat. They said they wouldn't let me go back to Yale. Back to her. God, what am I going to do?

"Sarah? Are you there?"

"Hey. Hi. Sorry." *Sarah suddenly felt an overwhelming urge to remind Dar of just how essential she was—how central their relationship was to her life.* "Do you…do you know how much I need you? How much I love you?"

"Of course I do," Dar said. "You tell me every day. And I love you, too."

Sarah swallowed hard and squeezed her eyes shut to rein in the tears. *"That's good. That's really good."*

"Are you okay?"

"No. Not exactly." She paused. *"Dar...something's happened."*

"What?" Darla's voice was suddenly edgy, apprehensive.

"They found out. My parents. About us."

"What? How?"

Sarah cringed as the memory replayed in her head. *"I left a chat window open by mistake on my computer, and my mom saw it when she came into my room."*

"Oh my God, do they know who I am?"

Sarah blinked at the unexpected question. *"Um, I don't think so."*

The line was silent for a moment. Sarah shifted uncomfortably in the seat, unconsciously drumming her fingers against the steering wheel. Dar sounded upset. *I've let her down.* Her heart thumped painfully and she pressed her free hand to the aching spot between her breasts.

"I asked you to be careful," Dar said. Her tone was distinctly accusatory. *"To protect us. And you—"*

"I know," Sarah interrupted. Her voice shook. *"I know. I'm sorry. I'm so sorry for being such an idiot. But they said they wouldn't let me go back to school and they're going to send me to a counselor and I couldn't stay there, I just couldn't."*

"Where are you?"

Sarah sniffled and realized she was crying. She scrubbed at her eyes angrily. *"At a rest stop off the highway."*

Darla didn't reply right away. When the silence grew, Sarah realized that she was going to have to ask. The epiphany made her stomach hurt.

"Can I...could I stay the night at your place? I don't have anywhere else I can go."

"No!" Darla sighed noisily. *"You know I wish you could, but... you're an open book, honey. My family would know about us just from looking at you."*

"What am I going to do?" Sarah whispered, unaware that she'd asked the question aloud. Disappointment knifed through her, sharp and bitter. What am I going to do? Where am I going to stay? In that instant, she realized what she had been hoping—that Dar would take this chance to come out to her own family. That she would stand up next to Sarah, proud and defiant, and together they would—

"Check into a motel for the night," Dar said. "Oh shit, hang on a sec."

Sarah heard distant voices through the phone—probably Dar's parents. She rubbed at her grainy eyes. It was hard to think. Her head felt fuzzy. What am I going to do now?

"I'm sorry," Dar said finally. "But I have to go. Family stuff. Call me tomorrow, okay? Promise?"

"Sure, okay." Sarah stared numbly out the windshield at the passing headlights—everyone traveling to or from somewhere. Except her. "Love you. G'night."

"I ended up just sleeping in my car," she told Corrie and Quinn. "It's big, fortunately—a big boat. It was my grandmother's. The back seat's pretty comfy." When she realized that she was babbling, she drank from her beer.

"I'm so glad you came here," Quinn said.

Sarah looked up and couldn't help but smile at the kind expression on Quinn's face. Corrie, she noticed, was pacing the length of the room like some kind of caged animal.

"I can't thank you both enough."

Quinn brushed the sentiment aside with a wave of her hand. "Have your parents called?"

"Yeah." Sarah took a longer sip and shifted her gaze back to the coffee table. "Dad called my cell in the morning. He asked where I was, and I wouldn't tell him. Then he said that if I didn't come home today, they were going to…to cut me off. Disown me."

"What?" Corrie exclaimed.

Sarah shrugged. "I told them I didn't care what they did. If they don't want me the way I am, then I'm not going back." She wanted her voice to stay steady, but it cracked a little on the last word, and she cleared her throat. "At that point, I drove around until I found a coffeehouse with 'Net access, and looked up your number."

"This is bullshit," Corrie muttered, her voice low and agitated. "Total fucking ridiculous *bullshit*. I'll call my parents right away and have them talk to yours. What the hell are they thinking?"

"No," Sarah said quickly. "Please don't do that. That's not what I want."

Corrie stopped in her tracks and frowned. "But why not? They need to see reason. My family has lived with my sexual orientation since I was in college. They're pros. And your parents will listen to mine. Sponsors at that damn club have clout."

Sarah rubbed her face with her hands and looked up at Corrie. "Look. I appreciate it—more than I can say. But they're kicking me out. They made that choice. I'm not going to beg. If they don't want me, fine. I don't need them. I don't." *Do I?*

"Why don't we examine your options, here?" Quinn said. "I'll even make a to-do list, okay? So we're organized."

She hopped up to get a pad of paper and a pen, and Corrie looked after her fondly. "Believe it or not," she told Sarah, "I've really come to appreciate to-do lists over the past year."

Sarah laughed. It felt good that she could still laugh, even in the middle of all this. At the beginning of it, even. Had it really only been twenty-four hours since the confrontation? It felt like a lifetime.

"The first thing I should do, I guess," she said, "is to call Yale and see whether there's any—anything. Any money they can give me, any advice. Any way that I can stay there." Her voice trembled a little at that last bit, but she kept her gaze firmly focused on the coffee table.

"Good idea," Quinn said. "Talk to a dean, definitely. More than one."

"I don't know what comes next, though." Even to her own ears, Sarah's voice sounded forlorn. "Everything else depends on that, really. On whether I can manage to stay."

Quinn nodded. "But even so, we may as well write a few things down. Like applying for loans. And finding a job, right?"

"And scholarships, too," Corrie put in. "There are tons of scholarships out there from large and small organizations. Every little bit will help."

Sarah nodded and took another long drink. The to-do list already felt overwhelming, and she was deathly afraid that she'd burst into tears at any moment. She could feel them burning behind her eyes and clogging her throat. *One step at a time. Just one at a time. And take deep breaths.*

"You should stay here with us for the time being," Quinn said. "Until you decide what to do next."

"Oh no, no," Sarah protested. "I really couldn't. You're—"

"For fuck's sake, Storm!" Corrie cut her off. "Stay. We have a guest room. It's no trouble."

Quinn rolled her eyes. "I think she's trying to tell you that we'd really like to help."

At that moment, a black cat trotted briskly into the room, paused to inspect Frog's tail, sneezed, and proceeded to jump into Sarah's lap. The feline meowed once before curling up on her thighs and beginning to purr.

"Why, hello there," Sarah said, trailing one finger along the line of white that ran from the cat's left ear, down past her neck. "You're a friendly one."

"See?" said Corrie. "Rogue clearly wants you to stick around. No more objections, 'kay?"

Rogue squinted up at her happily when Sarah scratched under her chin. "Okay," she said. A sudden sense of peace washed over her—unexpected and so very welcome. "All right. Thank you."

❖

Sarah looked down at the silver cell phone lying in her palm, its cover scratched and battered from being accidentally dropped, kicked, and occasionally even drop-kicked. It had survived all that abuse for years. Now, it was suddenly useless—canceled by her parents. They had worked fast. When she'd tried to call Yale at precisely nine o'clock in the morning, she'd heard instead a mechanical voice informing her that her phone was no longer in service. *Disconnected.*

Corrie had sworn like the sailor she was before handing Sarah the portable, and she'd refused to hear a word about being paid back for the long-distance call. After over an hour of conversation, all Sarah was certain about was that she wasn't going back to Yale next year. They'd been very kind, of course. The two deans with whom she'd spoken had talked to her in soft, compassionate, patient tones. They'd expressed their regret and their desire to help...and they had all given her the same advice. *Take a year off. Work. Apply for loans and scholarships. Write a letter to the financial aid office. Get your feet back under you. And then come back.*

"You'll still have a place here," one had said. "But there's nothing that financial aid can do on such short notice, with less than a month until the semester begins."

She pressed down with her right foot to open Corrie's trash can and turned her hand over, letting her useless cell slide off her palm and into the garbage.

"What's the word?" Corrie asked from behind her. Sarah turned toward the voice and smiled faintly at the sight of her benefactress, poking her head through her own kitchen window as though she weren't sure she was welcome inside her own house.

"Not so good," she managed.

"Hang on." Corrie let herself in through the sliding door and sat down on the love seat. Sarah took her by-now customary place on the couch. "Tell me."

"There's not much to tell. Nothing they can do for me financially. I should take a year off, they said." She looked over at Corrie and shook her head vehemently. "But that just feels so...so *wrong* to me. What if I take a year off and never manage to go back? And what am I going to do for a year anyway, without a degree?"

Corrie frowned. "Well...what if you keep taking classes

somewhere else, just to stay in the game? You'd only have to pay in-state tuition here at URI. And at least some of the credits will transfer, I bet, though you'd have to check."

"In-state tuition." Sarah leaned forward, suddenly hopeful despite her best judgment. "How much would that be, do you think?"

Corrie grabbed her laptop from the kitchen counter. "Dunno the exact number, but let's find out."

A few minutes later, Sarah was regarding the computer screen dubiously. "I know it's much, much less, but...it's still a lot." She turned to Corrie. "Besides, look—the transfer application had to be turned in months ago."

"Fuck that." Corrie got to her feet and started pacing again. "I can't guarantee anything, but this is *my* university, and I know people. If you want to do this, I'll see what I can manage about getting your app considered."

Sarah looked up at her in awe. It was suddenly hard to swallow. "Corrie. Why are you doing all of this for me?"

Instead of meeting her gaze, Corrie turned toward her deck and the view of the ocean beyond. "No matter what, I'd want to lend you a hand. But, Storm..." She turned back just enough for Sarah to be able to see her profile. "I can't help but feel responsible."

Sarah blinked, struggling to keep her jaw from dropping. She never would have expected Corrie to invoke the memory of their one, brief encounter. "It would have happened without you, though," she said. "I am...I am what I am."

"You're family, is what you are," Corrie said firmly. "Let me do what I can."

Sarah leaned back into the couch cushions and closed her burning eyes. Tears were threatening in earnest now, and she didn't want to break down in front of Corrie. *Tired. So damn tired.* She rested one hand on the slight swell of her stomach, wishing that it would settle down. *Am I going to feel this way forever?*

"Okay," she whispered, battling the tightness in her throat. "If you really don't mind. Thank you."

CHAPTER TWO

Three weeks later

Sarah walked briskly out into the late afternoon sunlight, pausing to wave a quick good-bye to one of her coworkers at the Billington Cove Yacht Club. While waitressing at the marina's clubhouse wasn't her dream job by far, it was steady work and the tips were good. *I'll need to find another job soon, though,* she reminded herself. As the sailing season drew to a close, the club would drastically cut back on their staff. If she didn't manage to land something else, she'd be unemployed by mid-October. Between tuition and housing payments, that just wasn't an option.

Sarah shoved her hands into the pockets of her cargo shorts and started down the sidewalk, heading back toward the bungalow. *I'm not going to worry about it. Not today, anyway.* When the ocean breeze ruffled her hair, she inhaled deeply and smiled.

Today was a good day. How could it not be? Dar was coming down for a visit, and with Corrie and Quinn out of town for the weekend, they'd have the house to themselves. It would be their first time together in several months. God only knew when they'd be able to see each other again afterward. School was starting for them both next week. Sarah hunched her shoulders at the pang in her chest that always accompanied the thought of not returning to Yale. She was still in awe—and so very grateful—that Corrie had managed to find her a spot at URI for the fall. And it wasn't as though the Kingston campus was far from New Haven—a two-hour drive at most. Sure, she wouldn't be able to crash in Dar's room whenever she wanted, but it wouldn't be difficult to visit. *We'll make it work, somehow. We have to.*

She looked down at her watch and quickened her pace. Dar was probably on the road already, and Sarah wanted the chance to clean up around the house and take a shower before she arrived. Everything needed to be perfect.

What would it be like, seeing her again? It had been almost three months since they had last seen each other, but Sarah's palms could still remember how it felt to cup Dar's face in her hands, and her lips still burned whenever she recalled their hungry kisses. This visit was long overdue. It didn't feel right to be away from Dar—to not be able to show her, every day, just how deeply she cared. Last year at school, Sarah had been able to indulge that need as often as she wanted. Snacks when Dar was studying, roses on her pillow, love notes tucked into her textbooks…it had been so easy to prove her devotion.

All summer, Sarah had been eagerly anticipating the day when life would return to normal—when she could do so much more than send text messages and virtual flower bouquets and love songs via iTunes. Now, what she had once considered "normal" was a pipe dream. The distance would remain. Somehow, she had to deal.

Oh, quit whining, she told herself firmly. *You're going to see her* today. *No brooding!*

Sarah smiled as she remembered the intensity of their last reunion, after winter break. They had only been apart for a month that time, but it had felt like forever. She had stopped in her room just long enough to throw her bags onto the bed before sprinting across campus to Dar's dormitory. Dar had opened the door as soon as she'd knocked, and they had stood still for a moment, just looking at each other. Sarah remembered feeling an all-consuming thirst for her—a desperate need to burn Dar's image into her brain before she had finally closed the gap between them and kissed her with all the passion that had been pent up inside her throughout those long, hungry weeks.

Dar had felt a little shaky after that kiss, she remembered. So Sarah had told her to sit down on the bed, and when she had…

Sarah pulled off Dar's shirt before dropping to her knees and wrapping her arms around Dar's waist. She sighed deeply as she pillowed her head on Dar's smooth, firm stomach.

"Missed you so much. So damn much." She pulled back just far enough to press light, sucking kisses along the arch of Dar's rib cage, slowly moving up toward her breasts. When she circled one nipple with her tongue, Dar murmured her approval. Sarah wanted to devour her, consume her, but she held herself in check and swirled her tongue gently, the way Dar liked her to.

When the need to taste Dar overwhelmed the urge to tease her, Sarah unzipped Dar's jeans and pulled them down her toned legs. She paused briefly to push her tongue in and out of Dar's navel, before moving down toward the triangle of blond hair between her legs. Dar's stomach muscles quivered as she leaned back on her elbows. When Sarah urged Dar's legs over her shoulders and gently parted Dar's lips with both thumbs, she was rewarded with a low moan.

"I love you," Sarah whispered as she dipped her head to tease Dar's opening. She savored the musky taste on her tongue—so familiar, so beloved. And then she licked slowly up, up and around Dar's clit, loving the way Dar's thighs trembled beneath her hands.

"So good," Dar whispered.

Her fingers tangled in Sarah's hair, sliding across her scalp. Sarah wanted to draw out their lovemaking—to bring Dar up so high and then keep her there forever—but it had been far too long. Her need to feel and hear Dar come eclipsed everything else, and she groaned softly against Dar's wet, swollen skin as she gently sucked Dar's clit into her mouth.

"Ohmygod, Sarah."

Sarah fluttered her tongue, and soon Dar was gasping incoherently. She was close. Sarah lost herself in her lover's passion, willing her lips to communicate the magnitude of her desire. Dar cried out as her entire body tensed...and then she was coming, and Sarah clung to her bucking hips, drinking her in.

The gritty guitar chords of Bon Jovi's "It's My Life" shattered Sarah's daydream. Pulse racing from the memory, she dug her new cell phone—a prepaid model that she had to "top up" every month—out of her pocket. *Dar.*

"Hey, sweetheart," she said, smiling broadly. "Where are you? How's the drive going? God, I can't wait to see you."

"Hi," Dar said. "About that...I'm still at home."

What? No! Sarah stopped in her tracks, heart pounding furiously. "What's wrong? Did something happen? Are you okay? Did your family—"

"I'm fine. No worries. I just...I got off work late, and it'll take a while to get down there, and I'm pretty tired right now."

Sarah felt a surge of relief so sharp that it made her dizzy. *At least she's okay.* But then the import of Dar's words registered, and anxiety returned. "So...what do you want to do?"

Dar was silent for so long that Sarah took the phone away from her ear to make sure that the call was still live. It was.

"Maybe this isn't the best weekend for me to visit," she said.

"What?" Sarah exclaimed before she could help herself. "But—but this is the perfect chance for us. We can be together, without any distractions." *Please!*

"Look, Sarah, I just—"

"What if I meet you halfway between here and there?" Sarah interrupted, her brain racing. "So you don't have to drive as far? We could stay in a hotel tonight." She forced out a laugh. "Nothing four-star, obviously, but I can afford one night in a Motel Six." *I need this. I need this so bad. Please.*

Another long pause. "I don't really know what to say," Dar said finally.

Sarah frowned in confusion. *Huh?* She decided to try out another laugh. "Well, you should say yes, obviously."

"I can't do this long-distance thing," Dar blurted.

The world shifted, sliding sideways as Sarah's throat closed and her head spun and her heart thumped furiously. She tried to inhale, but couldn't seem to take a deep breath. Her entire body felt as though it were shutting down. *Oh no. No, no, no. No.*

"What do you mean?" she whispered.

"Come on, Sarah. You're there. I'm here. We each have our own lives now."

"But I'm not even that far away." Sarah's voice sounded tinny to her own ears. *Say something, anything, anything to make her change her mind!* "I...I could see you every weekend. I'll drive up. You don't ever have to—"

"I don't want to do this anymore."

A rush of anger knifed through Sarah's shock. The claustrophobia of her panic disappeared in its wake. "You don't want to do this? Or you don't want me?"

"Both, I guess. I don't know." Dar exhaled heavily. "Look... I'm sorry about the timing, here. I know things are rough for you. But I think it's better that we end this right now, before it gets messier."

Sarah couldn't believe what she was hearing. She felt as though she had suddenly crossed over into a deranged parallel universe. How could Dar be acting this way? How could she be this callous? After almost a year together, how could she just decide one day that she'd had enough?

"*We* are not ending this. *You* are." *Maybe she was never in love with you*, she realized. *Maybe you were projecting your own feelings onto her.*

The anger coalesced in her gut. Had Dar really been pretending all this time? Tolerating Sarah as she waxed eloquent about the depth of her emotion, as she repeatedly brought Dar gifts like some kind of lovesick puppy? Barely putting up with her intensity instead of embracing it? *I was a fool. Such a fool.*

"But how can you possibly think this will work?" Dar's voice was shrill. "We live in totally different worlds now."

Sarah clenched her teeth against another white-hot burst of rage. "What? This is about me not coming back to Yale? About going to URI instead? Are you *kidding* me?"

"Sarah," Dar said. Her tone was condescending now—slow and soft and syrupy sweet. "I just don't think—"

"You've made it perfectly clear what you think." Cold. She felt cold, suddenly. How had this happened so fast? *How did I misjudge her so badly?*

"I'm sorry."

"No, you're not." The epiphany was liberating. Sarah took a deep breath, willing her voice to be strong and steady. "I have to go, Dar," she said. "Good-bye."

As she jammed her thumb against the Off button, another wave of anger tinted her vision crimson. She barely reined in the impulse to hurl her phone against the street.

"Goddammit!" she whispered, hands trembling at her sides. Hot tears spilled over onto her tingling cheeks. First her family turned their backs on her, then Dar. *Why? What the hell is wrong with me?*

She stood still for a long time, staring at nothing through burning eyes. As the rage seeped slowly out of her, it left a pervasive numbness in its wake. *I should have seen that coming,* she thought dully. *Should've known. Should've...* But even if she'd realized that Dar was slipping away, what could she have done? *I'm not what she wants anymore. I can't be what she wants. Maybe I never was.*

Above her, the clouds flared orange as the sun sank farther toward the horizon. It was an exquisite summer sunset, but all she noticed was the dying of the light. *I'm all alone, now—really and truly.*

Sarah continued toward the empty house. Sleep. All she wanted to do was sleep.

CHAPTER THREE

One week later

The late morning sunlight beat down on Aurora Song's shoulders as she perched on the flatbed of her friend Matt's truck and frowned at the huge box that held her television. She was worn out from a solid hour spent carting her belongings up to her dorm room. At this point, all she wanted to do was to curl up in one of her beanbag chairs, pop in a comfort movie—maybe *Beauty and the Beast*—and vegetate. Of course, she couldn't follow through on that plan with her TV still in the damn truck. Fortunately, Matt had volunteered to go in search of help.

Rory sighed and stretched her legs, wishing she had a bottle of water. She closed her eyes and tilted her head up to catch the slight breeze. *Junior year.* At the thought, Rory felt a twinge of nerves. Her course load wasn't going to be easy. The documentary class she'd signed up for would demand that she create a full-length film, something she'd never done before. Short films she could do. Commercial-length pieces were *easy* by now. But a full-length documentary? The prospect was daunting.

"Hey, Rory!" Matt's high-pitched shout forced her eyes open. "Look who I found."

Rory turned, shielding her gaze from the sunlight. When she caught sight of Matt's companion, she sucked in a sharp breath. *Oh shit. Jeff Lee.* Dismayed at her grimy jeans and sweat-stained T-shirt, she jumped down off the bed, quickly brushed off the seat of her pants, and curled a stray wisp of hair behind her left ear. *I'm going to kill you, Matthew.*

"May I present your knight in shining armor, milady," declared Matt with a flourish in Jeff's direction.

Jeff shrugged one shoulder, grinning slightly. He looked good in a pair of faded jeans and a tight black T-shirt. Hell, he looked good all the time.

"How's it going, Rory?"

"Hi, Jeff," she said, trying to play it cool. "Thanks for giving us a hand."

"Yeah, no problem." His eyebrows arched as he regarded the box. "That really *is* a monster. You won it, huh?"

He was clearly impressed, and Rory couldn't stop herself from smiling like a fool. "I see Matt's been talkative," she said. "What a surprise."

Together, they maneuvered the television off the truck and staggered toward the front door of Hutchinson Hall. Rory kept sneaking glances at Jeff as they waited for an elevator to take them up to the third floor. His shaggy dark hair kept falling into his eyes, and he smelled faintly of tobacco, and dammit, she could feel all of her old feelings rising up to clog her throat. *When the hell will I get over this silly crush?*

"So, uh," she said, "what'd you do over the summer, Jeff?"

"I was in Austria, studying at the Vienna Conservatory."

"Oh, wow," Rory said, instantly hating herself for letting that be her first reaction. Why did she always have to act like such a fangirl around him? "That sounds, ah, like quite an opportunity." *Idiot, idiot, idiot!*

"It was sweet," was all Jeff said as they pushed the box into the elevator and rode up.

By the time they reached the end of the hall and Rory's room, they were all gasping for breath. Rory's arms burned as she straightened up from depositing the TV in an unoccupied corner.

"All right," she said breathlessly. "Thanks, you guys. Come over and watch a movie anytime, okay?"

Jeff nodded absently as he looked around the room. "These corner suites are pretty decent," he said. "Who are you living with?"

"Sarah Storm."

Jeff's brow wrinkled. "Hmm. I don't think I know her."

"Me, neither," Rory said. "She's a random. My two closest female friends are studying abroad this year, so I decided to try my luck in the roommate lottery."

"That's brave of you."

"Guess so." Rory felt a spike of anxiety at Jeff's comment. Sarah seemed nice enough—at least, her voicemail messages did—but what if the two of them were completely incompatible? With an effort, she shrugged off the familiar worry. *I'll know soon enough.* "At the very least, she's got a cool name," she said.

"I still think it's ridiculous that you and I can't live together, Ror," Matt chimed in. "Dumbass heteronormative housing policy."

"It's probably for the best," Rory said. "I love you, and I don't mind Andrew Lloyd Webber in small doses, but…"

"Yeah, yeah yeah." Matt sighed dramatically. "I know. It would never work."

"Who *did* you find to room with?" Jeff asked.

"Me, myself, and I." Matt smirked. "Being an RA means I get to have a single. Can you say 'Party Central,' ladies and gentlemen?"

Jeff grinned. Rory felt her heart do a somersault. A full-fledged smile was a rare and beautiful thing where Jeff Lee was concerned. *I could make you happy, Jeff. Couldn't I?*

"Your parties are always chill," he said. "I'll look forward to them." He headed for the door and looked over his shoulder just before crossing the threshold. "See you 'round, Rory."

Rory nodded, barely managing to repress her urge to wave. "Yeah—see you. And thanks again." She sighed as the door closed behind him, and she slumped against her desk. Reining herself in around Jeff was exhausting.

"Am I the best best friend or what?" Matt said, triumphant.

"You are a rock star," Rory said absently, surveying the piles of boxes that littered her desk and floor. The place was a mess. *I should*

at least unpack some of this stuff before Sarah gets here tomorrow.
"All right, you—I think I'm going to do some unpacking. Want to meet up for dinner?"

"Definitely," Matt said, turning to leave. "Text me."

Once he had gone, Rory pushed herself away from the desk and squared her shoulders, determined to at least make a dent in the chaos. "Huh," she muttered. "Do I set up the TV first? Or the computer? Decisions, decisions…"

❖

Sarah stepped out of her car and looked up at the façade of Hutchinson Hall, her home for the next year. She already knew—from a colorful pamphlet sent to her by the Department of Housing and Residential Life—that it had been named for the dissident Puritan preacher, Anne Hutchinson. Sarah's lips curved in a fleeting smile. When Hutchinson had dared to challenge the religious establishment, she'd been kicked out of her colony.

"You and me both," Sarah murmured. She ran her fingers through her hair, still unused to how short it was. The day after Dar had broken up with her, Sarah had experienced an urge to make a change. As her hair had cascaded to the floor in the wake of the clippers, Sarah had felt a sense of lightness, of freedom. *I look like I'm supposed to*, she had realized as she'd stared into the mirror. *This right here—this is finally* me.

Her attention snapped back to the present as she noticed an attractive redhead walking toward her, carrying a milk crate full of books. An older man—presumably her father—followed in tow. The woman paused briefly as she drew alongside Sarah to look her up and down. Sarah blushed and quickly turned away to yank open the back left door of her car. She slung her backpack over one shoulder and grabbed her duffel bag full of clothing. *No milk crates for me,* she thought, realizing that she'd only need to make one additional trip to retrieve the lamp and the hot pot that Corrie and Quinn had given her.

Once inside the building, Sarah bypassed the line for the

elevators and headed toward the stairs. As she lugged her bags up three flights, she wondered whether her roommate had already arrived. She and Aurora Song, who apparently liked to be called Rory, had been playing phone tag for the past week. Rory sounded nice enough on voicemail, but Sarah had her doubts. Who still needed a roommate, junior year? Rory wasn't a transfer student, so why wasn't she living with one of her friends?

Sarah stopped in front of room 333, raised her hand to knock… and paused at the sound of shotgun fire. A string of expletives and a triumphant holler followed the blasts.

"You suck!" someone shouted from inside. The voice was high-pitched, yet masculine. "Oh my God, Rory, I *hate* you!"

Rory's reply was muffled and indistinct, but it earned a shrill laugh from the guy. Apparently she did have friends, after all. Sarah squared her shoulders, took a deep breath, and rapped twice on the door.

When it opened, she was face-to-face with an Asian woman dressed in baggy sweats and a Guns N' Roses T-shirt. Rory was only an inch or two shorter than Sarah, and when she smiled, the corners of her mouth dimpled.

"Hey, you must be Sarah." She stuck out one hand, and Sarah shook it. "How's it going?" She gestured into the room, where a lanky guy with bright red hair was lounging on a beanbag chair in front of the television. Which was…fancy. Forty inches, Sarah guessed, and high-definition.

"That's Matt," Rory said, gesturing toward her companion.

As Matt bounded up to shake her hand in turn, he dropped an Xbox controller onto the chair. "Great to meet you," he said. "Rory's just been schooling me at Halo 3. She's a killing machine!"

Rory rolled her eyes. "Comforting thing to know about your roommate, huh?" She flipped off the TV and turned back to Sarah. "So. Can we help you with your stuff?"

"Oh, that's okay," Sarah said as she dumped her bags on the floor next to the unclaimed desk. Rory's desk sat directly across the room, and it was already a mess. A computer screen overshadowed stacks of DVDs, papers, and random food products that had not yet found a home. A poster for a French film—something about a city and maybe infants, if Sarah was reading the title correctly—broke up the monotony of the beige walls. She forced a smile to her lips, trying to mask her self-consciousness at how few possessions she owned. "I only have one more trip to make."

"A light packer," Matt said. He elbowed Rory. "What a concept! It took three people just to lug this freaking TV up here."

"It's a really nice one," Sarah said.

"I got lucky," Rory said, shrugging. "Won it in a commercial competition sponsored by Samsung."

Sarah gaped at her. "Whoa. That's really cool."

Matt slung one arm around Rory's shoulders. "Hollywood's going to fall at her feet one day."

Rory snorted. "No, I'll be a starving artist falling at *your* feet, begging for handouts because I'm too poor to pay my landlord."

Matt threw back his head and started to sing about not paying this year or any year's rent, until Rory clapped one hand over his mouth. She grinned at Sarah apologetically. "I know better than to get him started. My bad."

Sarah, who had been watching their banter with interest, laughed. "Oh, I don't mind. I've never seen the actual show, but I loved the film."

Matt pulled away to give Sarah a bear hug. He looked over his shoulder at Rory. "This one's a keeper! Don't piss her off." In another moment, he was at the door. "And now, I'm outta here—far be it from me to interfere with roommate bondage. I mean, bonding." He winked. "So great to meet you, Sarah. See you soon."

Rory shook her head as he disappeared into the hall. "What a character. The beds are through there, by the way," she said, pointing. "Is it okay with you that I grabbed top bunk?"

Sarah took a quick look into the second room. It was narrow and contained only the beds, two battered wooden dressers and a closet. "No problem," she said. "I'll be back in a sec—going to grab the rest of my stuff."

On her way back from the car, Sarah stopped by the HRL office to pick up her room key. She also received a thick packet of materials, including course descriptions for the fall semester, and a book listing all of the university's student organizations. Between work and her classes, she didn't anticipate having much free time, but it would be nice to get involved in a group, if only to make a few friends. *Maybe the GLBT organization.* Its Web site, when she had Googled it once on Corrie's computer, had looked promising. And she had seen signs posted in the atrium of the building advertising an open house tonight.

I wonder if Matt knows anything about it, she mused as she trudged back up the stairs. *No way can he be straight.* It was encouraging that Rory was friends with him. Sarah had been anxious about how her roommate might react to news of her sexual orientation. She didn't want to spill the beans just yet, but at least there was hope that Rory wouldn't completely flip out. Of course, having a gay friend wasn't exactly on par with living with a lesbian. *I'll wait a few weeks. Get to know her first.*

When she shouldered open the door, Rory was bent over her desk, apparently trying to straighten it up. Her brisk movements were endangering the integrity of her stacks of DVDs, and Sarah kept a wary eye on them in case they began to topple.

"That's quite a movie collection you've got there," she said.

"Oh, thanks." Rory looked up and grinned. "These are just the ones I can't live without. I've got tons more back home."

"Are you a film major?" Sarah asked as she began to unpack her backpack. The laptop went on her desk for now, and the few favorite books that she'd salvaged from her childhood bedroom went on the bookshelf above it.

"Yep. How about you?'

"I'm pre-med."

"Ah, so you're the daughter my parents always wanted."

Sarah raised her head, startled, but Rory was smiling. "They wanted a doctor and they got the next Stanley Kubrick, if I have any say about it."

"Stanley Kubrick?"

"Film director—made *A Clockwork Orange, Lolita,* and *The Shining,* among many others. Pretty much my idol."

Sarah reached back into her bag, flustered by her own ignorance. "I've never seen any of those," she admitted.

"Well," Rory said, "if you're ever in the mood to sack out in front of a movie, then I've got your poison."

"Cool." Sarah was suddenly envious of Rory's evident passion for her subject of study. She'd never felt that way about any academic topic. School had always just been there, and she had excelled at it because she'd been expected to.

As she bent down to open a desk drawer, she noticed the time on her watch. "Oh, jeez. I need to go. To work," she added, answering Rory's questioning look.

"Where do you work?"

"Billington Cove—the yacht club there." Sarah patted her front left and back right pockets, feeling for her keys and wallet. "Anyway, it was good to meet you. See you later."

"See you." Rory gave her a little wave and then turned back to her sorting. Sarah's gaze was drawn to the way Rory's dark shoulder-length hair curled around the nape of her neck. She shook her head.

Straight girl. Not to mention your roommate. *Knock it off!*

She was just lonely. Which was yet another reason to attend the open house tonight. It would be a good chance to meet people. There were plenty of safe, fun, commitment- and emotion-free ways to find companionship, right? Dar had been her first and only girlfriend, but she'd watched many of her friends at Yale move from hookup to hookup, never settling into a relationship.

I could do that, she thought as she closed the door behind her, firmly ignoring the ache in her chest that materialized every time she thought about Darla. *Sure does beat the alternative.*

❖

The GLBT student center in Adams Hall was already packed with people by the time Sarah arrived, a few minutes before nine p.m. She found space to lean against one wall, just opposite a tattered couch. Sure enough, Matt was there, chatting animatedly with a petite redhead wearing a white sundress that left most of her tan legs visible. Sarah did a double-take as she recognized the woman who had given her the once-over in the parking lot earlier.

When she found herself staring, she quickly looked away and inspected the room. Rainbow flags and Pride posters covered nearly every inch of white space. Beneath them, shelves packed with books and movies rested against the walls. There was a television in one corner and a small refrigerator in another, with a microwave on top. A huge bowl filled with condoms sat on a small table near the door.

It was easy to tell the newcomers. Like Sarah, they were standing or sitting quietly, taking in their surroundings and listening to the chatter of their neighbors. Most of the silent ones looked so very young. *Freshmen*, Sarah realized. *God, they look like they belong in middle school.*

"All right, everybody, listen up!" Matt bellowed cheerfully. "Let's get this party started." He grinned, and Sarah watched nearly the entire room smile back in return. His enthusiasm was infectious. "I'm Matt, the treasurer of this illustrious organization. This," he said, pointing at the redheaded woman, "is our heartthrobby—and single, ladies!—president, Chelsea. She's the top around here."

Somebody wolf-whistled. Several people rolled their eyes. Matt favored the room with an exaggerated wink. "Give her a hand, ladies and gentlemen!"

"Thanks so much, Matt," Chelsea said dryly. She took a step forward and continued to address the room in a clear, confident voice. She was unarguably beautiful, and Sarah watched several of the women in the room eye her with undisguised appreciation.

"To those of you back for another year, it's great to see you again. And to those who are new, welcome. I'd like to start this meeting by having everyone introduce themselves, and then we'll move on to announcements."

When it was her turn, Sarah described herself simply as a pre-med transfer student. She felt a momentary spike of anxiety that someone would ask her where she'd transferred from, but the introductions continued around the room without a pause. *What are you afraid of, anyway? They'll think you failed out, sure, but so what?* Sarah looked down at her toes, tan against the black straps of her Tevas. Why couldn't she stop caring about what other people thought? Everything would be so much easier.

Up in the front of the room, Chelsea was again taking control. "The pizza will be here soon"—she smiled benevolently when a raucous cheer went up from several corners—"so I'll make these announcements brief. We have conversation groups every Monday and Thursday at nine. Come, hang out, chat with each other about anything and everything. Also, save the date—we'll be holding our annual formal on the Friday after Valentine's Day. I know that's still a long way off, but it's our biggest event of the year, so next week I'll be sending around a dance committee sign-up sheet."

"And last but certainly not least, GLAD—Gay and Lesbian Advocates and Defenders—is looking for student volunteers for their voting campaign. As many of you probably know, there's going to be a referendum in the spring on the proposed amendment to define marriage as between one man and one woman, and to ban the creation of civil unions." Chelsea paused for the chorus of boos. "Exactly. If you're interested in helping them, come see me after the meeting. I've got their contact information."

She looked over to the door, where Matt was paying for several boxes of pizza. "That's all for now. Enjoy, and remember to sign up to be on our e-mail list if you haven't already."

Sarah hung back as most of the room descended on the food. Chelsea's last piece of news, the bit about GLAD, had intrigued her. It would feel good to volunteer a bit, if she could find the time. Especially for such an important cause. Maybe if the vote in the spring passed, her parents would realize that being queer wasn't such a big deal—that it was just a part of her, like her eye color or her height. How could they continue to reject her if legally, Rhode Island accepted her? Suddenly resolved, she made her way over to where Chelsea was talking with another woman and waited. But before she could catch Chelsea's attention, someone came up behind her and clapped a hand on her shoulder.

"Sarah! Really good to see you."

"Hey, Matt," she said, turning around. She felt a sudden

compulsion to beg him not to tell Rory, and had to clench her teeth against the impulse. "So—treasurer, huh?"

He shrugged. "That's what I get for being an econ major."

"The real story is that he's secretly embezzling our money to fund his hair dye collection," Chelsea said. She looked at Sarah and smiled. "Sarah, right?" She cocked her head. "Didn't I see you in the parking lot earlier today?"

"Yeah, that was me," Sarah said as they shook hands. Chelsea's was soft and her nails brightly colored. Sarah hoped that her palms weren't sweating. "I, uh, just wanted to talk to you because I'm interested in volunteering with GLAD."

"Oh, great!" Chelsea reached into her bag and extracted a flyer. "Here you go. This has all of their info on it."

"Thanks." Sarah folded up the paper and slipped it into her front pocket. She was acutely aware that Chelsea hadn't stopped staring at her since they'd begun talking. The attention was simultaneously flattering and discomfiting. "Well…later."

She was about to turn toward the door when Chelsea reached out to touch her arm. "Thanks for coming tonight. See you soon."

"Definitely." Sarah managed a self-conscious smile and walked away. Her skin tingled where Chelsea's fingers had rested. *Oh, get a grip. So she's attractive and kind of flirty. That doesn't mean you have to get all awkward.*

She made her way toward the staircase and climbed it slowly. Chelsea reminded her of Dar, a little—sophisticated, feminine, poised. She tended to feel tongue-tied around such women until she got to know them. *I'm glad Rory's not like that. It's easy to talk to her. I think we'll be friends.* And Matt was fun. He made her laugh.

But when she came to a stop in front of her door, a sudden wash of loneliness flooded over her. What were her friends at Yale doing right now? Were they missing her at all, or were they too caught up in the beginning of the school year to even spare her a thought? And Dar—had she moved on yet? Or was she sizing up her prospects, now that—

Stop it. Stop it stop it stop it. Sarah clenched her fists at her sides and shook her head. *Knock it off. Be grateful for where you are, dammit. It could be so much worse.* Taking a deep breath, she opened the door and answered Rory's greeting as cheerfully as she could.

"How was work?" said Rory as Sarah closed the door behind her. "And I just made myself a cup of chai. Want some?"

"Sure," Sarah said. The uncomfortable pit in her stomach began to fade in the face of Rory's solicitousness. "It smells really good. Thanks."

"Another chai drinker! Sweet." Rory grabbed a carton from the mini-fridge and began pouring its contents into a URI mug. "May as well just come out and ask you: what music do you like?"

"Ah, I see—this is really an elaborate compatibility test." Sarah flopped into one of the beanbag chairs and arched both eyebrows. She hadn't felt like joking around very often during the past month, but Rory's bantering tone made it easy. "I'm on to you."

"You're smart *and* you drink chai. Killer combo." Rory winked. "I'm gonna be more specific: when I play Guns N' Roses, should I wear my headphones or not?"

"Definitely not."

"You are the perfect woman."

Sarah found herself belly-laughing. "And you're prone to hyperbole."

Rory whistled. "Great vocabulary, good taste in beverages, likes Guns N' Roses. What else should I know about you, Sarah Storm?"

Sarah's pulse jumped at the question. Rory had just given her the perfect opportunity to come out, and for a moment, she seriously considered it. But what if Rory freaked? It was a very real possibility. *Can't deal with that. Not today.*

"Um…let's see," she said. "Cheesesteaks are my favorite food."

"Yum. What's your restaurant of choice around here?"

"I don't know," Sarah said. At Rory's confused look, she decided to 'fess up. Her ignorance about URI was going to be blatant. *I can't keep* this *a secret.* "I literally just got here. I'm a transfer student."

"Oh? From where?"

Sarah took a deep breath. "Yale. So tell me, where should I order my cheesesteaks from?"

Rory blinked at her for a moment, then shook her head. "Kingston Pizza. Good stuff."

"Cool," Sarah said, relieved that Rory was apparently not going to ask why in hell she'd transferred out of Yale. "Thanks." When the ensuing silence stretched on for more than a few seconds, she started to feel anxious. "So…what classes are you taking this semester?"

Rory leaned back so that her front two chair legs were in the air. "I've got three fun ones and two pains in the ass," she said. "Film Theory, Documentary Film I, and Modernist Lit are going to rock."

"Modernist Lit? Why are you taking that?"

"English minor. That class is going to be *hard*, 'cuz modernism is some crazy shit, but I know I'll enjoy it."

"Fair enough," Sarah said. For the second time that day, she felt out of her depth academically. *Is it obvious that I have no idea what "modernism" means, the way she's using it?* "What about the ones you're not looking forward to?"

Rory's chair legs returned to the floor with a loud thump. She scowled. "Intro Econ, because I promised my parents. And Intro Bio, because I've been putting off my goddamn science requirement since freshman year."

Sarah laughed. "Do you ever wish you could trade credits with someone else? I've got plenty of science under my belt. You can have whichever you'd like."

"Oh man. I would so take you up on that." Rory stared dreamily into space for a moment, then shrugged. "Anyway. How about you? What are you taking?"

"Physical Chemistry, Inorganic Chemistry, Advanced Genetics, and Bioethics." Sarah shrugged. "I still need three more credits, though. Do you have any ideas for a good class?" When she looked up, Rory's mouth and eyes were open wide. "What?"

Rory shut her mouth with a click. "So what you're telling me is that you're a brainiac."

"No, I just want to be a doctor." Rory's compliment was nice, but Sarah didn't exactly feel as though she deserved it. "Help me out with my fifth class, will you?"

Rory tossed over a copy of her course guide for the semester. "Sounds like you need something non-scientific. I took a really good women's studies class last year—interesting and pretty easy."

Sarah opened the book toward the back and leafed through the course descriptions. She'd never taken a women's studies class at Yale, though many of her friends had. It was yet another area that she knew practically nothing about. *And I really should.*

"Which one did you take?"

"Current Topics in Women Studies," Rory said. "It's offered every year, but the content changes depending on what's going on in the real world. Same prof every year, too. She's cool."

Sarah flipped to the relevant page and skimmed the description. The class promised to teach her about how contemporary laws and social practices impacted women and the field of women's studies. It did sound interesting, and it'd be a nice break from the rest of her course load.

"All right," she said. "Sold." She got to her feet, went to her desk, and flipped open her laptop. "I'm going to register for it right now."

"And I," Rory said, "have had enough of all this school talk." She dropped to the floor in front of the television and grabbed one of her controllers. "Will it bug you if I play video games for a while? I can always put the TV on mute."

"It won't bother me," Sarah said as she loaded up URI's homepage.

"Wanna play? The two-player version is really fun."

"If you knew how much I suck at video games, you never would have asked me that."

Rory made a dismissive sound. "It's just a skill, like any other. I'll teach you someday, if you want."

Sarah laughed again. "Make sure it's a someday when you're feeling very patient."

After signing up for her class, she opened up her e-mail program. She had promised Corrie that she'd check in. Once she was finished, she spun in her chair to watch Rory's progress. Rory's tongue poked out slightly between her teeth, and the tendons in her forearms jumped as she pounded buttons. The olive tone of her skin contrasted with the dark fabric of her T-shirt, which hugged her torso like a second skin. Her gray sweats were a little baggy, of course, but—

She's got a really nice ass. The thought was unbidden and unwanted. Sarah gritted her teeth and mentally slapped herself. Rory was kind, funny, and smart—that much was apparent even after only a few hours of living with her. She was also the only person at URI with whom Sarah had had more than a passing conversation. Sarah was lonely right now—lonely and searching for human connection. It would be far too easy for her to read more into their fledgling friendship than was really there. Besides, she and Dar had only been broken up for a week. *I'm just rebounding. That's all. Looking for a connection anywhere I can find one.*

Suddenly exhausted, Sarah rubbed her burning eyes and pushed her chair back from her desk. It had been a long day, and those kinds of thoughts were proof positive that her brain needed a rest. "I'm going to bed," she said.

"Okay," Rory said. "Sleep tight." She looked over her shoulder briefly and smiled—a quick, easy smile that made Sarah feel warm inside.

Sighing, she pulled the bedroom door shut and wrestled her sheets onto the bottom bunk. The mattress was a little harder than the one she'd gotten used to at Corrie and Quinn's, but it felt good to have a bed that she could truly call her own again.

As she did every night, Sarah worked on wiping her mind clear of every troubling memory and anxiety about the future. Often during that last month of the summer, she had lain awake for hours, her heart thumping painfully as she tried over and over to figure out what to do next.

Now, mercifully, the faint sounds of Rory's game lulled her into sleep within minutes.

Chapter Four

Three weeks later

Rory used her fork to prod the mysterious vegetable that had been served up alongside her macaroni and cheese. *Suspicious.* Was it spinach? Kale? Green bean mush? Deciding not to risk it, she shoved it as far to the side as possible.

"You know I love watching movies with you," she told Matt, who was devouring his hamburger as though it were the last he'd ever eat. "But I can't tonight. Sarah said she'd help me study for my stupid bio exam. She's kind of a whiz at that stuff."

"How are things going with her, anyway?" Matt asked.

Rory shrugged. "Fine, I guess. She's not around much. Her job keeps her pretty busy when she's not in class."

"Yeah, every time I've seen her, she seems like she's on the go." Matt slurped from his soda. "But she's a good roommate?"

"Neat, quiet, and she doesn't eat my cereal. Almost too good to be true." Rory took a bite of her dinner. "I think she's kind of lonely, though."

"What makes you say that?"

"Couple of things. She brings a lot of meals back to the room. And if she's made any friends, I haven't met them." Every time they were in the room together, Rory tried to draw Sarah into conversation, but she hadn't gotten very far over the past few weeks. There was a lot she wanted to know, starting with why the hell

Sarah had transferred to URI from *Yale*, of all places. What was her story? And why did she look so damn sad, sometimes? Sarah was happy to talk about how her classes were going, or to share a funny anecdote about some table she'd waited on at work, but she had yet to volunteer any deeply personal information. *Can't seem to get past the surface with her.*

"Well," Matt was saying, "I can tell you right now that I know of at least three women who would *love* to fix her loneliness problem." Suddenly, his eyes widened and he covered his mouth with both hands. "Oh shit," he mumbled. "Fuck."

For a second, Rory was confused by Matt's sudden interjection. Then she realized what he had said and several of the puzzle pieces fell into place. Sarah's tomboyish look made a different kind of sense now. *So that's what's beneath the surface. Huh.*

She leaned forward. "Did you just out my roommate to me?" When Matt nodded miserably, looking utterly stricken, she rolled her eyes. "Bad form, dude."

"Well, it's *you*! I mean, it's hard to be careful around you because obviously, duh, you're cool with it, but Sarah doesn't know that."

Rory frowned. "Does she think I'll flip my shit or something?"

"How should I know?" Matt's voice always screeched when he was upset, and he drew several looks from those sitting at nearby tables in the cafeteria.

"Chill," Rory said. "It's not a big deal."

"You're not going to bring it up, are you?"

"We'll see." Before he could start squawking again, she changed the subject slightly. "So she's got some admirers, does she?"

Matt, always a sucker for gossip, latched on to the new topic with gusto. "Every lesbian, bisexual, and bicurious freshman, of course." When Rory began to laugh, he held up one hand. "That's small potatoes. The real news is that *Chelsea* has the major hots for her."

Rory let out a low whistle. She had never heard of Chelsea crushing on anyone before. It was usually the opposite. "Sarah the stud, huh?"

"You have to ask?" Matt sounded indignant. "What are you, blind?"

"Rhetorical question," Rory said. "Yes, I find her attractive, okay? Handsome. And her eyes…I've never seen eyes that blue."

"Duh. She's totally smokin' in that hunky butch way, and it's like she doesn't even know it. Hell, sometimes she gives *me* twinges, especially when she wears jeans and a polo shirt…"

Rory laughed at the dreamy note in Matt's voice. "My roommate can pass for a hot guy. Wow."

Matt blinked as though he were waking up. "Don't you dare ever tell her that last thing I just said."

"What?" Rory said, grinning mischievously. "That even you have a crush on her?"

"I do not!"

"Yeah, you sorta do."

"I'm *gay*, for Christ's sake!" Matt bellowed. The entire dining hall went silent. "What?" he said, looking around belligerently. "It's not like all you people didn't know that already!"

Rory bit down on her lower lip in an effort not to laugh. "Y'know that book *Coming Out Every Day*? That's your life."

Matt flashed her a cheesy smile and reached for a few of his fries. "Loud and proud, baby."

"Anyway," Rory said, "back to Sarah." As soon as Matt had mentioned Chelsea's interest, Rory had visualized them as a couple. *They'd look great together.* "I think we should set her up with Chelsea."

Matt rolled his eyes at her. "Of course you do. Emma."

"Hey! Emma was *bad* at matchmaking. I'm good at it."

"Uh-huh, right. That must be why Dan and I are still together."

Rory narrowed her eyes. This was familiar territory. "I still contend that you guys were an excellent fit for each other."

"And I still contend that the fact that he dumped me on my ass pokes serious holes in your argument!"

Rory sighed heavily. "Fine. You're entitled to your opinion. It's just…think about it. Wouldn't Sarah and Chelsea make a good couple?"

Matt chewed slowly as he considered the question. "Depends on Sarah's personality. Chelsea's a handful. Think Sarah would mind how clingy she gets?"

"At least she wouldn't be lonely," Rory pointed out. "Maybe Chelsea's neediness will be good for her."

"Maybe." Matt looked down at his watch and frowned. "Hey, don't you have to get to class?"

"Shit, yeah." Rory grabbed her tray and pushed back her chair. "Thanks. See you later."

As she headed toward the double doors, she tried to decide how she'd broach what was clearly a sensitive subject with Sarah. There was no question in her mind that she had to say something. She didn't want Sarah to have to continue hiding. Rory felt a sudden flash of anger. What was her deal, anyway, with not being out from the very beginning?

Do I not read as queer-friendly, somehow? How the hell is that possible? My best friend is a flaming gay boy!

But Rory's irritation subsided as quickly as it had come. Maybe Sarah had had some bad experiences with coming out. And it wasn't as though they were more than friendly acquaintances who shared the same living space. But that was going to change. *I'm going to get to know her better, dammit,* Rory pledged. *I'm going to be her friend. And bringing this up will be the first step.*

❖

All throughout their evening review session, Rory tried to come up with a good way to steer the conversation toward the pink elephant that had taken up residence in their room. She was still racking her brains, though, when Sarah announced a few minutes before nine o'clock that she needed to leave for another study date at "the library." Rory had to struggle not to smile. Matt also always had something going on at nine o'clock on Mondays, and it had nothing to do whatsoever with hitting the books.

By the time Sarah came back around ten thirty, Rory had decided that bluntness was the way to go. So she scraped back her chair, curled her feet underneath her, looked Sarah in the eyes, and said, "I know that you weren't just at the library—that you were at one of those talk-group-things over at the GLBT student center. I know you're a lesbian and I don't care. I'm not going to freak out." She paused to grin up at Sarah, whose eyes and mouth were open wide. "And I also happen to know that you, roomie, are being crushed on by *many* women."

Sarah sat down hard. She blinked at Rory. "How did you—"

"Matt. It was an accident. He didn't mean to tell me, and he feels awful about it."

"Huh." Sarah rested her elbows on her knees and stared down at the frayed carpeting. "Guess that explains why he avoided talking to me tonight."

"Don't be mad," Rory said quickly. "It only slipped because he knows—as do you, now—that I'm totally cool with it."

Sarah's smile was tentative. "Really?"

"Yeah. And I don't even mind if you stare at me while I'm undressing. I'm a hottie, it's just a fact."

Rory felt a surge of relief when Sarah laughed. It was a good sound, and one that, she realized belatedly, she hadn't heard very often.

"Good to know," Sarah said. She reached both hands up to rub her neck and shoulders. Rory fleetingly thought of offering a massage, but decided that in the present context, it would come off as weird.

"So, dontcha want to know about these girls who are falling all over themselves for you?" she teased.

"Uh, you were serious about that?" Sarah looked genuinely surprised.

"Well, you really should talk to Matt," Rory said. "But he gave me the impression that you're considered…what was the word he used? *Hunky.*"

"Hunky?" She sounded incredulous. "Are you sure he wasn't joking?"

"Oh, I'm sure." Rory found herself surprised in turn. Had Matt been right? Did Sarah really not know just how attractive—*scratch that, hot*—she was? How could she not know? Sure, Sarah was no willowy blond supermodel, but she was tall and lean and striking. And she radiated a sort of barely contained intensity, a tautness in her bearing that was subtly charismatic. *Like gravity.* Rory had no doubt that Sarah was the proverbial talk of the town among the queer women on campus. And if she really was blind to all of the attention, that would make her even more attractive.

"What about you?" Sarah asked.

Rory frowned. "What about me, what?"

"I just realized…" She faltered. "I mean, I guess I don't know. Do you have a boyfriend?"

Rory decided to let Sarah change the subject, and allowed herself a self-deprecating laugh as she got up to snag a soda from their mini-fridge. She tossed one to Sarah, too. "Ah, no. I'm a hopeless romantic. I want…I need grand passion, you know? It's all or nothing for me."

"Grand passion. Like, feelings that are all-consuming?"

"Yeah." Rory was suddenly unable to meet Sarah's intent gaze. She focused instead on a nick in one leg of her chair. "I want to love someone with everything in me, and I want them to love me back the very same way."

When Sarah didn't reply for several seconds, Rory looked up. Sarah had a distant expression on her face—as though she were looking at something far away. Something that made her sad.

"I get that," she said. "Have you ever had it?"

Rory decided that this conversation had gotten much too serious. "Naw," she said, flicking open the tab of her soda and taking a long sip. "I specialize in unrequited love. Like, for a little over a year now, I've been carrying a torch for Jeff Lee. How unoriginal, right?"

"Who's Jeff Lee?"

"Senior. Music major. Fucking brilliant violinist. One of those broody artist types—smokes and drinks too much, but you don't care because he's an incredible listener and a goddamn genius. I fell head over heels for him freshman spring, when we were in the same study group for a class on nineteenth-century novels—" Rory suddenly realized that she was saying more than she'd meant to, and shrugged off a familiar pang of longing. "I want to save him from himself, you know? Me and about a thousand other women." She met Sarah's sympathetic look and cracked a half-smile. *She's a good listener, too.*

"He sounds cool. Maybe you can introduce me someday." When Rory nodded, Sarah took a deep breath. "And look, I'm sorry I didn't tell you earlier. About me. It's a tricky thing, you know?"

Rory nodded again. She wanted to ask Sarah her story—how she had realized, when she had come out, what that had been like. But now didn't feel like the right time. "I can imagine" was all she said.

"Yeah. So…back to work?"

Rory blew out a heavy sigh. "Ugh. No thanks."

"Still studying bio?" Sarah got up to look at the papers scattered on Rory's desk. "Anything I can help with?"

"Not bio right now. Taking a break from the cramming to brainstorm for my documentary class. I'm totally stuck."

"Hmm," Sarah said, leaning her butt against the desk and folded her arms across her chest. In that position, her resemblance to James Dean was positively spooky. "What do you have to do?"

Rory twisted the tab on her can. "It's a yearlong class. First semester's all about history of the documentary, technique, stuff like that. Second semester is spent creating a film and workshopping it with the rest of the class." She slouched down in her chair. "Sounds so great in theory, right? Thing is, the prof wants us to write up a proposal of what we want to do by next week. And I don't have a clue."

Sarah frowned in thought. "Well, is there anything you *don't* want to do?"

"Plenty," Rory said. "I don't want to do anything on, like…like saving the fucking whales, you know? Not that saving the whales isn't a good cause, because I'm sure they deserve it, but I want to make a film about something really pertinent. Relevant to my life, my friends." She rubbed her tired eyes. "Nothing I can think of seems right." *And I am seriously running out of time.*

She started as Sarah propelled herself away from the desk and spun back around, clearly excited. "I know—GLAD!"

"Glad?" Rory shook her head, puzzled. "What? Like sandwich-bag Glad?"

Sarah laughed again. "No, no, the acronym. G-L-A-D—Gay and Lesbian Advocates and Defenders. They're an organization. I volunteer for them. They have all kinds of projects going on throughout New England, but right now they're especially vested in campaigning against this referendum in the spring—"

"Oh, yeah, Matt was telling me about that. Some bullshit proposal to limit the definition of marriage, right?"

"Yeah, and to make it so that Rhode Island wouldn't be able to create civil unions or anything like them. GLAD has this subcommittee that's trying to get the word out to Rhode Island students to vote against the bill. They're splitting time between here and Providence, trying to hit as many schools as possible."

"Very cool." Rory nodded as the idea sank in. *Important— check. And the timing is perfect. Jeez…this could actually work.* "How did you get involved with them?"

"Chelsea made an announcement at the GLBT student center open house," Sarah said, "and I decided that it'd be a good thing to do. I mean…it's not just about getting married, you know?" She was staring off toward the darkened window now, clearly lost in thought. "What if I had a partner someday, and she was hospitalized for some reason, and her family wouldn't let me see her?" She shuddered. "Or…did you know that there's no clear law on the books in Rhode Island about joint gay adoption? One parent is allowed to adopt, but it's all murky as to whether the other can, and how awful would it be if you were blocked from doing that?"

Rory touched Sarah's arm lightly, wanting to offer comfort.

There had been real pain in her voice, and fear. "Yeah. That would really, really suck."

Sarah grinned—a little sheepishly—and took a step away from the desk. "Sorry. I got a little carried away, there. I guess…I mean, if some*one* doesn't like that I'm queer—fine. That's their problem. But the state and federally sanctioned discrimination is just plain unconstitutional. Volunteering with GLAD lets me fight the good fight."

Rory nodded. "And you think I should make a film about them?"

"Oh, I'm not telling you what to do," Sarah said quickly. "But it does seem to fit your criteria."

"That it does." Rory turned back to her computer. "They must have a Web site, right? I'll check it out."

"Look, why not just come along with me tomorrow night when I go to volunteer? We're going to put up posters all over campus about an info session that's being held next week. Someone from GLAD's Boston office will be there to give us the posters and help out. You can talk to them and scope out the whole thing."

"Sure, all right," Rory said. She looked over her shoulder at Sarah and gave her the thumbs-up. "Sounds great. Thanks."

Sarah smiled in return and went back to her desk. A moment later, Rory heard her shuffling papers. Resolutely, she turned back to her biology textbook and flipped it open. Earlier, her discouragement about the documentary had been a distraction, but now that she had settled on a topic, she felt that sense of quiet purpose that made doing any task easier. Including studying for this goddamned exam.

❖

The group that gathered on the stairs outside Roger Williams Dining Hall the next evening was small. When everyone greeted Sarah by name, Rory realized that she had been fundamentally wrong earlier about Sarah not having any friends. *It's not just me. People are drawn to her. Good energy.*

"Hey, everyone," Sarah said. She withdrew one hand from

the pocket of her windbreaker to gesture at Rory. "I brought my roommate."

Sarah introduced Nancy, the GLAD representative, first. She was a lawyer from Boston who looked to be in about her mid-forties and had very impressive piercings along the shell of her right ear. *Cool. Ow, but cool.*

"That's Travis, and there's John," Sarah continued. She turned to Chelsea, who was, as usual, dressed to the nines.

I've never seen her without heels on, Rory realized. *Kinda scary.*

"And this is—"

"Oh, Chelsea and I go way back," Rory said, grinning. "We suffered through our freshman seminar together."

"Hi, Rory," Chelsea said, sparing her a quick glance before honing back in on Sarah.

Rory would have bet her collector's edition copy of *Dr. Strangelove* that the only reason Chelsea was volunteering tonight was because she had known that Sarah would be there. *Perfect chance for me to play Yente.*

Nancy called their small meeting to order by handing each of them a stack of flyers and a box of tacks. "Before we head out," she said, "I thought I'd give you all a heads up on an exciting development that will be announced next week. Given the spring referendum here, GLAD has decided to create an organization called Fair Rhode Island that will be exclusively devoted to the Vote No campaign. Your GLBT center has decided to fund a paid internship as part of this new initiative."

"Really?" Sarah asked eagerly.

It was clear that she was fascinated by the opportunity. Rory fleetingly wondered how Sarah was going to find time for yet another job, in addition to classes and all this volunteering that she apparently did. *You are some kind of superstar, Sarah Storm.*

"So the internship is for students?"

Nancy nodded. "Only URI students can apply. And I'm here tonight because GLAD has made me the Fair Rhode Island point person for URI. I'm getting the lay of the land. Literally." She rubbed her hands together. "So let's pair up and divide the campus into thirds."

Rory saw her opening and seized it. Sarah was going to spend the evening flirting with Chelsea, if she had anything to say about it. Or being flirted with, at any rate. "If you don't mind me as a partner, Nancy," she said, "I have some questions that I'd like to ask you about GLAD. For a school project."

"No problem. Let's take the west side."

Rory suppressed a grin as she watched Chelsea turn to Sarah. *Bingo. Checkmate. Yahtzee.* But just to shorten the odds, when Chelsea moved away briefly to pick up her bag, Rory made sure to lean in close to Sarah, under the pretext of adjusting the collar of her shirt like a helpful roommate.

"She likes you," she muttered. "Don't be dense." And then she quickly turned toward Nancy, pointing toward a cluster of buildings across the quad. "Shall we start over there?"

The groups drifted apart into the cool night. "So," Nancy said as they began walking. "You said you have some questions. What's this project that you're working on?"

"It's for my documentary film class," Rory said. "At the end of the school year, I need to submit a documentary of my own. I've been racking my brains trying to figure out my topic."

"And you're thinking of choosing the upcoming election?"

"Yeah. When Sarah—she's my roommate—told me about the whole Vote No campaign, it sounded great on a number of levels. Pertinent issue, perfect timing." Rory slipped her hands into the front pocket of her hooded sweatshirt. *Ball's in your court. Fingers crossed.*

"So what is it exactly that you need from me?" said Nancy. "I have to tell you, the prospect of having a film chronicler is exciting to me on several levels."

"Oh?"

"This is all speculation, of course," Nancy said, "but for one thing, I could imagine asking you to let us use parts of the piece for television advertising early next year. Assuming you'd have some workable material by that point, of course."

Holy shit! Rory thought. *How cool would that be?* "That won't be a problem," she said. "If you give me the green light, I'm hoping to start filming as early as next month."

"How much of the campaign would you be able to document?"

"All of it, I hope. The referendum is in mid-April, right?" At Nancy's nod, Rory shrugged. "My deadline will be around the same time. It'll be tight at the very end, there, but I work best under pressure."

"All right, then. This all sounds good to me."

"Does that mean I officially have your permission?" said Rory.

"It does indeed," Nancy said.

Yes! Rory didn't bother trying to hold back her excited smile. She couldn't believe that it had been so easy. This entire plan had come together in a matter of days. *Like clockwork. Really good call, Sarah.*

"Need me to fill out a form?" Nancy asked. "Paperwork is effortless for us lawyer types."

"There will definitely be release forms. Everyone in range of the camera will have to sign one." Rory rolled her eyes. "I get the point, but it's a pain in the ass. Pardon my French."

Nancy just laughed, her breath misting in the air. She had a good laugh—throaty and genuine. *She's fun. Thank God. I won't mind hanging around her for the next several months.*

"Why not just drop off the forms at our office, sometime in the near future?" Nancy said. "That way, you can get familiarized with how we work. Meet people, too."

"Sure, that sounds good. Where is it?"

Nancy gave her the address and Rory paused to write it on the back of one of the flyers, which she then stuck in her pocket.

"How many staff members do you have there? I'll want to interview them all, as long as they're willing. And attend all of your events. Planning meetings, too, if that's okay."

Nancy laughed again. "Oh, you're certainly welcome to come to any and all functions. We're always looking for larger attendance numbers. As for interviews, I have a feeling that anyone affiliated with GLAD and FRI will be more than happy to give you their two cents." She grinned. "We're advocates and defenders. Not exactly a reticent bunch."

"Excellent." Nancy's encouragement was only making Rory feel more enthused about the project. *This is really going to work. And it'd be so sweet to get part of the film on television. That'd be a helluva line on the résumé.*

"Oh, but you asked about numbers. It's a small operation— myself, my assistant, and whoever ends up interning with us."

Rory nodded, wondering if it would be appropriate to plug Sarah for the job. *Aw hell, why not? Can't hurt.* "About that," she said. "I'm sure you'll get a lot of candidates for the position. I'm also sure that Sarah will apply. So just know that she's awesome and deserving and such a hard worker..." She trailed off. "Point is, you can't go wrong with her."

"You're dating her, aren't you?" Nancy said dryly.

"Huh? What?" Rory spluttered. "Um, no. She's honestly *just* my roommate. Don't hold it against me, but I'm a straight chick."

"No need to worry." Nancy briefly rested one hand on her shoulder. A smile played around the corners of her mouth. "Unlike plenty of other organizations, we don't discriminate on the basis of sexual orientation."

Rory made a show of wiping her forehead with the back of one hand, then gestured toward the set of double doors that they were about to pass. "That's a residence hall."

"And it looks sorely in need of postering." Nancy led the way up the steps, then held open the front door. "Let's get to it."

Chapter Five

One week later

D^o I look okay?" Sarah smoothed the front of her pink oxford shirt and fiddled with the positioning of her belt buckle.

Rory paused her movie, turned, and raised her eyebrows. "Oh yeah. Smokin'."

"I'm trying to look professional. Not hot."

"Well, too bad. You look professionally hot." Rory ducked when Sarah sent a crumpled piece of paper flying at her head. "I bet that the powers that be over there will offer you the position on sight."

Sarah looked at her watch and started pacing. "Seriously, though, I'm up against some tough competition, and they all know this university a lot better than I do. I need to be sharp."

Rory got to her feet and stretched. The movement exposed a tantalizing sliver of olive-toned skin. *Soft*, Sarah thought, before she quickly looked away. She had expected her initial attraction to Rory to wear off, but the feeling had only grown stronger. It was disconcerting, especially since she had no basis for comparison. None of her roommates at Yale had ever affected her this way.

"Listen," Rory said, oblivious to the scrutiny. "I don't think they'll be quizzing you on URI trivia. They probably want what every employer wants—someone who's passionate about the project and will work hard, you know?"

"Yeah, I guess."

"Relax," Rory insisted. "Nancy has a good sense of humor. Have a good time, will you? Joke around with her."

"Good time. Right." Sarah grabbed the miniature basketball from underneath her chair and halfheartedly aimed a shot at the small hoop that Rory had attached to the back of their door. The ball hit the rim and nearly knocked over the trash can. "Oops."

"More arc. You totally straight-armed that."

Sarah rolled her eyes. "Thanks ever so much, Coach."

"Maybe you should do some suicides to get those jitters out of your system."

This time, Sarah laughed. *How does she always have the perfect comeback?* "I'll pass. Besides, it's time for me to go."

"Good luck. Knock 'em dead. Don't pick your nose."

"You and your pearls of wisdom." Sarah opened the door and looked back over her shoulder. "Thanks. See you later."

❖

Nancy's assistant—*Kelly*, Sarah reminded herself—emerged from the inner office and beckoned to her. "We're ready for you now."

Sarah followed her inside and took the indicated seat at a small, round conference table. Nancy sat across it, a file folder and legal pad on the table before her.

"Hey, Sarah. Good to see you again. How are you?"

Relax. Joke around. Rory's advice echoed in her ears, but she'd never been much of an improv comedian. *Best to stick with being polite.* "I'm doing well, thanks. And you?"

"Just fine." Nancy smiled. "We appreciate your coming in today."

Sarah tried to smile back. She was pretty sure that her expression looked sickly. *Relax!* "Well, thanks for having me."

"This shouldn't take long," Nancy said. "We just want to get to know you face-to-face and give you an opportunity to ask us some questions, okay?"

Ah, the "this is not a test" speech. Right. Sarah nodded. "That sounds great."

Nancy looked down at the papers on her desk. "Really interesting résumé you've got here. You're a sailor, huh?"

The question caught Sarah by surprise. She had expected some reference to her two years at Yale, but not about her position on the sailing team. "Was. I don't have time for it here, unfortunately." She resisted the urge to rub her suddenly sweaty palms on her slacks.

"Do you sail?"

"Oh, I've only been out a few times. I'm a rank amateur." Nancy clicked her pen and jotted something down on the legal pad. "Tell me, what made you decide to transfer out of Yale?"

Sarah's stomach lurched, despite the fact that she had anticipated the question and had an answer prepared. "Finances," she said. "My circumstances changed after sophomore year, and I couldn't afford tuition any longer."

Nancy was frowning slightly as she looked across the table, and Sarah wondered whether she suspected the truth. It would be so easy to elaborate, but... *No. I won't play that card.*

"How are you liking URI so far?" was Nancy's next question.

"Oh, I'm enjoying it quite a bit. Especially the GLBT student center."

"It looks like you've gotten very involved there already," Kelly chipped in.

"There's so much going on, and the people are fun." On a whim, Sarah decided to try for some humor, after all. "Very persuasive, too. Somehow I ended up on the dance committee, despite the fact that I have two left feet and no aptitude for interior decorating."

When they both laughed, Sarah felt relieved. She leaned back in her chair and took a deep, slow breath. *All right, Rory. Good call.*

"So," Nancy said, "why don't you tell us a bit about why you applied for this internship?"

Sarah had anticipated this line of questioning, too. She leaned forward slightly. "I know that I don't really have much experience— academic or practical—with the kind of work I'd be doing as your intern." She shrugged. "That probably doesn't make me the most attractive candidate on the planet. But I'm taking a women's studies course right now that's cross-listed with political science, and I'm really enjoying it."

Kelly looked like she wanted to say something, but Sarah continued on before she could be interrupted. "Also, I have to admit that my own coming-out process wasn't exactly smooth. I'm not looking for pity, and I certainly don't think I'm unique. I guess what I'm trying to say is that the fight for equal rights isn't only intellectual to me. It's personal, too. I'm really vested in it."

"I feel exactly the same way," Nancy said.

She had, Sarah noticed, written several more notes down on the paper. *Sure wish I could see what they say.*

"You just talked a lot about your interest in our project," Kelly said. "What other personal qualities do you have that you feel make you a good fit for this position?"

Sarah smiled. This was an easy one. "I'm a hard worker. When I got to Yale, I found out that high school had been a real breeze for some of my peers—that they had barely tried. That was never true for me, and I don't mind admitting it. I wouldn't feel right if I didn't try my hardest at anything I commit to."

"Your transcript is certainly impressive," Nancy said.

Sarah nodded. "I'm planning to go to med school. It has to be."

"Dr. Storm." Kelly raised both eyebrows. "That has a dramatic ring to it."

"Sounds like a character on *General Hospital* to me," Sarah said, grinning.

"Well," Nancy said, "that's about all we need from our end. But if you have any questions for us, please don't hesitate to ask."

"I do have a few, actually." This part was, Sarah knew, just as important as her responses had been. Having no questions, or asking only about superficial matters, would hurt her application. But posing insightful and penetrating questions would show Nancy and Kelly that she wasn't just interested in a line on her résumé— that she cared about Fair Rhode Island and its mission.

She asked them about the precise relationship between GLAD and FRI. She asked about their purpose in creating the internship, and about the nature of the intern's duties. She asked about their priorities and concerns with respect to the referendum. And when she finally sat back and announced that she was out of questions, she had at least as many notes written down as did Nancy.

"Thanks again for coming in," Nancy said as they walked her to the front door of the small office suite. "We'll get in touch with you within the next few days to let you know."

"Will do." Sarah shook her hand, then Kelly's. "Thank you both."

She blew out a long sigh as the door closed behind her. *Whew, all right. That didn't go half bad, I think. Now all I can do is—*

"Sarah, hey! There you are."

"Chelsea?" Sarah blinked in the bright sunlight as Chelsea gave her a swift hug and a light kiss on the cheek. "This is a surprise. What are you doing here?"

"Well, you seemed really worried about this interview. So I thought I'd meet up with you afterward and treat you to ice cream."

"Wow, thanks. That's really nice of you." Sarah rocked back and forth on her heels, uncertain of what to do next. *Can't believe she was here waiting for me.*

"There's a Coldstone Creamery around the corner," Chelsea said. She reached for Sarah's hand and tugged her forward. "C'mon."

When Chelsea didn't relinquish her hand, Sarah decided to just go with it. It felt nice to be close to someone again—someone who clearly wanted her company. Who had sought her out. They'd been crossing paths frequently—on the quad, in the chem building, in the dining hall. Sarah had figured that it was coincidence, but suddenly, she wasn't so sure.

Maybe Rory was right after all. Maybe she does like me. But despite some pretty solid evidence, Sarah couldn't quite believe it. *Chelsea could have anyone at this school. Everyone says so. Why the hell would she pick me?*

"I thought about working in a Coldstone one summer," Sarah said in an attempt to break the slightly awkward silence. "The singing for tips thing really threw me for a loop, though."

Chelsea laughed. "You don't like to sing?"

"Oh, I like it just fine…when I'm in the privacy of my own car with the radio drowning out my very mediocre alto voice." Sarah grabbed the door and held it open. "How about you?"

Chelsea grinned over her shoulder. "I'm in an *a cappella* group here."

"Oh, yeah? That's cool. Which one?"

"Afterhours. It's a co-ed group. We're performing this Friday at the KKG house. You should come."

"Okay, sure."

Once they had ordered, Chelsea led the way to a small table in the back corner. Sarah couldn't help but admire the way her low-cut jeans hugged her butt and thighs. *Hot.* When they sat down, Chelsea sipped at her smoothie and rested one hand on Sarah's left arm. *And okay, she's definitely flirting with me.* It felt nice, sure, but also a little scary. Given how her relationship with Dar had ended, was she really ready to get back on the metaphorical horse?

She's not asking you to marry her, idiot. Chill out and enjoy this. Just…go with it.

"So," Chelsea said, "tell me all about the interview."

Sarah summarized it briefly before turning the subject back to Chelsea's musical aptitude. It was so much easier to be a good listener than to carry the conversation herself. Chelsea was more than willing to talk about her passion for music, her major, and her career plans, topics that lasted them until they were standing outside of Hutchinson.

"I have just been talking your ear off, haven't I?" she said, taking a step closer to Sarah.

"I like hearing about your interests," Sarah said, resisting the urge to move away. *What's wrong with you? Flirt back!*

"One of my interests happens to be you," Chelsea said, looking up intently.

"Oh?" Sarah's mouth felt suddenly dry.

"Yeah." Chelsea reached up to put her arms around Sarah's neck. "Have I told you yet how hot you look today?" When Sarah shook her head slightly, Chelsea rose onto her toes. "You look really, really hot," she whispered into Sarah's right ear.

Sarah shivered at the feeling of their bodies pressed together and Chelsea's warm breath against her face. For a split second, she was disoriented by the unfamiliarity of the embrace. Dar had been—

No! she thought savagely, angry that the memory of Dar had intruded into this moment. Dar had no place in her life, and no place in her head. *She's gone. She didn't want you. But Chelsea's here, and she* does. *Get on with your life.*

Taking a deep breath, Sarah let her hands come to rest on Chelsea's waist. "You're one of the most beautiful women I've ever seen," she said, wishing she'd had more practice at situations like this.

Chelsea's response was to kiss her. Sarah felt her entire body jolt at the combined sensation of Chelsea's lips and tongue against hers. *Whoa.*

"Mmm," Chelsea said when she pulled away. "That was nice."

"Yeah." Sarah cleared her throat "Yeah, uh, thanks. For the ice cream and…everything."

Chelsea's smile was bordering on smug. "See you soon," she said, before spinning on one heel and sashaying away. Sarah watched her go. She still felt a little dazed.

Well. That was…interesting. Her pulse was racing and she desperately needed a drink of water. There was something incredibly attractive about a person who just took what she wanted like that. But on the other hand… *I barely even know her.*

"So get to know her," she muttered as she turned toward the door, wishing she could leave her lingering doubts behind. *Take Rory's advice. Date. Have a good time. Be normal, for Christ's sake.*

❖

The call came on Sunday night, while Sarah was halfheartedly studying for her inorganic chemistry midterm. Bored and restless, she was more than happy to be interrupted by her cell phone.

"Hello?"

"Sarah, this is Nancy, from Fair Rhode Island."

"Oh hi, Nancy." Sarah looked over her shoulder in time to see Rory turn in her desk chair and wave two sets of crossed fingers in the air.

"I'm calling to offer you the internship," Nancy said. "What do you say?"

"Really?" Sarah blurted.

"Yes, really." Nancy sounded amused. "Does that mean you accept?"

"Of course, yes. I'd love the position!" Sarah watched a huge smile break out on Rory's face. She grinned back.

"Excellent. Why don't you come down to the office tomorrow to fill out some paperwork. It'd be great to have you start by the end of this week, if that works for you."

"Definitely. Thank you so much, Nancy. See you tomorrow, then."

Rory war-whooped as soon as Sarah flipped her phone shut. "That's so fantastic!" she said, jumping out of her chair to give Sarah a quick, fierce hug. "Congratulations!"

"I can't really believe it," Sarah said. "God. This is so very cool."

"No more waitressing for you, roomie. You've got a bona fide internship—oh!"

"Oh? Oh, what?"

"Hey, would you mind if I got this moment on film?" Rory said. "I think it might fit in to the documentary."

"Ah, no," Sarah said, surprised and a little bit flattered. "I don't mind. Though…I can't act worth beans."

Rory took her by the shoulders. "I'm making a *documentary*, genius. You're not supposed to act."

She went to the closet, then, and rummaged around briefly.

When she turned around, she was holding a small video camera that she expertly trained on Sarah. "Sarah Storm has just discovered that she's been selected as the student intern for Fair Rhode Island," she said, setting the scene for her future audience. "How do you feel, Sarah?"

"Uh," Sarah said, abruptly self-conscious. Now that Rory was standing there filming her, she realized that being the protagonist of this documentary meant that she'd be seen—and frequently—by many people once the film was finished in the spring. *I may not have to act, but I'd better not look stupid.*

"I feel great," she said, trying to relax. *Forget the camera. Act like this is just a conversation with Rory.* "I can't believe they picked me. I'm really honored. And excited."

"Tell me a little about what you'll be doing in the internship," Rory prompted.

Sarah focused on Rory's face and immediately felt better when she smiled encouragingly. "I'm sure I'll find out more tomorrow," she said. "But based on what I know so far, it sounds like I'll be working primarily to raise awareness on the URI campuses about the proposed amendment and to encourage my peers to vote—hopefully 'no'—in the April election." She shrugged. "If that's going well, I'd also like to work on getting the word out to the broader community."

"Sounds like you'll be busy," Rory said. "Would you mind talking a little about why the Vote No campaign is so important to you?"

"Well, as a lesbian, this campaign has personal significance to me," Sarah said. When she realized that she had just come out on camera, she felt a twinge of panic that subsided as quickly as it had come. "Someday I'm going to fall in love with a woman who feels the same way about me. And when I do, I'm going to want to marry her. Not in Massachusetts or in Canada—*here.*" She couldn't help thinking of Dar, and quickly changed tacks.

"But there's more to my involvement in FRI than my own sexual orientation. Limiting the definition of marriage is unconstitutional. If the proposed amendment passes, the state of Rhode Island will be discriminating against many, many people on the basis of their sexual orientation." The familiar anger at her parents burned in her chest, and she sat up straighter. "That's not just, and I'm going to do everything I can to convince the people of Rhode Island to vote no."

Rory lowered the camera slowly. "You've got my vote," she said, looking thoughtful. "You're really eloquent when you get all fired up, you know that?"

Sarah slumped back into her chair, relieved to be out of the spotlight. "Seriously?"

"Yeah. You're going to be good at convincing people."

"I hope so," Sarah said. She gestured toward the camera. "Was that what you wanted?"

"Yeah, that was excellent," Rory said, leaning against her desk. "I'm thinking that I'll use interviews to contextualize the other footage that I get."

Sarah nodded. She didn't know the first thing about making a movie, but she had seen a few documentaries that worked that way. "Sounds good."

"Thanks for letting me put you on the spot," Rory said. "Especially since you'd probably much rather be celebrating." She pointed to Sarah's cell and waggled her eyebrows. "Don't let me keep you any longer. Call Chelsea up right now. Go have yourself a good time."

Sarah looked at her phone where it lay on the desk, then back at Rory. *I don't want to go out,* she realized. *I want to stay in.*

"I'll tell Chelsea tomorrow," she said, raising one hand to forestall Rory's protest. "What I really feel like doing right now is watching a movie with you."

"Yeah?"

"Yeah. So why don't you pick out something for us—one of the many films I haven't seen but really should."

Rory nodded. "All right, I can do that. As long as you start boiling water for cocoa in that hot pot of yours."

Sarah grinned. "You've got a deal," she said. "I like the way you think."

Chapter Six

Two weeks later

R aise your arms."
When Sarah did, Chelsea whisked off her shirt, then quickly shed her own. Sarah felt her pulse speed up as she took in the lines and curves of Chelsea's naked torso. *Beautiful.*

"I like the way you look at me," Chelsea said. "Now—lie back."

Again, Sarah did as she was told. The sensation of Chelsea's palms brushing over her nipples made her gasp. When Chelsea rolled both between her fingers and lightly pinched them, Sarah's hands moved to Chelsea's shoulders.

"Good?" Chelsea whispered. They were in her room, on her bed. Moonlight streamed in through the window, tinting pale skin silver. Chelsea was on top, and the things she was doing with her talented hands sent bursts of pleasure down Sarah's spine. The sensations settled between her legs.

"Yeah," Sarah said hoarsely. She leaned up to capture Chelsea's lower lip, first sucking on it, then tracing it with her tongue. When Chelsea responded by pinching harder, Sarah's hips bucked.

Chelsea pulled her mouth away and scooted down to use her tongue on Sarah's breasts. Sarah's back arched as Chelsea sucked on one nipple. "God, yeah—"

Chelsea raised her head and looked down at Sarah. They were both breathing hard. "You are so damn hot."

"You're making me crazy."

"I mean to."

Chelsea returned her mouth to Sarah's breasts and let her hand slide down so that her palm was resting over the fly of Sarah's jeans. The pleasure ebbed, suddenly, as Sarah tensed. *Not like this.* But Chelsea clearly misunderstood the reaction and began to nimbly unbutton Sarah's pants.

"No," Sarah blurted.

Chelsea froze and pulled back enough to meet Sarah's gaze. "What's wrong?"

I don't know. Sarah took a deep breath, struggling to come up with an explanation. *Everything was feeling great until it suddenly... wasn't.*

"Your roommate might come back," she said lamely.

Chelsea grinned and went back to popping buttons. "She won't come in. I put our code for 'do not disturb' up on the whiteboard on the door."

Sarah smiled but moved one hand to rest firmly over Chelsea's, halting her progress. "I just...I'd like to wait, if it's okay."

"Oh." Chelsea moved her hand out from under Sarah's and turned onto her side. Sarah moved in to spoon her, pressing a soft kiss against the nape of her neck.

"I've disappointed you. I'm sorry."

Chelsea's laugh was rueful, but she snuggled back against Sarah's body. "Maybe a little. Sorry if I was moving too fast. My ex and I slept together on our very first date, so I guess two weeks feels like a long time."

Sarah closed her eyes, uncertain of what to say. She hadn't waited very long before sleeping with Dar, either. *So what's wrong with me now? Chelsea wants me. She's incredible at foreplay.* Sarah buried her face between Chelsea's shoulder blades, glad that her bedmate couldn't see her face. *Why can't I just relax and have a good time? Why can't I just be like Corrie?*

One thing was certain: nothing more was going to happen tonight. *Way to kill the mood, champ.*

"Hang in there with me," she whispered. "Okay?"

Chelsea pulled Sarah's arm more tightly around her. "No problem." She laughed softly. "I think it's sweet that you want to wait, actually."

Sarah decided not to reply. Better for Chelsea to believe her sweet, or old fashioned, or noble, than for her to know the truth.

I'm afraid. How messed up is that?

❖

Half an hour later, Sarah zipped up her jacket as she left Chelsea's dorm. She walked across the quad slowly, kicking at fallen leaves and wondering what the hell was wrong with her.

I like her, I really do. But maybe that was the problem. She had fallen head over heels for Dar. Even now, despite how that relationship had crashed and burned, Sarah could remember the profound depth of her emotion. *So intense. So crazy intense.* While she was attracted to Chelsea and found her fun to be with, that kind of passion was definitely missing.

Everyone who knew about the breakup, and even some who didn't, had encouraged her to get out, meet new people, date. It had certainly seemed like a good idea a few weeks ago. But now, Sarah was starting to have doubts. *What if that's not how it works for me? What if I'm incapable of...dating?*

She blew a long sigh into the mid-October night and watched her breath dissipate into the air. As she turned toward Hutchinson, she found herself wishing that it were really that easy to blend into her surroundings, seamlessly becoming part of everything around her.

It's been less than two months. You're still settling in. Give yourself some time. The funny thing was that for all intents and purposes, her life looked good. She was doing well in school. She was dating *Chelsea*, of all people. Money was tight, but she was managing. Just yesterday, Nancy had remarked on how many student volunteers she was bringing in to FRI. By all counts, she was successful, and should be happy. *So why do I feel so...off?*

Sarah shook her head and walked faster, as though she could

outpace her existential crisis. *I'll feel better when I'm back home.* Rory's sharp wit and acerbic tongue always made her laugh.

❖

Sarah opened the door to find Rory pacing the length of their room, holding the telephone to her ear and speaking rapidly in Korean. Her voice was elevated slightly—the conversation didn't sound exactly comfortable. Once in a while, an English word stuck out in her speech, like a boulder breaking the flow of a whitewater river. Most of what Sarah could make out seemed to pertain to Rory's film classes.

Sarah went to her desk and sat down. She couldn't offer Rory privacy, really, but she could at least try to just go about her business and not pry. She cracked open her physical chemistry textbook to the week's chapter but was unable to move past the first paragraph on the page. Instead, she was mesmerized by the cadence of Rory's voice.

So cool. I wonder which she learned first. Does she dream in Korean? Sarah was impressed. She had taken several years of Spanish in high school, but it had never really stuck. *Admit it. You never really tried to become anything more than proficient. How amazing would it be to be fluent in another language?*

"Yeah," Rory said. "Uh-huh, okay. Bye." She set the phone back in its cradle, rolled her eyes at Sarah, and flopped down into one of the beanbag chairs in front of the television with a heavy sigh. "Parents."

No kidding. Sarah's stomach rolled the way it always did when she thought about her family. In over two months, she hadn't heard a word from them. She swallowed down the anger and worked to change the subject. "Maybe this is a weird thing to say, but listening to you speak Korean is really cool."

Rory laughed. "That's hilarious. My Korean is for shit." She picked up an Xbox controller and began fiddling with the buttons. "My older sister, Michelle, now *she* can speak it. I suck."

"Well," Sarah said stubbornly, "it sounds beautiful to me."

"If you say so." Rory shrugged, "I just wish they'd leave me alone sometimes, you know? Their pestering drives me crazy." She looked up at Sarah. "Yours never call. Mine should take a page out of their book."

Sarah felt like she'd been punched in the chest. Her heart lurched crazily, and she couldn't take a deep breath. She stayed very still and tried to act like everything was normal, but Rory must have seen something in her face, because she sat up and frowned.

"What? What is it?"

Sarah shook her head. Sudden tears burned behind her eyes. She wanted to speak but couldn't. *Pull yourself together!*

"Sarah? Did I—I mean…what's wrong?" Rory scooted forward and tentatively rested her hand on Sarah's knee.

"Don't wish that." Sarah felt as though the words had been pulled from her throat.

"I'm sorry," Rory said. She looked confused, and worried. "Look, whatever it is…you don't have to tell me, 'kay? No pressure."

Her voice was soft and the heat of her palm soaked into Sarah's skin, warming her. Anchoring her. *Feels so good.* Suddenly, she could breathe freely again.

I should tell her. She had been keeping the truth from Rory to avoid pity. But what use was there in hiding it now? Rory was her friend—the closest friend she had. She had proven that. *And I'm tired of carrying this all by myself.*

When she felt relief, Sarah knew that she had made the right decision.

"I don't talk to my parents anymore," she said quietly, focusing on a small coffee stain on the floor next to Rory's feet. "This past summer, they found out that I'm queer. They were going to put me in counseling, and refused to continue paying tuition for Yale. When I left home and told them I wasn't coming back, they disowned me. That's why I transferred here."

She paused, but Rory didn't say a word. Sarah didn't trust herself to look Rory in the eyes, so she focused on the warm pressure of Rory's hand on her leg and took an unsteady breath.

"I haven't spoken to them since they cut me off. Fortunately, loans and my job are bringing in just enough money to keep me afloat."

Rory took her hand away and got to her feet. Sarah instantly missed her comforting touch. She looked up to see her pacing, from the door to the television and back again.

"I'm angry," Rory said suddenly. Her voice was low and tight. She didn't stop walking, and she didn't meet Sarah's gaze. "I know that doesn't help you, but I am. Really, really angry."

Sarah felt her lips twist in something like a smile. She suddenly wanted to shelter Rory—to protect her from the same feelings that she was still fighting.

"I know what you mean. And it does help." She caught Rory's hand as she passed by, arresting her progress across the room. "Thank you."

Rory squeezed her fingers. "I am so, so sorry that I brought it up."

"You didn't know. It's all right. And frankly, it feels good to tell you." Sarah let go of Rory's hand to massage the back of her neck. *So tense, these days. Always so damn tense.* "I'd rather not have anyone else—"

"I won't tell a soul," Rory said immediately. "Not even Matt. Please don't worry about that."

"Okay. Thanks."

Rory flopped back down onto the beanbag chair. When she looked up at Sarah, her face was troubled. "If there's anything I can do, anything at all…tell me, okay? Please?"

In an instant, Sarah's relief soured into guilt for burdening Rory with her problems. *You idiot. Why didn't you just let it go when she gave you the out?* She shook her head firmly. "No worries. I'm doing just fine, really. And I shouldn't have laid all that on you. I'm sorry."

"Sarah."

The way Rory said her name—so very gently—made Sarah blink back more tears. *Shit.* Rory's gaze held hers, even though she wanted to look away.

"Please don't apologize. I wanted to know. It's no burden."

Sarah nodded. Miraculously, even her inner skeptic was convinced of Rory's sincerity.

"Now," Rory continued, switching to her usual, teasing tone. "I dunno about you, but I'm suddenly in the mood to blow shit up." She gestured toward her Xbox. "How about a little Halo action?"

Sarah laughed even as she swiped the back of one hand across her eyes. "I told you, I'm abysmal at video games. Hopeless. Never even had a Nintendo when I was a kid."

"Oh, what, you're such an old dog that you can't learn any new tricks?" Rory tossed her second controller to Sarah and gestured toward the unoccupied beanbag chair. "Get down here. I'll teach you."

Sarah rolled her eyes, but followed Rory's orders. While the game loaded, Rory explained the functions of each of the buttons and both joysticks. The more she said, the more apprehensive Sarah felt.

"I'm going to suck at this," she warned, holding the controller gingerly. "Are you sure this is going to be cathartic and not incredibly frustrating?"

Rory bumped her shoulder and pressed the Start key. "You're not supposed to be a genius at it right away, child prodigy. It's a *game*. No frustration allowed. Now hit 'A'."

Rory cycled through a series of options on the screen that left Sarah feeling dizzy. "What are you doing?"

"Choosing weapons and a place to fight," Rory said. "We're each going to have a shotgun. I'm going to stand in the middle of everything and you're going to practice on me. All right?"

"Um, sure."

Sarah manipulated the joystick clumsily and watched her avatar move back and forth across the screen with jerky movements. "See? I'm sucking already. And I feel kind of seasick."

"You're doing fine," Rory said. "Just run over here. Good. Now, make sure your gun sight is on me. Yeah, like that."

"Now what?"

Rory grinned ferally. "Pull the trigger."

When Sarah did, Rory's screen started blinking and alarm bells went off. "Nice shot!" said Rory. "Now do it again."

Sarah obliged, and Rory's heavily armored avatar fell to the ground. "Whoa," she said. "That thing packs quite a punch."

Rory held up her hand for a high five. "Cathartic, yeah? Like I said."

"Look at the size of this gun," Sarah said, playing along. "How…phallic and empowering."

Rory laughed and leaned toward Sarah, her dark eyes glittering. "C'mon, Storm, let's go again, and this time I won't be quite so easy on you."

The innocent appellation made Sarah freeze momentarily. *Storm.* Her friends at Yale had called her that. But hearing her last name now, out of Rory's mouth, didn't produce the nostalgic pang she had expected. It just sounded good. *I'm exactly where I want to be.*

"Bring it on, Song," she declared, relaxing into the competitive banter. Right here, right now, she didn't feel out of place at all. "Let's see what you've got!"

CHAPTER SEVEN

One month later

Rory, perched in the corner of Nancy's office behind her tripod, zoomed out on the three women sitting at the conference table when Nancy finished her summation of FRI's financial situation and sat back in her chair.

"Okay—anything else, before we quit for the day?"

"I have an idea that I'd like to run past you both," Sarah said. Rory shifted the camera angle slightly and zoomed back in, focusing on Sarah. "I've been doing some research into how organizations in other states have worked to protest similar amendments. In Wisconsin, they organized a candlelight vigil at the Capitol building. Apparently that was well attended by students and community members alike."

Rory smiled as both Kelly and Susan leaned forward eagerly. Sarah had run the idea by her on their way to the FRI office earlier this afternoon, and Rory thought it was brilliant. Now, as she watched Sarah begin to pitch the vigil to her superiors, she felt proud of her creativity and persuasiveness.

She really is a professional, Rory mused, keeping an eye on the camera to ensure that Sarah hadn't moved out of its field of vision. On second thought, Rory zoomed out again, wanting the audience to be able to see just how convincing Sarah could be. No one could resist her. Over the past few weeks, Rory had watched her transform even the most apathetic GLBT students and allies into burgeoning activists. Rory was certain that even if she hadn't been documenting the Vote No campaign, Sarah would have gotten her involved.

"So, if you think this is a good plan," Sarah was saying, "I'll go ahead and get in touch with student leaders at Brown and Providence College to see what they think."

"That sounds great," Kelly said. She looked to Nancy, who was nodding enthusiastically.

"I agree," Nancy chipped in. "Excellent idea. I may be able to get us some pretty high-powered speakers, too, depending on the date."

Sarah smiled brilliantly at the praise. Rory felt her own lips curve up. It was impossible not to be affected by Sarah's happiness. The only thing better than seeing that expression was being the cause of it.

"I'll make some phone calls tomorrow to get the ball rolling," Sarah said. "If Brown and PC are on board, I'd like to set a date before we hit the Thanksgiving holiday."

"Good," Nancy said. She pushed her chair back. "Okay. I think we're done for the day."

Rory turned off her camera and made a few notes about the afternoon of filming. Some of her earlier footage would work well in a montage, while the staff meeting might be something to show in pieces, interspersed with a few interviews. She waved good-bye as Kelly left the office, then she folded up her tripod and slid it into its carrying case. Yawning, she meandered over to Sarah's desk, where Sarah was frowning intently at her computer.

"Didn't you hear it's closing time? Whatcha doing?"

"Updating the Vote No Facebook page." Sarah looked over her shoulder and smiled. "We broke five hundred members today."

"That is kick-ass!"

"Yeah, it really is." Sarah turned back to the computer. "How'd filming go?"

"I got some excellent office footage. Your staff meeting, you on the phone, you printing flyers. Good stuff."

Sarah looked skeptical. "Sounds kind of boring, actually."

"Yeah, well, it'd be less boring if you took my suggestion to wear leather to work. You know, like Kate Beckinsale in *Underworld*." Not for the first time, Rory considered just how ridiculously hot Sarah would look in that kind of outfit. *She has the perfect body for it.*

Sarah burst out laughing and spun around in her chair. "And what kind of message would that send, exactly, about this campaign?"

Rory smirked. "The sexy kind."

"Hmm." Sarah leaned back and steepled her fingers beneath her chin. "I can see the slogan now: 'It's sexy to vote no.'"

"Exactly!" Rory poked Sarah in the shoulder. "It's all about the marketing. You're learning quickly."

Sarah rolled her eyes. "You are so crazy."

"Yeah, and I'm also starving. Want to hit the dining hall?"

"Sure. I'm done here."

Rory slung the tripod case and camera bag over one shoulder while Sarah zipped up her backpack. She would have preferred to eat at her favorite Thai restaurant in downtown Kingston, but it was kind of expensive, and Sarah would insist on going dutch. *Caf food it is, then.*

As they walked back toward campus, they passed a wide variety of storefronts. The window displays were universally Thanksgiving-themed. Rory cast a sidelong glance at Sarah, who hadn't yet mentioned her plans. Rory hadn't wanted to bring it up, but at this point, with just over a week until the holiday, she had to say something.

"You should come home with me for Thanksgiving," she said, deciding that bluntness was the best strategy. "I bet you've never had a Korean-American turkey dinner before."

Sarah turned her head and smiled, but the expression never reached her eyes. "Thanks, that's really nice of you. But I'm all set—going to stay with some friends in Wakefield. The ones who put me up after I left home."

"Cool, okay." Rory wrestled with her disappointment. She had just assumed that Sarah had nowhere else to go, and would be a part of her Turkey Day experience. *Dammit—should have asked her earlier. Idiot.* "Are you going there for Christmas, too?" she asked.

"I'm staying in the dorms, actually."

"What?" Rory swung her head around so quickly that her neck hurt. *The hell you are!* "No way. You can—"

Sarah held up one hand. Her smile was genuine now. "Don't worry. I'm going to Corrie's on Christmas Day. I just decided to stay here because I have a lot to get done."

"FRI stuff?"

"Yeah. I have to work on pulling together the big debate we're having in January. And I also need to complete a bunch of applications. For Yale, for scholarships…feels like there's a billion, and they all have deadlines of early next year."

"Oh. Gotcha."

They continued on in silence, but Rory's brain was working furiously. *Of course she's going back to Yale, dumbass. Why wouldn't she?* Suddenly, she was uncertain about whether she wanted dinner after all. Her stomach felt queasy.

"Thanks for inviting me to your place," Sarah said. She bumped Rory's shoulder with her own. "That really means a lot."

As always, it was easy to take refuge in teasing banter. "I didn't realize how popular you were," Rory countered. "Should've invited you sooner."

"Ha ha ha." Sarah kicked at a rock on the sidewalk and sent it spinning into the gutter. "You know, I've decided that the silver lining about being disowned is that you don't have as many presents to buy."

"I see what you mean," Rory said, deciding to play along. "Maybe I should try that tactic. I'm stumped on what to get my mom."

Sarah chuckled, but it sounded forced. *Good try, babe*, Rory thought. The wound was clearly still too fresh to be a laughing matter. Watching her stride along, shoulders hunched as though she were facing down some kind of invisible wind, made Rory's heart flip-flop in sympathy. And then suddenly, she had an idea.

"You're in no rush, right?"

"Huh?" Sarah looked up, surprised. "No, not really. Got a dance committee meeting at nine, but nothing before then. Why?"

"I want to show you something. It's nearby, don't worry." *This will be perfect.*

"Feel like divulging more details?"

Rory grinned. "Nope. You're gonna have to trust me."

Sarah heaved a sigh. "Looks like my life is in your hands, then."

Rory led her west a few blocks, into one of the residential areas of Kingston. Then she turned left, up a narrow, winding street. At the hill's crest was a small park, nestled between two colonial style homes. It sported a swing set, a jungle gym, and a sandbox that looked like it could use some refilling.

"Here." Rory set her bags on the ground and sat down in one of the swings.

"Here?" Sarah stood with her arms crossed under her breasts. The setting sun made it impossible for Rory to see her face, but she sounded dubious.

Rory pointed to the swing next to her as she rose into the air. "How long since you've been on one of these?"

"Not since elementary school, I guess." Sarah sat, then pumped her legs once. "Just like riding a bike."

"Feels good, doesn't it?" Rory swung higher, until her butt lifted slightly off the seat at the apex of each pass. She looked over to see Sarah grinning widely.

"It really does."

"That's what I like about swinging. You have to smile, at least once. No matter what the fuck is going on in your life." She watched as Sarah leaned back, her face turned up toward the sky. For once, she looked carefree.

"Yeah. I get that."

They swung for a while in silence. Rory breathed in the crisp November air and felt her stomach settle. *Exactly what I needed.* "There's just something peaceful about it," she said finally.

"Could be the rocking motion. Reminds us of the womb, maybe?"

"There's a thought." Rory pumped hard to regain some lost momentum. "But it's exhilarating, too, you know? When you close your eyes, it almost feels like you're flying."

"Whoa, yeah," Sarah said, a moment later. "That's cool."

"Tell me something. If you could have a superpower—any superpower—what would it be?"

Sarah laughed. "Have I ever told you how much I enjoy the way your brain jumps from random topic to random topic?"

"No," Rory said. "And you haven't answered my question, either."

"You're such a taskmaster. And I guess...I think I'd want to be able to heal. Any disease. Be the ultimate doctor."

Of course you would. Behind her closed eyes, Rory had a sudden glimpse of Sarah as a pediatrician, talking in a gentle voice to an anxious young child. The imagined scene made her stomach feel strange again.

"I think you'd be a very busy lady," she said, swinging higher in an effort to shake off the odd feeling.

"Well, how about you?' Sarah challenged. "Oh wait, I know. You'd make movies that could tell the future. Sort of like that painter in *Heroes*."

"The one who gets his head ripped open and his brain eaten?" Rory screwed up her face. "Yuck. No thanks!"

"Well, what then?"

"I want the ability to make the world's best frozen margarita." *But I'll settle for the power to crack you up.*

When Sarah laughed again, Rory was certain that it had been a good idea to show her this place. It had never occurred to her to tell anyone about it before—not even Matt. She tilted her head back and exhaled slowly, watching the naked arms of the surrounding trees sway in the breeze. Somehow, the world made sense when she was here. *Wish I could just stay like this forever.*

"Do you come here a lot?" Sarah asked, snapping her out of her reverie.

"Once in a while. Mostly when something's bugging me." Rory

turned her head to meet Sarah's curious gaze. "Some people go to therapy. I swing."

"Free, fun, and mildly aerobic." Sarah grinned. "Sounds good to me."

Rory looked back up in just enough time to catch the instant when the orange and pink faded from the clouds, rendering them black in a cobalt sky. For some reason, witnessing that moment made her heart thump painfully.

"Do you believe in the soul?"

"Yes. Why?"

Rory could feel Sarah looking at her, but kept her own eyes fixed on the darkening horizon. "This will sound weird, but when I'm swinging, it's like...I can feel my soul. Actually, honest-to-God feel it sort of burning inside me."

There was a long moment of silence. *Great*, Rory thought. *Now she thinks I'm really psychotic. Nice job, Song.* The disappointment from earlier returned, tenfold. *And I was sure she'd under—*

"I know what you mean," Sarah said quietly. "I've felt the same thing, sometimes. Mostly it happens to me when I'm out on the water, sailing." She scuffed her feet along the ground, decreasing her speed. "Never told anybody before, though."

"Me, neither." Rory took a deep breath before jumping off her swing. She twisted in midair to face Sarah when she landed. "It'll be our secret, yeah?"

Sarah nodded as she slowed to a halt. "Okay." A second later, her stomach growled loudly, breaking the somber mood that had settled over them. "I think my stomach is telling us to get food, posthaste."

Rory shouldered her bags. "Sounds like." She turned toward the sidewalk, but paused when she felt Sarah's hand on her arm.

"Thank you for this," Sarah said. "I have a feeling I'll be back soon."

Rory opened her mouth to reply, but the shrill ring of Sarah's cell phone cut her off.

"It's Chelsea." Sarah put the phone to her ear. "Hey. What's up?" She paused to listen. Rory couldn't make out any of the words, but Chelsea's voice had an edge to it.

"Oh, I'm sorry," Sarah said. "Didn't realize. I've just been hanging out with Rory. We're heading to the dining hall now. Want to meet us there?"

Huh. Wonder if she's jealous. It was an amusing and oddly satisfying thought. Chelsea was a good person, but the way she'd latched on to Sarah was starting to irk Rory. *She's high maintenance, and Sarah's already got more than enough on her plate.* Not for the first time, Rory wondered whether she had done the right thing in pushing that relationship to happen.

"See you soon," Sarah was saying. "Bye."

Rory arched an eyebrow. "You in trouble?"

"Apparently I managed to foil her surprise. She'd planned for us to have dinner off campus tonight." Sarah sounded contrite. "She seemed kind of mad, but how was I supposed to know?"

"And now she has to settle for the decidedly unromantic ambience of Roger Williams." Rory patted Sarah on the back. "Nice going."

Sarah looked at her balefully. "I don't need you laying on the guilt trip, too!"

"Yeah, because you should *totally* feel guilt over this. You're her girlfriend, not her Ken doll." She cocked her head and narrowed her eyes. "Though come to think of it, you sort of look like Ken—"

"Oh be quiet," Sarah said, poking Rory just below the ribs.

"Um, news flash: you are the ticklish one. Not me." When Rory poked her back, Sarah squawked. "Now c'mon, let's hustle." Rory picked up her pace, grinning cheekily over her shoulder. "Don't want to keep Barbie waiting."

❖

Later that night, Sarah opened her door to the sight of Jeff Lee leaning over Rory, while both of them watched something on her computer. She was glad that neither had turned to look at her, because she was sure that her expression was one of shock. *What is* he *doing here?*

"I don't have much so far," Rory was saying, "but hopefully it's enough for you to get a feel for the project."

"Yeah, definitely." Jeff stood up straight and scrubbed a hand through his short, spiky hair. "You're going to follow the whole campaign?"

"All the way up to the referendum in April." Rory looked up at him. "So? What do you say?"

Sarah took off her jacket and moved further into the room. She settled into one beanbag chair with her bio textbook, but couldn't resist casting furtive glances toward Rory and her crush. Sarah had only seen Jeff from afar, when Rory had pointed him out one day near the beginning of school. He was about her height and was dressed in low-riding jeans and a dark, long-sleeved shirt.

"I'll do it," he said.

"Excellent!"

Jeff smiled. He had a great smile, Sarah realized. A great smile and really big, expressive eyes. *No wonder she's into him.*

"How about I come up with a few possible themes and try them out on you after Thanksgiving? They'll be really basic, but at least I can get a sense early on of what you'd like."

"Sounds great," Rory said. Sarah could tell that she was simultaneously very excited, and trying to keep her cool. It was cute. And for some reason, it made her stomach hurt.

"By the way," Rory continued, pointing at her, "this is my roommate, Sarah. Sarah, meet Jeff."

Sarah got up to shake Jeff's hand. His fingertips were callused— no doubt from hours spent with his violin and guitar. "Good to meet you," she said.

"Jeff's just agreed to do the score for my documentary," Rory said. She turned back toward him. "I really can't tell you how much I appreciate this."

"Well hey, it's not like I'm being totally selfless." Jeff shrugged on a black jacket and shouldered his bag. "Gets me some publicity, and I might even be able to pitch this as a final project for one of next semester's courses."

"Sweet." Rory got to her feet and stretched. Her shirt rode up, as usual. Sarah thought she might be doing it on purpose this time. Sure enough, she caught Jeff looking at that tantalizing sliver of skin. A wave of pure fury rendered her suddenly breathless.

What the hell? Sarah berated herself, disgusted at her reaction. *This is ridiculous. Quit it.* She clenched her teeth and focused hard on regaining control of her emotions. *They're talking about school. It's not like he asked her out on a date or anything. And even if he did...so what? Rory's straight. And I'm happy with Chelsea.*

Oh yeah? her internal skeptic asked snidely. *Then why are you still putting her off whenever she wants to have sex?*

Sarah gritted her teeth and mentally slapped that annoying voice. *I'm just not ready yet. It's too soon after Dar. That's all.*

Jeff's "See you later" interrupted her internal debate, and she looked up in time to wave as he headed for the door. When it closed behind him, Rory pumped one fist in the air.

"I cannot *believe* he said yes!" She paced the length of the room, gesticulating wildly as she spoke. "He is so fucking talented. You'll see. Or, well, you'll hear. It's just insane that he's actually going to do it. Insane."

Sarah couldn't have stopped herself from smiling even if she'd wanted to. Rory's enthusiasm was infectious. "That is so great," she said. "And I don't think it's insane at all. Clearly he wants his music to be associated with a high-quality film."

Rory frowned at her. "Seriously? You really think?"

"I really know." Sarah straddled her desk chair and fixed Rory with the most serious look she could muster. "You're the one who keeps saying how brilliant he is. Seems obvious to me that he can recognize genius, too."

Rory sat in the other beanbag chair, still beaming. "I hope you're right," she said.

"And he's good-looking," Sarah prompted. She felt a fierce and sudden need to know whether Rory's long-carried torch for Jeff was still burning brightly.

"Well, duh."

Sarah's stomach lurched. "So you still like him?" She wondered why she was pushing, even as she did.

"Yeah, but it's completely hopeless," Rory said. "Utterly and completely. He has no idea I exist, that way."

"Oh, I don't know," Sarah said, remembering how Jeff's gaze had wandered over Rory's body. "I wouldn't be so sure."

Rory, probably thinking that she was spouting meaningless platitudes, changed the subject entirely. "Enough about me. How was your meeting?"

Sarah thought for a moment about not letting Rory get away with it, but she didn't want to risk making her mad. "Same old, same old. We still can't agree on a color scheme for the decorations."

"Well, you still have plenty of time. The dance is in February, right?"

Sarah nodded. "And you're coming, right?"

"Wouldn't miss it."

"You should ask Jeff to be your date," Sarah said, unable to resist the opening. *What if it weren't hopeless, Rory? What then?*

Rory looked at her as though she had announced that she were going to start wearing dresses and applying makeup. "What part of 'completely hopeless' do you not understand? And besides, I don't think silly college dances are Jeff's style." She batted her eyelashes and smiled too sweetly. "You're just gonna have to deal with me third-wheeling as always."

"What? You are not a third wheel." *And if I've ever made you feel that way, then I am seriously doing something wrong!*

"Hmm," Rory said, flipping on the television. "So you say. Now shut up and come watch last week's *Bionic Woman* with me."

This time, Sarah let Rory change the subject for good. She stretched out next to her on the floor and pillowed her chin on her hands. "Yes, boss."

CHAPTER EIGHT

Early December

Rory knocked lightly on the door to Professor Danser's office, and opened it when he told her to come in. She was a little nervous about this interview, since Professor Danser, on the verge of retirement, was probably the most famous member of the English department faculty. Fortunately, she had done well in his introductory theory course last year and was fairly certain that he liked her. He was also, Rory thought, quite possibly the most charming man she had ever met. Tall and slender, impeccably well dressed and sporting a refined British accent, he was sophistication incarnate.

"Hello, Rory," he said in a deep baritone. "Nice to see you again."

"Thanks for making time for me, Professor," Rory said, easing her bags onto the floor across from his desk. "I know you're busy."

"Not too busy for a good cause," he said. "Will that far corner do for your equipment?"

"That'll be fine." Rory set to work assembling her camera and tripod, trying desperately to think of small talk. Fortunately, Professor Danser made it easy for her.

"My partner and I have been following Fair Rhode Island's campaign with a great deal of interest, as you can imagine," he said. "How did you become involved?"

Rory stifled a smile, wondering if that was Prof D's roundabout way of asking her if she was queer. "My roommate is the student intern for FRI," she said. "When she explained their mission to me, I realized that the campaign was the perfect topic for my documentary."

He nodded and Rory went back to fiddling with the orientation of her camera and thinking of Sarah. As the semester had begun to wind down, they had both become even busier, and Rory missed the days when it had been normal to hang out in the room with Sarah for a few hours every night. Now, she was either studying in the Biology building, studying in the library, or working in the FRI office. What little free time she did have went by default to Chelsea. Not for the first time, a wave of jealousy broke over Rory, causing her hands to fumble at the familiar controls. She bit back a sigh and leaned closer, exasperated at herself for letting their relationship get to her. It was just that for some reason, the more she saw Sarah and Chelsea together, the more she didn't like Chelsea. Which was strange, because she had considered Chelsea a friend—if not a *close* friend—for years now.

"All right," Rory said, struggling to focus on the task at hand. She pressed the Record button and nodded to her audience. "I'm all set, Professor. I have a list of questions that I can ask you, of course, or we can just have a conversation about what Fair Rhode Island's campaign means to you and why you feel that it's important."

"Well," Professor Danser said, a slight smile curling his lips, "since I am a professor, why don't I go ahead and profess, and you can interrupt me with questions or comments as you see fit."

Rory laughed. "Fair enough. That makes my job easy."

Professor Danser cleared his throat, adjusted his tie, and looked straight into the camera. "I have been a scholar of literature for over forty years," he said. "I am not a lawyer, nor am I a politician, nor a theologian. I am in no way an expert on marriage. But I *am* an expert in loving my partner, another man, with whom I have shared a bed and a home for thirty-five years."

Rory felt goose bumps rise on her forearms at the strength of emotion behind Professor Danser's words. "Have you and your partner ever wanted to get married, Professor?" she asked.

He nodded. "We've wished for that option since the beginning. And like any two mature people who intend to build a life together, we deserve to have our relationship sanctioned by *this* state. We deserve to be able to co-own a house without having to add special clauses to the title. We deserve the right to visit each other in the hospital in the case of an emergency—God forbid—without filling out power of attorney forms that may not be respected anyway."

Rory zoomed in closer as he spoke, wanting her future audience to become as caught up in the cadence and substance of the professor's words as she was. "What would you say to those who are in favor of the proposed amendment?"

Professor Danser arched his snowy eyebrows. His expression was mild, but his tone was quietly vehement. "I would have them remember that it was not so long ago that interracial marriages were illegal in most states. When we look back on those laws, we call them—and their makers—racist and bigoted." He paused, staring down the camera as though it were the lawmakers in question. "The issue of gay marriage is not qualitatively different. It will become a reality—if not next year, then the year after that. Or ten years after that. I would ask the state of Rhode Island to be forward-thinking, courageous, and compassionate *now*, when our position on this question can truly make a difference."

Rory let out her breath slowly. *I've got to use part of this in my commercial,* she thought. *He's an incredible speaker, and he'll probably appeal to the older demographic.*

"I couldn't agree more, Professor," she said. "Before I stop recording, is there anything you'd like to add?"

Professor Danser smiled briefly, still focused exclusively on the camera. "Vote no."

Rory grinned back. How could she be anything less than optimistic, given the professor's testimonial? *I can't wait to show this to you, Sarah,* she thought as she packed everything up. *You're going to love it.*

❖

Sarah paused near the classroom door as her women's studies professor rifled through the tall stack of papers on her desk. Professor Torrey was a willowy woman whose long, silver hair reached almost to her waist. She ran a casual, lively class that Sarah had been enjoying since the first day of the semester.

"Here you are, Sarah," she said, handing over Sarah's paper face-down. "And actually, do you have a few minutes to talk right now?"

Sarah's heart trip-hopped in her chest at the question. *Oh jeez. Did I really botch up the assignment?* Professor Torrey didn't look upset or disappointed, though. In fact, she was smiling. *That's got to be a good sign, right?*

"Sure thing," Sarah said. She dropped her backpack onto a nearby chair and leaned against the desk attached to it. While the rest of the class filed out the door, Sarah flipped her paper over to see the grade.

Relief blossomed in her gut. *Oh thank God,* she thought, looking down at the bright red "A" next to her name.

"All set," Professor Torrey said. "Thanks for waiting around."

"Of course."

The professor began putting books into her bags as she spoke. "I just wanted to tell you in person how impressed I was with your paper's treatment of the politics around the upcoming referendum."

Sarah flushed at the compliment. "Really? Thank you!"

Professor Torrey slung her bag over one shoulder and nodded. "Most people would have approached this issue much more canonically," she said. "They would have assumed that two and only two monolithic entities are involved—the 'straights' who want an amendment passed, and the 'gays' who want it shot down."

Sarah shook her head. "I hear that perspective often, at work. I think it's really problematic to discount the gray area."

"I couldn't agree more," Professor Torrey said. "And that's why your discussion of how banning civil unions will be detrimental to heterosexual couples is so smart and thoughtful."

Sarah grinned. The praise—from someone she respected so highly—was intoxicating. "I'm glad that you think so."

"What's your major?" Professor Torrey asked, looking at Sarah intently.

"Chemistry," Sarah said. "I'm pre-med."

"Ah." Professor Torrey moved toward the door, indicating for Sarah to walk with her. "It's clear that you're highly motivated, and I'm sure you'll make an excellent doctor. But I can also see that you're passionate about the law, and about social justice. More than that, you're a strong, effective writer." She paused at the stairwell near the end of the hallway. "If you ever decide that the medical profession isn't your heart's desire, I'd encourage you to consider going to law school. I think you'd find it illuminating."

Sarah was surprised. It had never occurred to her to study law. *But why not? You're surrounded by lawyers at FRI. What they're doing is so important.*

"Thanks, Professor," she said. "I'll keep that in mind."

Professor Torrey nodded. "Have a good weekend, Sarah."

"You, too."

Sarah thought about their conversation as she walked back to her room. She had wanted to be a doctor for as long as she could remember. *I've never even considered another profession—not seriously.* And yet, she was getting passionate about this referendum, and the politics around it, in a way that she'd never experienced before—so much so that she was thinking about taking a political science course next semester. *Law school. Huh.*

But as she turned into the stairwell and jogged up toward the third floor, reality set in. She already had student loans that needed paying off, and whatever professional school option she chose would just create more debt.

"Oh, shut up," she muttered to her inner pragmatist. "Let me dream."

Sarah got out her keys as she approached her room, but tried the handle first. To her delight, the door swung open. *Rory's home.* Eagerly, she stepped inside, brandishing her paper. "Check *this* out!"

"Hey, you." Rory said. She swiveled around in her desk chair and gave Sarah that welcoming grin that always made her feel like a million bucks. "What's up?"

"Look what Prof. T gave me on the most recent paper," Sarah said, proudly displaying the A for Rory. "And she thinks I should go to law school."

"Law school?" Rory raised her eyebrows. "Sarah Storm, Esquire?"

Sarah grinned. "Sounds sophisticated. What do you think?"

"I think you should totally be a public defender. Like in *My Cousin Vinny*."

Sarah rolled up her paper and smacked Rory in the shoulder with it. "No way. I'd go civil, not criminal." She rested her palms on Rory's desk and leaned in to look at her computer screen. "What are you working on?"

When Rory leaned her head against Sarah's arm for a moment, Sarah had to fight the sudden urge to kiss her on the forehead. She blinked hard. Those little compulsions were happening more and more frequently, and they rattled her. She had to stay in control. The last thing she wanted to do was make a stupid, careless mistake that would estrange her from Rory.

"I just so happen to be editing footage of my favorite roommate," Rory said, pointing toward the spot in the frame where Sarah was frozen in the act of distributing flyers outside the dining hall.

"I'm your only roommate."

"D'oh!" said Rory. "You caught me. And, hey, remind me to show you my theory professor's interview at some point, okay? It was incredible."

"Cool. I will." But as she stood looking at the paused video, Sarah had an idea that had nothing to do with FRI or the amendment. The conversation with Professor Torrey had left her feeling cheerful, and she was in the mood to have some fun. *I know just the thing.*

"Hey, are you slammed tonight? Do you have a lot of stuff to get done for tomorrow?"

Rory shook her head. "Just working on this damn commercial, but that doesn't have to be done until the end of the month. Why?"

"Let's have a movie marathon."

Sarah was rewarded by a wide smile from Rory. "I'm always up for that and you know it. What do you have in mind?"

"Lesbian films. Ever seen one?"

Rory frowned in thought. "I saw *Kissing Jessica Stein* in the theater. Wasn't impressed. Other than that…can't think of any."

Sarah gasped melodramatically. "Here you are, making a queer movie, and you haven't even seen a representative sample?"

Rory hung her head. "I'm delinquent."

"For once," Sarah said, "I'm going to give *you* a film lesson." She grabbed the Kingston Pizza menu from their corkboard and thrust it into Rory's hands. "You order us dinner. I'll run to the video store. Meet back here at…" Sarah consulted her watch. "No later than 1800 hours."

Rory saluted. "Yes, ma'am."

Sarah put her coat back on, patting the inside pocket to make sure her wallet was there. "This is going to be fun," she said as she opened the door. "I promise."

"Hurry home, stud," Rory called after her.

Sarah knew that Rory was just joking around, but the compliment still felt good. *I wonder if she really* does *find me attractive?* She shook her head and quickened her pace. It was silly for her to even think that way. *Why would it ever matter?*

❖

"You are a prince among men, Matthew," Rory said as Matt set down a twelve-pack of beer. She handed him a wad of cash. "Thanks for the speedy delivery."

"No problemo," Matt said. His hair was a fluorescent pink today, and it clashed spectacularly with his red jacket. "What's the occasion?"

"Movie marathon. Pizza's on its way. I'd invite you, but it's roommates only."

"Sounds kinky."

Rory rolled her eyes and pushed him into the hall. "You have yourself a good evening, perv," she said as she firmly shut the door in his grinning face.

She whistled as she stashed the beer in the fridge and arranged the beanbag chairs directly in front of the television. Just half an hour ago, she had been anticipating an ordinary night—working on her commercial until she couldn't stand it anymore, and then playing video games or procrastinating on Facebook. Now she was fidgeting as she waited for Sarah to get back. She couldn't think of anything she'd rather do than spend the rest of the day sitting next to her, cracking jokes about the films and critiquing them as they played.

An insistent buzzing noise interrupted her train of thought, and she turned toward the source of the sound. It was Sarah's cell phone. She'd left it on her desk. *Probably Chelsea. I'd better remind her to check it when she gets back.* Rory felt a sudden flash of anxiety. What if Chelsea wanted Sarah to do something with her tonight? Would their movie night be called off?

At that moment, Sarah barged into the room, brandishing three discs. Rory felt her heart stutter in her chest, the way it had taken to doing whenever Sarah looked happy. It was beautiful. *She* was beautiful—beautiful and handsome all at once. A mélange of feminine and masculine—exquisitely androgynous.

"What?" said Sarah. "You're looking at me funny."

Shit, Rory thought, realizing that she'd been caught staring. She mentally shoved those thoughts to one side and summoned her best insolent grin. "Yeah, well," she said. "You're funny lookin'."

"Ha ha." Sarah shed her coat and headed for the bedroom. By now, Rory knew her routine. As soon as Sarah was in for the night, she changed into what she called "grungy clothes." It was a cute tradition.

"Two comedies and a mob movie," Sarah called. "How does that sound to you?"

"Lesbian mafia? Seriously?"

Sarah emerged wearing a long-sleeved URI shirt and black sweats. She looked soft and young and carefree. Rory's heart lurched again, and she quickly turned toward the fridge to avoid Sarah's scrutiny.

"Not exactly," Sarah said. "You'll see."

When Rory turned back, she was holding two beers. She opened one and handed it to Sarah. "Congrats again on rocking that paper, roomie."

Sarah looked surprised. "Where'd this come from?"

"Matt, of course." Rory winked. "He's my supplier until you turn twenty-one."

"Oh, I see how it is. Come March, I'll be your errand girl?"

"You know it." Rory gestured toward the TV. "Which are we watching first?"

"*Red Doors.*" Sarah inserted the first DVD and settled back into her chair. She stretched out her long legs in front of her and crossed her ankles. "I guess I'd call it a dramatic comedy. It's about a Chinese-American family."

"Cool." Rory flopped down next to Sarah on the floor as the opening credits rolled. Sarah had clearly been thinking about her in the video store, trying to choose at least one film that she could relate to. *You're sweet*, she thought as they shared a smile. *Often brooding, sometimes moody, but fundamentally sweet.*

"Hey," she said, as the camera revealed the entire family sitting at dinner. "This is giving me an idea. You should come over sometime during Christmas break. Meet my parents." She glanced at Sarah, who looked surprised. "What do you think?"

"You really want me to?"

"Um...duh," Rory said, exasperated. "I just said I did." Sometimes, Sarah's insecurities grated on her. *Just believe me already, will you?*

"Okay then," Sarah said. She took a long sip of her beer. "That sounds really fun. Thanks."

Rory nodded, pleased. A visit from Sarah would make the holidays much less boring. *And it'll be good for her, too—to get out of the dorms and see people.* She took a sip from her beer and gestured toward the screen. "So. Which of the sisters is gay?"

Sarah rolled her eyes and playfully pushed one of Rory's feet with her own. "Not going to tell you. Watch the movie."

❖

When *Red Doors* faded to black, Rory immediately scrambled to her feet and headed for her desk.

"That was really fucking good," she said. "I need to look it up on IMDB." As she searched, she heard Sarah gathering up their beer bottles. "Hey, can you get me another?'

"Sure. And I'm glad you liked it." Sarah set a newly opened bottle near Rory's right hand and paused to look at the computer screen. "The end always makes me teary. Don't tell anyone, okay?"

Rory snorted. "What am I going to do, hijack the campus radio station and make a public service announcement?" She took her hand off her mouse to pat Sarah on the shoulder. "Your secret is safe with me...holy shit!"

"What?"

"Okay, that movie was the director's *first* full-length project. Seriously." Rory whistled. "And it won three awards. One from *Tribeca!*" She shook her head. "I am fucking impressed."

"If I admit to not knowing what Tribeca is, does that mean I'm uncultured?"

"Naw," Rory said. "Just ignorant." She winked. "It's a film festival in New York City."

"I may not know much about film," Sarah said, "but I do know that the next one on our list was made by the same guys who made *The Matrix.*"

"The Wachowski brothers? Cool. Bring it on." She sat down, but Sarah hovered near the television, twirling the DVD in her hand.

"This is the mob movie. And I just want to warn you...the beginning is sexy, and the middle and end are violent."

Rory arched her eyebrows. Sarah was blushing, and it was

adorable. "Don't worry," she said. "I'm a video-gamer, remember? Totally desensitized already."

Sarah looked like she didn't believe her, but hit Play anyway. "Well, if any of this makes you feel weird, just say the word and I'll turn it off."

Rory smiled at Sarah's needless concern. But as the plot of the film unfolded, she began to rethink her declaration. The obvious sexual tension between the two female protagonists was making her hot. She'd seen women flirting before, of course, but never with the kind of barely controlled ferocity that she was witnessing onscreen. And one of them—Corky—looked kind of like Sarah.

She shifted in her chair, trying for a more comfortable position, but there wasn't one to be found. *I guess I need some quality time with my right hand,* Rory thought, amused at her body's unexpected reaction. But her attention was drawn back to the television when the tension between the two women ratcheted up another notch. Rory leaned forward, spellbound. It really looked like Corky was about to fuck Violet…right there on the couch.

And then the strangest thing happened. Rory suddenly found herself wondering what it would be like to tease Sarah, the way Violet was teasing Corky onscreen. How long would Sarah hold back before finally succumbing to Rory's seduction? Would her kisses be gentle, or fierce? *How would she touch me?* Rory could feel herself getting wet, and somewhere in the depths of her brain, an alarm bell was pinging insistently, but she was enthralled by the combined force of the film and her fantasies.

On screen, the camera spun in a circle above a mattress. Rory stopped breathing. *Holy shit.* What would it be like to touch Sarah? To skim her palm between Sarah's breasts and along the plane of her abdomen…to trace the lines of her torso as they converged. To slide one finger deep inside—to watch as Sarah's body tensed and her head snapped back.

Rory's breathing was quick and shallow, and her face felt hot. Every muscle in her body was clenched tightly, held taut in the grip of desire. *Oh my God. I want her.* Rory wanted to look at Sarah—to see her reaction to the scene—but she stayed absolutely still, afraid that her eyes would betray what she was thinking. She kept her gaze on the television but couldn't seem to focus on anything. She had never felt like this before—had never experienced this sudden and intense a reaction to something. *No, not something. Someone.* The movie might have triggered her daydreams, but it was Sarah that she wanted. *Sarah. Fuck, this is insane.*

When a knock sounded at the door, Rory started. As Sarah got up to answer it, Rory rubbed the back of her neck and took two long gulps from her beer. She needed to settle down, and quickly. But when she heard Chelsea's voice, guilt jolted through her like an electric charge. *Oh, knock it off,* she told her conscience. *I don't have anything to feel guilty about. Thoughts are just thoughts.*

"I've been so worried about you," Chelsea was saying. "I called and left a bunch of text messages. You didn't get them?"

Rory watched Sarah's head turn toward the phone on her desk. "Damn, I'm sorry. I guess I haven't checked in a while." Sarah put her hands on Chelsea's waist, leaned in, and kissed her. "I'm really, really sorry for worrying you. I must not have heard my cell." She indicated the television. "We've been watching movies."

Rory wondered whether Chelsea recognized the film on her TV, and if so, what she was thinking. Then again, she seemed so completely wrapped up in Sarah that she didn't have eyes for anything else. When they kissed a second time, Rory's grip on her bottle tightened. *Chelsea knows everything I don't.* The feel of Sarah's lips, the texture of her skin, the—

She quickly jumped to her feet and squeezed past Chelsea to open the door. "Bathroom," she explained. "Back in a minute."

Once she reached the sanctuary of the ladies' room, Rory splashed cold water on her face. She clutched the edges of the sink and stared into the mirror, trying to focus on her reflection instead of on the vision of Chelsea and Sarah, naked in bed together, that was playing on the wide screen of her brain. *Fuck fuck fuck. What am I going to do?*

"You're going to not be an idiot," she muttered. *So I'm in lust with my roommate, so what? Every lesbian on campus is, too.*

The thought brought Rory up short. She watched as the expression on her face shifted from anxious to surprised. "Jesus. Am I queer?" She had never believed that she was a zero on the Kinsey scale—more like a one. *But you just got hopelessly turned on thinking about Sarah. About* fucking *her. You're at least a three, kiddo.*

"Yeah, well, so what?" Rory stared at her reflection defiantly. So what if she was having a revelation? It didn't change anything. Not really. Sarah had a girlfriend. End of story.

She slumped against the counter and buried her face in her hands. Her head felt like it did every summer after she got off the Teacups ride at the local fair. *Holy fucking fuck. How did this happen so fast?* And if it had to happen at all, why couldn't she be jonesing after someone single?

If it's women you want, there are plenty others out there. But Rory didn't feel like she wanted "women" at all. She quickly cycled through her female friends. Was she attracted to any of them? *No... no, no. And no. Huh.* So what made Sarah different? And why was she having an epiphany *now*? The end of her first semester junior year was not a convenient time. And if she was going to have all of these inconvenient feelings, why couldn't they at least be directed toward someone who would reciprocate? Why couldn't she just feel a general attraction to all things...womanly?

But no. I want a woman. Just one. The one fucking living in my fucking dorm room. Fuck.

She reached for a paper towel and dried off her face and hands. It was past time for her to go back. Sarah might think that something was wrong. And it was imperative that she be absolutely, positively, utterly and completely ignorant about this new development. *I'll spend time thinking about this later,* Rory vowed. *Right now...I just gotta get through tonight.*

As she marched back down the hallway, Rory prepared herself to find Sarah and Chelsea snuggling. But when she opened the door, Sarah was alone, sitting in her beanbag chair, a beer dangling from her right hand. She had that pensive expression on her face, but smiled when she saw Rory.

"You all right?" she asked.

"Never better," Rory said, glad that she was so good at lying through her teeth. "Where's Chelsea? I figured she'd stick around."

"Oh, she had a lot of work to do." Sarah twisted the bottle idly, and Rory felt her gaze drawn to Sarah's fingers. They were long, and slender, and dammit all to hell, she was *not* going to imagine what they'd feel like inside her.

"Okay," Rory said, uncertain about whether she should feel relief or panic that they were alone again. She retrieved her own drink. "Want to keep watching?"

"If you do," Sarah said. But if you're not liking *Bound*, we can just switch to the next movie. *D.E.B.S.* It's a parody."

"I want to see how this one ends," Rory said. "The camera work is fucking brilliant." And then, because she figured it was something that her old self would have said, she added, "That love scene was *hot*. H-a-w-t hot."

Sarah's answering laugh sounded relieved. "Glad you thought so. I was a little worried that it might, y'know, weird you out."

"No way, babe," Rory said, mustering all her bravado. She settled back into her chair and focused on the television. "Didn't faze me. Not one bit."

CHAPTER NINE

The next day, Rory sat in her biology class, completely ignoring the professor's lecture on mitochondria and instead trying to figure out whether she was attracted to any of the other women in the class. The one sitting at the end of her row had a classically beautiful, heart-shaped face. She probably could have been a model if she had been taller. The one sitting two rows in front of her had well-toned arms, though Rory was mystified as to why she insisted on wearing a tank top in December. Then there was the woman in the front row with the long, slender legs—very shapely. Oh, and the girl slouching in the back corner had cool hair—spiky and dramatically highlighted.

Rory sighed as she dutifully copied down the terms that her professor was scrawling on the board. She didn't understand herself. How could she be attracted to only bits and pieces of the women in this huge lecture hall, while simultaneously lusting after every inch of Sarah? And if Sarah was the only woman to whom she was attracted, then did that really make her a lesbian?

What about Jeff? she thought suddenly. She sat back in the uncomfortable wooden seat, trying to figure out whether her feelings for him had changed. *I still think he's hot. And incredibly talented.* But in the past few weeks, she hadn't thought of him much except in the context of her documentary's soundtrack. *Maybe I'm finally over that crush.*

If so, what did that mean for her sexual orientation? *What am I?* If she and Sarah were ever to date, people would assume that she was at least bisexual. Rory frowned at her notebook. Not that she cared what people called her, really, but the whole phenomenon of labeling was interesting. And mildly disturbing. For the first time, she understood why so many of her queer friends were loath to identify with one specific group. *If you're still confused, it must not feel very good to have someone put you in whatever box suits their purpose.*

Rory shrugged, trying to loosen the knot of tension that had developed between her shoulders. She thought briefly about cornering Matt and telling him all about what was going on…but he would have definitive ideas, and she wanted to be able to figure this out for herself. Now that she knew she was capable of wanting another woman, she couldn't help but wonder whether any of her friendships in middle and high school had been based on a deep-seated, unrecognized attraction. *Holy crap. Did I have crushes on all my friends without knowing it?*

Mercifully, at that moment, the professor dismissed class. Rory gathered up her belongings and left the room, intent on getting home as quickly as possible. She was tired of overthinking this. Her head felt like a hamster wheel. If she could just immerse herself in working on the FRI commercial, she would be able to escape the unwelcome questions stewing in her brain. For a while, anyway.

❖

"Don't you want to get lunch?" Sarah asked as Chelsea pulled her away from the dining hall. "I only have an hour until Bioethics."

Chelsea shook her head, steering them toward her dorm. "I'm starving," she said, her voice husky, "but not for food."

Sarah's gut somersaulted. Although they'd been together for almost two months now, she and Chelsea still hadn't made love. Sarah didn't know why she was so reluctant, but hadn't been able to stop dragging her feet. Fortunately, she had been so busy during the past few weeks that the issue hadn't really come up. Now, though, it looked like Chelsea was taking matters into her own hands.

As they rode up to Chelsea's room in the elevator, she backed Sarah against the wall, leaned in, and kissed her deeply. Sarah couldn't hold back a soft moan as Chelsea's tongue tangled with her own. She pulled Chelsea close, praying that for once, her brain would just shut off so her body could take over.

"You're an incredible kisser," Chelsea whispered as the elevator came to a halt.

"It takes two," Sarah said, smiling. The desire that Chelsea had awakened seethed inside her, making her restless. But something was holding her back from just giving in and letting it take over.

"I never get to see you anymore," Chelsea said as they entered her room. She kicked off her shoes and sat on the bed, beckoning to Sarah. "I don't want to whine and complain, because I know that you're busy for good reasons, but...I've been missing you." When Sarah sat next to her, Chelsea gently pushed until Sarah was on her back and she was lying on top. "And just thinking about you makes me horny," she murmured, trailing kisses down Sarah's throat.

Fear rose sharply in Sarah's gut. This was getting out of control too fast. "Kiss me again," she said, pressing one hand to the small of Chelsea's back. When she obliged, Sarah reached between their bodies and brushed her knuckles over Chelsea's nipples.

"Oh, God," Chelsea murmured against Sarah's mouth.

Relieved that the distraction had worked, Sarah twisted her hand so she could torment Chelsea's breasts with her fingers. She shifted so that one of her legs was resting between Chelsea's, and gently pressed her thigh up into Chelsea's body.

"Sarah—" Chelsea gasped, grinding down against her. "Baby, yes."

"No talking," Sarah ordered before deepening the kiss. Chelsea was wild above her, panting into her mouth as Sarah twisted her nipples and rhythmically pumped her thigh against Chelsea's sex. When Chelsea tossed her head back to expose her throat, Sarah arched up to kiss the throbbing pulse in her neck.

Without any warning, she thought of Rory. What would Rory's breasts feel like against her palms? They'd be heavier—more full. Would she be sensitive? Would she give as good as she got, pressing her knee into Sarah and teasing Sarah's nipples, even as she approached climax? Would she lean down to kiss Sarah, pulling hard on her hair as her tongue—

And then, with a tiny cry, Chelsea came. Guilt burned in Sarah's chest, but she continued her movements, only stopping when Chelsea collapsed against her. She wrapped her arms around Chelsea, pulling her closer when a series of tiny aftershocks made her shiver. *Oh God,* she thought. *What's wrong with me? Why the hell did that happen?* Struggling to put Rory out of her mind, she tightened her hold on Chelsea and kissed her forehead lightly. "Wow."

"No shit," Chelsea said, raising her head to smile lazily. "You're incredible. And I was *so* wound up." She pressed a series of nipping kisses to Sarah's jaw line, ending at her ear. "Your turn now," she whispered throatily, sending a shiver down Sarah's spine.

But although her body reacted, panic flooded her brain. *No.* She struggled to sit up in the bed. "I can't," she said, trying to stay calm. "Class soon." She refused to consider what it might mean that Rory had invaded her thoughts, earlier. *It didn't mean anything. Only happened because we watched* Bound *yesterday.*

Chelsea frowned at her. "Your class isn't for another half an hour," she pointed out. Sitting back on her heels, she regarded Sarah with an accusatory look. "Why won't you let me touch you?"

Sarah blinked at the direct confrontation. Frantically, she tried to come up with a valid reason. Any reason at all. *I can't tell her that it just doesn't feel right,* she thought desperately. *I'll hurt her.* But just as Chelsea was starting to look really upset, inspiration struck. *Dar.*

"My ex," Sarah said hurriedly, taking a deep breath when Chelsea's expression transformed into sympathy. "She was my first, and things heated up between us really fast. I never saw the breakup coming." Sarah felt hollow inside as she thought back to that day— not too long ago, still—when Dar had so unexpectedly called it quits. "I guess…I guess I'm afraid to become that serious again."

She had begun speaking just to say *something*, anything, but now that the words were out there, Sarah thought they might actually be true. The idea of letting someone get close enough to hurt her the way Dar had was terrifying. *Maybe that really is why I'm keeping Chelsea at arm's length.*

Chelsea reached for Sarah's hand, nodding. "Okay," she said softly, rubbing her thumb over Sarah's knuckles. "I understand. Thank you for telling me. I can wait a while longer." She leaned in for a gentle kiss. "When I finally do make love to you, Sarah Storm, I don't want you to feel anything but pleasure."

❖

Rory's pulse sped up when she heard the door open, but she stubbornly remained hunched over her desk, staring at her computer screen.

"Hey," Sarah said. "Missed you at the office today. What have you been up to?"

Missed me? She missed me? Rory bit her lip to keep from grinning like an idiot, and instead shifted her cursor to highlight several seconds' worth of footage. "Hey, yo," she said as nonchalantly as she could manage. "I've been working on first cuts for this damn commercial all afternoon."

"Nice," Sarah said, coming to stand directly behind her. Rory silently begged her for a shoulder massage, but sadly, Sarah kept her hands to herself. "How's it going?"

Rory shrugged. "Eh. I should have started working on it earlier. Nancy needs it in two weeks, so it's just one more thing on my plate besides finals."

"Rotten timing," Sarah agreed. "Anything I can do to help?"

All kinds of inappropriate answers jumped to the front of Rory's brain, but she settled for shaking her head. "Unless," she added a moment later, spinning around to face Sarah, "you want to save me half an hour and bring me back some food from the caf."

"I can do that." Sarah checked the calendar hanging from their corkboard and laughed. "Apparently it's Asian cuisine night at Roger Williams. Any special requests?"

Rory stuck out her tongue. "Asian cuisine my ass," she said.

"My mom could cook circles around those noobs." She sat up straighter then, suddenly remembering a conversation she'd had with Matt this morning. "And speaking of my mom…do you still feel like coming over during winter break?"

"Yeah, sure," Sarah said. "I think that would be really fun, if you want."

"How about for New Year's? Matt only lives about half an hour away from me, and he just told me today that he's going to throw a party. So if you want, you can come over on the thirtieth and then we can head to his place together." A sudden thought caused her stomach to lurch crazily. "Unless you're going to hang out with Chelsea—"

Sarah held up one hand, forestalling Rory's caveating. "Chelsea's family is spending that week in Hawaii," she said. "It'd be great to meet your parents and go to the party with you."

Rory knew that Sarah was speaking only in the platonic sense, but her stomach got all fluttery anyway. "Excellent," she said, turning back to her computer so that Sarah wouldn't see her face. "It's a date."

Chapter Ten

December 30

S arah turned into Rory's driveway, cut the engine, and stared up at the brick façade of Rory's house. Black shutters lined the windows, and a large wreath covered much of the dark gray front door. Without the heat blasting, the winter chill seeped quickly into her car, but Sarah made no move to get out. Despite the fact that she had been looking forward all week to spending New Year's Eve with Rory, she was suddenly apprehensive about meeting her family.

I don't really know much about them, she realized. Were they liberal or conservative? Religious? Rory had never even mentioned what her parents did for work. And what if they objected to their daughter being friends with a lesbian?

Sarah looked down at her clothes—a black long-sleeved shirt that she'd found on sale in the men's section of Old Navy, men's cargo pants, and Doc Martens. She sighed. *No way do I read as straight.*

"Why couldn't I have turned out femme?" she muttered as she shoved the door open. She stepped out onto the pavement and quickly grabbed her bag from the trunk, wincing at the bitter cold of the metal against her fingers.

She hesitated again, looking between the front door and her car. It wasn't too late to turn around—to call Rory and tell her that the plan had changed. *I could just meet her at Matt's house tomorrow night for the party. Skip the family thing altogether.* The idea was tempting. But when Sarah realized that she was letting her own family's reaction to her queerness scare her off, she squared her shoulders and marched up the front walk. *Be polite. Be charming. They'll like you just fine.*

When Sarah rang the doorbell, she was greeted by a slender woman of average height with salt-and-pepper hair. Rory's mother was wearing a red and green apron, and she eagerly ushered Sarah into the high-ceiled foyer. A faux-pine garland wound its way around the railing of a half-spiral staircase, and through a window at the end of the hall, Sarah caught a glimpse of a sparkling Christmas tree. The décor and ambience felt so much like that of her childhood home that for a moment, she couldn't catch her breath and had to blink hard against unwelcome tears. *Goddammit.*

"So," Rory's mother said as they made their way down the hall, "did you have a good Christmas?"

Sarah cleared her throat. "Yes, thanks. And you?"

"Oh, it was busy—very busy with so much family here." Rory's mother led her into a large, bright kitchen. Whatever was cooking smelled amazing. "Please, sit," she said, gesturing to the kitchen table. "Rory should be up soon. Would you like something to drink?"

Sarah requested a soda and was just about to ask what was on the stove when Rory barged into the room. She looked soft and rumpled in a pair of scrubs and a URI sweatshirt, and Sarah felt a quick surge of affection for her.

"Hey, you," Rory said, immediately wrapping her in a big hug.

Sarah closed her eyes and let out a deep breath. *Feels so good.* She had to resist the urge to pull Rory even closer, and stiffened at the impulse. *Jeez. Take it easy.*

"Glad you made it," Rory said as she stepped back. She grinned broadly before punching Sarah in the shoulder. "Merry Christmas!"

"Ow." Sarah tried to scowl, but the corners of her mouth

twitched. "Is that how you pass along season's greetings around here?"

"You know it." Rory jerked her head toward the doorway. "C'mon, let's go hang out in the basement. I have something to show you."

"Okay, sure." Sarah followed Rory into the family room and then down a flight of stairs. The basement floor was covered by a thick, spongy carpet, and a partition divided the room in two. The half she could see was clearly Rory's favorite place to hang out. Two battered couches faced an entertainment center, and the shelves that framed the television were packed with DVDs. Video game cartridges and several different species of controllers were strewn on the floor near the TV.

"Look!" Rory said triumphantly, pointing to a thin white box next to the DVD player.

"Um...what is it?"

Rory rolled her eyes. "Oh my God, you must live in a hole. It's the new Nintendo—the Wii!"

"Oh," Sarah said. "I've heard of it. Just didn't know what it looked like. Very cool."

"I think you'll love it," Rory said. "Especially the sports games. Here, I'll show you."

Sarah watched Rory fiddle with one of the controllers as the game booted up. It was such a familiar scenario, and a sudden wave of happiness broke over her. *God, I've missed this—just hanging out. Being in the same place.* Living in their dorm room without Rory simply hadn't felt right.

"So," she said, sitting back against the couch and pulling up her knees. "How was your Christmas?"

Rory shrugged. "Eh. Spent it trying to avoid all the members of my extended family who think I should change my major. How about you? Did you have fun at your friend's place?"

"Yeah, definitely." Sarah smiled at the memory of how Corrie and Quinn had pulled out all the stops to ensure that she had a good day. "I learned how to cook a duck."

"Nice." Rory flipped through a series of menu options on the television. "And how about all those apps you were working on?"

"Finished and in the mail," Sarah said proudly.

"You, my friend, are a rock star. Have you seen Chelsea at all?"

"Nah. Her family went to Hawaii for the holiday. They're not coming back until next week." Sarah cocked her head. She didn't want to know, but for some reason, couldn't stop herself from asking the question. "How about you? Seen Jeff?"

Rory let out an exasperated sigh. "Why the hell would I see him? How many times do I have to tell you there's nothing going on?"

"Mmm-hmm." Sarah refused to buy it. *Why is she being so insistent? I know she likes him.* "Is he going to be at Matt's tomorrow?"

"I have no idea, and I don't give a fuck," Rory said firmly. She held up two white gadgets that were linked to each other by a thin wire. "Enough nonsense. How good are you at boxing?"

"Huh?"

"Watch closely. This is the remote. This other thing is the nunchuk. You hold one in each hand, like so." Rory stood in front of the television and held both hands in front of her face. "Now, check it out. I'm gonna box against the game, by moving my arms and shifting from side to side."

Sarah leaned forward as Rory began to play. Sure enough, every time she lashed out with each fist, her avatar onscreen did the same. And when she ducked to the right to avoid an incoming punch, it whistled past her virtual head ineffectually.

"Whoa," Sarah said. "This is cool!"

"And aerobic," Rory said, slightly breathless. She jabbed hard with her right hand and succeeded in knocking out her opponent. "All right. Your turn."

Unlike her clumsy attempt at playing Halo, Sarah took to Wii-boxing immediately. She even managed to work up a sweat as she punched, blocked, and shifted from side to side. When she finally collapsed onto the couch, proclaiming that her arms were tired, Rory fished another set of controllers from a drawer and challenged her to a bowling match.

They bowled, they golfed, they played baseball. At one point, Rory's mother came downstairs with more drinks and a platter of gimbap, which Sarah thought was sushi until Rory explained the difference.

"Like it?" Rory asked, her mouth full.

"Yeah," Sarah said, reaching for another piece of the roll. "Especially the sesame flavor."

"Wanna take a break for a bit? See what's on TV?"

"Sure," Sarah said. "My arms feel all wobbly."

Rory stopped channel-surfing once she found the Rudolph the Red-Nosed Reindeer cartoon film. She flopped back against the couch cushions and rested her head on Sarah's shoulder. In another second, she had pulled away and was reaching for a nearby pillow.

"You're too bony," she said as she propped it between Sarah's arm and her head.

Sarah knew that she said something in reply, but couldn't for the life of her remember what. The sensation of Rory cuddled up against her was comforting and made her pulse speed up, all at once. *It doesn't mean anything*, she told her restless body. *Not like that. Just enjoy this for what it is.*

But even as Sarah forced herself to pay attention to the television, she knew she wanted more.

❖

An hour later, Rory's mother opened the basement door and called down that dinner was on the table. Rory stood up and stretched. Sarah missed her immediately.

"Ready for family supper?"

Sarah's anxiety returned, fluttering in her gut. "Bring it on," she said with false bravado.

"Prepare yourself for twenty questions," Rory said as they

made their way up the stairs. "Especially from Dad. He's a doctor, and I've told him that you're pre-med."

"Okay."

"And Mom will probably ask if you have a boyfriend." Rory looked back over her shoulder and leered. "Can't wait to hear your answer to *that* one."

The idea was so absurd that Sarah didn't even feel panicked. She laughed. "Seriously?"

"Seriously. They're totally clueless."

Thank God, Sarah thought. She took a deep breath and felt the pit in her stomach loosen. *That's a relief.*

When they walked into the kitchen, Rory's mother was depositing a large bowl of steaming rice onto the table, and Rory's father was opening a bottle of white wine.

"Can we help with anything?" Sarah asked immediately.

"No, no," Mrs. Song said. "Please just sit. Would you like some wine?"

"Absolutely," Rory said. But when her father put two glasses in front of them and then added an ice cube to each, Rory visibly cringed. She stuck her spoon in the glass and fished out the ice. "So freaking embarrassing," she said under her breath. Sarah had to bite her lip to keep from laughing out loud.

"Please, start," Rory's mother said as she sat down. "We're glad you can be with us, Sarah."

"Thanks for having me," Sarah said. "Everything smells delicious." Next to her, Rory muttered something about kissing up.

Sarah ignored her and started passing bowls. She didn't recognize any of the dishes, but they really *did* smell good, and she was excited to try some new things. Once she saw that everyone at the table had their food, she reached for her fork...only to discover that there was no such implement anywhere on the table.

Chopsticks. Uh-oh. Gingerly, she picked up the slender pieces of wood. *I'm going to look like an idiot.*

Rory nudged her with one elbow. "You're looking at those things like they're going to bite you."

"We have forks," Rory's mother said, rising from her chair. "Let me—"

"No no, it's okay. Please." Sarah motioned for her to stay put. "I want to try it. I'm just going to need some instructions."

Rory raised her chopsticks and effortlessly scissored them. "Hold one like a pencil, and then use the other one to make a pinching motion."

"Got it," Sarah said. But when she tried to latch on to a piece of meat, one of the sticks fell out of her grasp and clattered onto the plate. "Oops."

"The bottom chopstick should remain stationary," Rory's father offered. He also demonstrated, expertly grabbing a shrimp. Sarah tried again, frowning as she concentrated.

"That's it," Rory's mother chipped in. "Now use the top one to pinch—good!"

Sarah grinned triumphantly around her first bite. "Thanks for the pointers," she said after swallowing. Emboldened by her success, she latched onto a large leaf of what looked like cabbage.

"Uh, watch out for that," Rory said. "It's kimchi. Wicked spicy."

"I'm not afraid," Sarah said, just before putting the entire leaf in her mouth. Immediately, her eyes began to water and her nose started to run. She chewed quickly, and took a large gulp of wine as Rory laughed.

"Told you."

"I'm such a wimp," Sarah said, chagrined. *But at least I made everyone laugh.*

Rory's father leaned over the table to refill first her wineglass, and then his own. "So, Sarah, Rory tells us that you aspire to be a doctor."

"That's still the plan, yes," Sarah said. "Though I'm not sure what kind, yet."

"Rory has several cousins in medical school," Mr. Song said. "She can put you in touch with them when it's time for you to apply, if you'd like any advice."

"Wow, thanks," Sarah said. "That's really generous." She tried for the third time to grab a portion of vegetable-laden rice with her chopsticks, and failed once again.

"Do you need me to feed you?" Rory whispered.

"Shut up," Sarah muttered back.

Oblivious to their banter, Rory's mother was changing the subject. "Where does your family live, Sarah?"

Next to her, Rory froze, chopsticks poised between the plate and her mouth. Sarah felt her pulse jump and reached for her glass of wine. "They're in Newport," she said.

"Very nice. And what do they do?"

A sudden rush of white-hot anger made the glass tremble in Sarah's hand. *Apparently they disown their daughter because she happens to be queer.* She took a long sip and cleared her throat. "My mom is a homemaker," she said, concentrating on keeping her voice steady. "And my dad is a vice president at a biotechnology company."

"Oh?" said Rory's dad, clearly interested. "Which one?"

"Amgen," Sarah said. Silently, she begged Rory to change the discussion topic.

"So, hey," Rory said, just as her father was opening his mouth to ask another question. "I don't think I told you all—part of my documentary project is going to be aired in February in a commercial!"

Beneath the table, Sarah found Rory's foot with her own and pressed down lightly. *Thank you,* she thought. "Whoa," she said aloud. "That's so cool."

They chatted about Rory's film for a while, and then about movies in general. Rory's father opened a second bottle of wine and became increasingly jovial as the evening progressed. By the time Sarah got up to help Mrs. Song clear the table, he was decidedly tipsy.

"I'm going to set up the karaoke machine for us," he announced, just prior to disappearing into the family room.

"What?" said Rory to her father's back. "Oh, no. We are not

singing karaoke." When he didn't turn around, she followed him, continuing to protest. "Dad, c'mon, Sarah and I have to—"

"No excuses!" Mr. Song bellowed. "We are singing, and that is final!"

"Fuck," Rory said as Sarah caught up to her. "I am so sorry. Maybe we can get away after a round."

Sarah watched as Rory's father set the machine on the coffee table and fiddled with several controls. "I've never seen one before," she said. "Kind of cool."

Rory looked at her as though she were crazy. "Cool? Clearly, you've never heard my parents—oh crap." Rory's expression was one of horror as the opening bars of "Unchained Melody" floated from the speakers.

"I love this one," her mother called on her way in to join them.

Rory sat down hard on the love seat and stared at the floor as her father began to sing. Sarah sat next to her and patted her knee. "There, there," she said. "It'll be all right."

Rory glared. "Are you ever going to let me forget this?"

Sarah grinned cheerfully. "Nope!"

Rory groaned and buried her face in her hands while her father continued to regale her mother in a rather strained tenor voice about how much he needed her love. She kept her head down when her mother chose "I Will Always Love You" as a companion piece.

"I'm going to die," she said through clenched teeth.

"I dunno," Sarah said, nudging her with one elbow. "I think it's kind of cute."

"All right, Rory," her father announced after his wife's valiant— though warbling—effort. "Your turn."

"No," Rory said, shaking her head. "Absolutely not. No way."

"Let's sing a duet," Sarah said quickly, before a full-blown argument could erupt. "How about...'Sweet Child O' Mine'?" She glanced sidelong at Rory. "You have to mime the guitar riffs."

Rory laughed. "I'd need more than a couple glasses of wine to do *that*!"

Sarah walked over to the couch and accepted the microphone from Rory's father. "Come on," she cajoled. "Let's go for it."

Rory made a show of dragging herself over to stand next to Sarah. But once the song began, she leaned in close to the microphone and let loose. When Rory's rich soprano filled the room, Sarah realized that she had never before heard her sing. *God. She's really good!*

As soon as Izzy Stradlin's last chords faded, however, Rory grabbed Sarah's hand and pulled her toward the foyer. "Promise kept," she said over her parents' protests. "We're out of here." She led Sarah up the half-spiral staircase, down a hall, and into a room on the left. After closing the door behind her, she flopped onto the bed. "Whew. I think we're safe now."

Sarah perched on the desk chair and slowly spun in a circle, taking in the décor of Rory's childhood bedroom. Film posters plastered the wall. There was barely any white space to be seen. Just opposite the foot of the bed was a small television, and Rory's shelves were jam-packed with both books and DVDs.

"You have a really good voice," Sarah said. "I had no idea."

Surprisingly, Rory blushed. "Eh. It's okay." She pillowed her chin on her arms and regarded Sarah with a serious expression. "Hey...I am so sorry about my parents bringing up your family, earlier."

Sarah shrugged. "It's all right. Makes sense that they would. Thanks for changing the subject, though." She smiled. "Your parents are fun."

"Fun?" Rory scoffed. "My dad is a lightweight and has embarrassing habits, and my mom is a gossipmonger."

"Yeah, well, they're your parents. You have to talk about them like that."

Rory rolled onto her back and stared up at the ceiling. Her dark hair fanned out on the white bedspread, and Sarah was fascinated by the contrast. Suddenly, her fingertips itched with the desire to feel, not just to look. Her rebellious brain flashed to an image of herself on top of Rory, combing her fingers through Rory's hair while she kissed her insistently.

"The night is young," Rory said. "What do you want to do?"

Sarah blinked, trying not to betray her inner turmoil. *Distraction. I need a distraction. Stat.* "Cards? A movie?"

"Let's do the latter," Rory said, "since Matt's party is all about sitting around drinking and playing cards or board games." She flipped back over onto her tummy. "What are you in the mood for?"

Something that'll keep me from thinking about how much I want to kiss you. "I vote for an action flick."

Rory pointed toward a bookshelf to the right of the desk. "How about *Transformers*? Cheesiest movie ever made, and full of exploding shit."

Sarah grinned, relieved. "That sounds perfect."

After Sarah put in the DVD, she turned to find Rory patting the space next to her on the bed. "Best seat in the house." The bed was narrow, and when Sarah stretched out on her stomach, the length of her body was in contact with Rory's. Sarah had to fight not to press even closer. It was all well and good when Rory got cuddly, because that was clearly innocent, but Sarah didn't trust herself.

Rory bumped her as the opening credits began to play. "I'm really glad you came over."

"Me, too," Sarah said. She hesitated before deciding to be honest. About this much, at least. "I've missed you."

"Oh, I know," Rory said. "I'm eminently miss-able."

"Egomaniac."

"Damn skippy."

Resolutely, Sarah focused on the movie, rather than on how good Rory smelled and how exhilarating it was to be close to her. Sarah had long since made her peace with the fact that she was attracted to her, but tonight, those feelings were much stronger than usual.

You're just a little lonely, she thought. It made perfect sense, really. She had gotten used to having Chelsea around. Once school started up again, everything would go back to normal. Until then, she just had to watch herself and be sure not to do anything to make Rory freak out.

❖

Sarah should have been having a blast. Most of her friends were in the room—talking, watching TV, or playing games. The chatter was loud and frequently punctuated by laughter. It was New Year's Eve, for Christ's sake—the consummate party night. But Sarah was unable to relax into the festive atmosphere. Across the room, Jeff was flirting heavily with Rory. And it bugged her.

She took a long sip of her beer as she watched the two of them confer over their Trivial Pursuit question. They were sitting next to each other on the floor, and Jeff was resting one hand on Rory's knee as he leaned in close to examine the wording on the card that she held.

They look good together, Sarah thought dully. She felt her gut twist at the realization and tilted the can back for another sip, only to discover that it was empty. *Dammit.*

She got up from the couch, stalked into the kitchen, and yanked open the refrigerator door. It probably wasn't a good call to have another drink at this point, but that only made the idea sound more appealing. *Why can't I just be happy for her?* Rory had had a crush on Jeff for a long time. If those feelings were finally being reciprocated—and that's certainly what it looked like—then why wasn't she excited for her friend?

You're not allowed to be jealous of Jeff. You're with Chelsea, and Rory's straight, and that's the end of it. By now, it was abundantly clear that she'd managed to develop a crush on Rory after all, but those feelings had no place in their relationship. *I'll get over it.* The real problem was that Jeff was a tease. A player, even. *I bet he's just out for a good time. And Rory's going to get her heart broken.* Sarah couldn't stand to think about Rory getting hurt like that.

"Anyone want to help me with the champagne?" Matt bellowed from the living room.

Sarah checked her watch. Sure enough, midnight was approaching. She grabbed another beer and walked across the hall. "I'll give you a hand."

"You're a lifesaver," Matt said. He passed over a bottle and went back to working the cork out of the one he'd been holding. "So? You having fun?"

"Yeah," Sarah lied.

"It's too bad Chelsea couldn't make it."

"Yeah."

Chelsea, Sarah knew, would have kept her occupied all night. While normally that might have started to bug her, Sarah wished for the distraction right now. She topped off the last of the plastic champagne flutes and gestured toward the den. "I'll start handing these out."

By the time everyone was holding a drink, only five minutes remained until midnight. Sarah lounged against the wall near the sliding door to the deck, watching everyone gather around the television to listen to Ryan Seacrest count down to the advent of the new year.

Rory and Jeff stood next to each other on the edge of the small crowd. Suddenly, Sarah knew exactly what would happen when the ball dropped. The champagne toast, of course, and then someone was certain to start an off-key rendition of "Auld Lang Syne." But before any of that, there would be kissing. And she did *not* want to see Rory and Jeff kissing.

Quietly, she reached for the handle of the sliding door and slipped out into the chill night. Her teeth began to chatter almost immediately, and when she sucked in a breath, the air sliced her lungs. But at least out here, she didn't have to pretend.

❖

Rory had lost track of Sarah. Earlier, she'd been sitting on the couch, and just a few minutes ago, Rory had seen her handing out some champagne flutes. Now she was nowhere in sight.

Rory nodded absently as Jeff made some comment about the broadcast from Times Square, and craned her neck as she looked around the room. *Where are you? And why have you been avoiding me all night?* Rory thought she knew the answer to the second question. Clearly, Sarah thought she was doing her a favor by leaving her alone with Jeff.

Across the room, the crowd shifted and Rory caught a glimpse of Sarah hovering near the door to the deck. "Be right back," she told Jeff, not sticking around to wait for his reply.

I don't want him, you idiot, she thought at Sarah as she squeezed between her friends. *I want you. But if I told you, things would get weird. And besides...you're happy with Chelsea.*

Just as she reached the far side of Matt's den, she saw Sarah slip out onto the deck. Rory paused for a moment, uncertain about whether or not to follow her. Clearly, she wanted to be alone. *But the ball's going to drop any second now, and dammit, I will* not *let her be in a blue funk tonight.*

Rory threw back her shoulders, grabbed hold of the sliding door handle, and pulled hard. She stepped out into the night and coughed as soon as she breathed in. *Fuck, it's cold out here.* As her eyes adjusted, she saw Sarah leaning against the far end of the deck. Shivering.

"Brooding on New Year's Eve?" Rory shook her head and extended one hand. "No way, roomie. C'mon."

Sarah stayed put. "Hey, I'm fine," she said, obviously trying to sound cheerful. "Get inside. It's almost midnight!"

Rory took a few steps closer. "You don't fool me. And I'm not going in there without you."

Sarah's eyes glittered in the starlight as she frowned. Rory cocked her head, staring back at her defiantly. *Say whatever you want. I'm not leaving.* And then a cheer went up from inside the house as the ball dropped in Times Square and the new year began.

Rory felt the stubborn expression on her face dissolve. She quirked a grin at Sarah and took a few steps forward. "Happy new year, dork," she said as she pulled Sarah into a hug.

"Happy new year," Sarah whispered against Rory's temple.

Rory pressed her face against Sarah's neck. God, she felt so good—lean and warm and strong. Rory knew she should pull away, but Sarah wasn't moving, either. In fact, her hands were roaming up and down Rory's back. She wondered if Sarah realized what she was doing. *She's never touched me like this before. Why now?*

Suddenly needing to see her face, Rory leaned back and tilted her head slightly. Sarah was looking down at her with an unfamiliar expression—needy, and a little sad. *Longing.* Not guilt, not fear, not pity. Rory felt a frisson of shock course under her skin. *Holy shit. She wants me, too.*

She should have backed off, but Sarah's magnetic gaze was enthralling. Slowly, Rory raised her left hand to cup Sarah's cheek, curling three fingers around Sarah's jaw and pulling gently. *I need this. Need you. Damn the torpedoes.* As the gap between them began to narrow, Rory watched Sarah's eyes flutter shut and her lips part.

And then the sliding door flew open.

"What are you guys doing out—whoa!"

Sarah jerked her head away and immediately released Rory. She took a few steps back, hunching her shoulders. Rory barely managed to restrain herself from reaching out. Instead, she turned toward where Matt stood, silhouetted in the doorway. She couldn't see his face very well, but had no doubt that his mouth was wide open. *Goddammit.*

"Nothing to see here, Matthew," she said firmly. "Move along."

Matt paused for another few seconds before wordlessly closing the door. Rory returned her attention to Sarah, who was now rocking back and forth on her heels, scrubbing both hands through her hair. She looked sick with guilt.

Shit shit shit. What have you done? Rory felt an overpowering urge to take Sarah by the shoulders, kiss her hard, and then confess everything. *I think I'm falling for you.* But what if she didn't feel the same way? What if their near kiss had been only a momentary lapse?

A burning pressure pushed against the backs of Rory's eyes at the thought. *I couldn't stand it.* That left only one recourse. Humor had never yet failed her as an escape route. Now it would save her yet again. She forced her lips to curve up in a bright grin, and even managed to arch one eyebrow.

"Oh, quit looking like a deer caught in the headlights," she said. "I'm just a hottie, and that's a fact. Not your fault you can't resist."

And then, because her lips were still tingling in anticipation, Rory took a few steps forward, rose onto her toes, and delivered a light kiss to Sarah's cheek. The soft skin was hot beneath her mouth. "Now," Rory said, somehow maintaining her false bravado despite the hollow space that had opened in her chest. "How about some champagne, hmm?"

❖

Sarah heard Rory speaking, but it was hard to focus on what she was saying. *My God. I almost kissed her.* If Matt hadn't barged in on them, she would probably *still* be kissing her. Absently, Sarah raised one hand to the place that Rory's lips had touched. It burned.

But then Rory's words—and her familiar, bantering tone—sank into Sarah's addled brain. *Not your fault you can't resist. Not your fault you can't resist.*

She was just going to laugh it off? Just like that? Sarah suddenly wanted to scream. How? How could Rory *possibly* be acting as though everything were normal?

"Um," she managed. "Yeah. Champagne."

"C'mon," Rory said, reaching for her hand and tugging. Sarah watched their fingers entwine and felt a jolt all along her arm as their palms met, but Rory didn't even bat an eyelash. "Let's get back in there before we turn into popsicles."

Sarah followed obediently. She felt shell-shocked. *What does this mean?* she asked, accepting a plastic champagne flute from someone and automatically raising it in a toast.

It doesn't mean anything, her rational brain offered. *You're buzzed and you miss Chelsea. It's no more complicated than that.* Sure, she had some feelings for Rory. But how could she not? Rory was the closest friend she had. It was perfectly natural to develop a harmless little crush on her. As long as she kept those feelings under wraps so they couldn't hurt Rory or Chelsea, there was no problem. *Right?*

"Yeah," she muttered as the crowd began to sing. When Rory slung one arm around her shoulders as though nothing out of the ordinary had happened, Sarah polished off her drink, trying desperately to relax. *Right.*

CHAPTER ELEVEN

Late January

Independence Auditorium buzzed like a swarming hive. The venue could seat over two hundred people, and Sarah had no doubt that there would be standing room only tonight. She raised her eyes to the stage, where several faculty members sat behind a long table. This panel on the proposed amendment to Rhode Island's constitution had been funded by the women's studies department, but the GLBT student center had done most of the legwork. *Scratch that,* Sarah thought, smiling faintly. *I did most of the legwork.*

She squinted, double-checking that everything was in order. All four of the panelists were chatting amiably at the moment, but Sarah had no doubt that once the presentations were over, the meeting would become a heated debate. She focused on the two professors who were arguing the Vote No side—Professor Torrey from women's studies and a male professor from URI's law school. Speaking in favor of the amendment were another law professor and a sociologist. *I hope we win,* Sarah thought, despite knowing that it was naïve to expect a clear intellectual victory or defeat here tonight.

Having reassured herself that all was ready, Sarah allowed her attention to shift to Rory, who was manning the video equipment. A small pocket of space in the very center of the hall had been allocated for filming. Sarah watched as Rory fiddled with the height of the tripod, then put her eye to the viewfinder to test her adjustment. The sight of Rory working always intrigued her. She was single-minded when filming—an artist absorbed in her medium.

Not for the first time, their almost-kiss over New Year's replayed in Sarah's memory. She'd had many days alone in her dorm room to ponder, overanalyze, and worry about that moment, before Rory had returned for the spring semester. She had even prepared a little apologetic speech. But when Rory had opened the door two weeks ago, she had acted as though nothing had changed, tossing her bag on the floor and immediately enveloping Sarah in a bear hug. *Like Matt's party never happened.*

Most people, Sarah knew, would have been thankful for the opportunity to just let the whole thing go. But Sarah wasn't most people. The memory plagued her. How could Rory walk around acting like everything was normal between them? Why didn't she want to talk about it—to figure out what it meant?

Sarah pressed the heels of her palms against her forehead. *And why the hell can't I stop thinking about it?* Her brain ached and her stomach hurt. *A clean slate, that's what I want. No memories. Tabula rasa.*

"You okay, baby?" Chelsea asked, hovering at her elbow.

Sarah's stomach churned guiltily, but she managed to smile. "Fine. Just a little tired." She looked down at her watch. It was nearly seven o'clock. "Think we should sit?"

"I'll sit. You need to start this event, remember?"

"Oh yeah." Sarah had almost forgotten that she was responsible for introducing the panelists.

Chelsea stood on her tiptoes, threaded her arms around Sarah's neck, and kissed her. "You look so good tonight. Don't be nervous."

Sarah kissed Chelsea back automatically. But even as she responded, she couldn't stop from wondering how it would be different with Rory. Would Rory's lips be firm or soft? How would she taste? Would she demand the lead from Sarah, or melt into her, or...

Chelsea pulled away and laughed softly. "Maybe we should

save the make-out session for later, when we're not surrounded by strangers?"

Sarah felt her face turn red. She knew that Chelsea would assume she was embarrassed by their public display of affection, but that didn't bother her in the slightest. *Thinking about your roommate while kissing your girlfriend. How much more messed up can you get?*

"I'd better go," she said, indicating the podium. Hopefully, the speeches and debate would be thoroughly engaging, so much so that she'd be distracted from thoughts of Rory. Hopefully. But she doubted it. "See you soon."

❖

Rory watched Sarah ascend to the stage and take her place behind the podium. She tried to focus on adjusting the camera angle, breathing deeply and unclenching the tiny muscles of her jaw that had cramped up when she'd seen Sarah kissing Chelsea. *This is an important event to get on film,* she reminded herself. *Don't fuck it up.* But God, it was hard to think with jealousy raging through her blood like that virus from *28 Days Later.*

She had returned to campus determined to ignore what had happened—or rather, almost happened—on New Year's Eve. *It was just a fluke,* she thought for the thousandth time. Sarah had wanted to kiss her. She was certain of that much. But she had also been in one of her pensive moods, and buzzed besides. *That moment was about Chelsea, not about me.*

As always, though, her internal devil's advocate refused to stay silent. What if she was wrong about Sarah? What if Sarah *wasn't* happy with Chelsea? Rory had watched them closely since school had started again. Chelsea was as clingy as always, and Sarah as solicitous. Nothing seemed to have changed between them. *But what if Sarah's been discontent all along?*

Rory grimaced at the irony. She had shoved Sarah into that relationship, and now it was coming back to bite her. The fact was that Sarah was dating one of the most desired women on campus.

Nobody ever broke up with Chelsea; she broke up with them. *And if she hurts Sarah, I swear to God I'll—*

For a moment, Rory stared sightlessly through her camera's viewfinder. She was in the impossible position of both wanting and not wanting Chelsea to end that relationship. *Now* that *is fucked up.*

"Good evening, everyone," Sarah said from the podium. "And welcome. We're going to get started."

Her voice was loud and clear. Compelling. *She* was compelling, dammit—crisply handsome in her starched pink oxford shirt and gray slacks. Rory's fingertips itched with the need to slide through Sarah's short, dark hair—to massage her scalp as their lips clashed, tongues battling and teeth scraping together. It would be the kind of kiss that poets immortalized in verse and rock stars in song. The kind of kiss that would change her life forever. The kind of kiss that—

Oh my freaking God, Rory thought, suddenly disgusted. *I'm mooning over her like a twelve-year-old girl over Orlando Bloom.* She scowled at the viewfinder as she focused in on Sarah's face. These feelings were nothing new. Unrequited love was all-too-familiar territory. She had to suck it up and deal, just like always. *I'm a pro at this.*

And Sarah was a pro at public speaking. She looked sharp, relaxed, confident. *Hot.* She had this cleft in her chin—a tiny indentation that was, quite simply, adorable. Her face was perfect—finely chiseled like a Greek sculpture. What would it feel like to cup that face in her palms, to slide one thumb over those lips? Sarah's tongue would dart out and taste her skin, and she would shiver at the warmth and wetness, and—

The applause startled Rory, so much so that she almost knocked over the tripod. *Shit!* She recovered quickly, zooming out and panning away from the podium, toward the panelists. Out of the corner of her eye, she saw Sarah take her seat next to Chelsea, who reached for her hand. The jealousy rose again, coiling inside her like a solar flare. Would Sarah's palm be clammy? Would she rub her thumb over Rory's knuckles? Would she rest their joined hands on her thigh?

Stop it. The thought was savage. *You're making yourself crazy.* Resolutely, Rory turned back to her camera, vowing to concentrate on her work and not on the pipe dream of how Sarah's fingers would feel entwined with her own.

❖

Sarah walked faster as she neared the door of Adams Hall. She had needed to stay after the panel for a few minutes to thank the speakers and help clean up the stage area, but now she was hustling back toward the GLBT student center to debrief with the other students. The debate had been high-powered and controversial, and she was eager to hear what people were saying about it.

She was still several yards away when she picked out Matt's voice in a descant over the low buzz of the room.

"Was anyone else, like, totally freaked out by some of those people who asked questions?"

Sarah paused in the doorway, surveying the scene. The most active LGBT students on campus—about ten of them—lounged on the couch and on the floor. Two open boxes of pizza steamed enticingly on the work table, and Rory was perched on a chair in the corner, filming. Sarah waved, then took a place on the floor at Chelsea's feet.

"Yeah, there were some nut jobs there tonight," John said. He briefly rested his head on his boyfriend—Travis's—shoulder. "T kept telling me to just squeeze his hand when I *really* wanted to stand up and ream them out."

"Yeah, yeah," Matt said. "Like how about that guy who asked the question about people marrying their pets? I mean, what the fuck?"

Sarah rested her cheek against Chelsea's knee as she watched her friends' collective outrage. They were angry and passionate, and in that moment, she loved them fiercely. *God, I hope we win this. We deserve to win this.*

"Yeah, that was bullshit," one of the freshmen girls said. "Like my family dog could sign a marriage certificate. Right."

"That lawyer did have an interesting point about people abusing the system," Chelsea said. "People marrying their roommates for tax breaks and such."

Matt shook his head violently. "First of all…what straight boy is going to marry another straight boy, even if it *does* save them money? I think they'd rather starve. And even if they did, so what? People abuse the institution of marriage right now. All the time."

"I understand that, Matthew," Chelsea said sharply. "I was just saying that he had a point."

"Y'know what I don't understand?" Travis said into the slightly awkward silence. "I don't get everyone in that room who made comments about 'those people.' Like the woman who wanted 'those people' to stop making such a big deal out of this amendment. Could she not see that at least half the audience was queer?" He hunched his shoulders. "Made me feel weird."

"I don't know how Professor Torrey stayed as calm as she did," Sarah chimed in. "Seeing as she's one of 'those people' too."

"Why do they hate us so much?" John said quietly. "It's not like we're asking for special treatment. Just the same right as everybody else."

Sarah felt her heart lurch in empathy. She'd been asking the same thing, ever since that summer night at her parents' kitchen table. *Why won't you accept me? Why won't you be fair?* There was never an answer, and the constant questioning added to her fatigue.

"What do you think, Sarah?" another freshman was asking. "What's going to happen in April?"

Sarah ran both hands through her short hair. "I have no idea," she said. "I'm hopeful, you know? Because there's so much good stuff happening at FRI and in other organizations around the state. But…" She shrugged. "We have to remember that the amendment passed in both the House and the Senate. It has a lot of support."

"If it fails, I vote we all transfer to a school in Massachusetts," Travis said, half grinning.

"Screw Massachusetts," Matt said. "I'm emigrating to Canada."

Chelsea got to her feet and stretched delicately. "Well, I'm going to emigrate to my room," she said. "It's been a long day. And don't forget—dance committee meeting at noon tomorrow. We need to make posters." She looked down at Sarah. "Walk me there?"

"Absolutely." Sarah stood up and immediately yawned. Her eyes felt like sandpaper. But she couldn't afford to sleep yet. She had a response paper due first thing in the morning for her political science class.

Sarah paused at the door, her attention drawn to Rory. She was slowly packing up her camera, and there was a strange expression on her face—part sadness, and part something else that Sarah couldn't quite recognize. *She looks tired, too.*

"Hey Ror, I'll be home soon," Sarah said. "Will you be there?"

"Yeah," Rory said. She flashed a little smile, but that looked sad as well. "See you in a bit."

Wonder what's going on, Sarah thought as Chelsea reached for her hand and tugged. *I'll have to remember to ask her later.*

"Okay," she said aloud. "See you."

❖

Rory stared sightlessly at her computer screen. She should have been working on her English paper, but she'd pulled up Facebook instead. Even that wasn't an adequate distraction, though. She kept listening for the sound of Sarah's return—kept wondering whether perhaps Sarah had decided not to come home after all. She had never yet spent the entire night in Chelsea's room, for whatever reason, but what if today proved to be the exception?

Soon. Sarah had said she'd be back soon, but that had been almost two hours ago. What if Chelsea's roommate hadn't been home and Chelsea had taken the opportunity to push Sarah onto the bed? What if she had undone each faux-pearl button of her shirt until she could slip her hands inside and slide her thumbs over Sarah's nipples? What if, suddenly impatient, she'd reached down to finger Sarah through her slacks, kissing her hard until she came? What if—

The door opened, and Rory jumped. Resolutely, she continued to stare straight ahead, afraid that Sarah would be able to read her expression if she turned.

"Hey, yo."

"Hey," Sarah said. "I'm surprised you're still up. I can barely see, I'm so tired. I went to the library after I walked Chelsea home so I'd be forced to finish my paper."

The relief was so strong that it made Rory dizzy. She dared to spin so that she could watch Sarah move around the room, first hanging up her coat and then dropping her backpack next to her desk.

"And? Did you get it done?" Sarah looked over and nodded. Fuck, but she was hot in her slightly rumpled dressy clothes.

"Yeah, all set. It's not brilliant, but it'll do." She cocked her head. "What have you been up to?"

"Trying to work." Rory shrugged and stood up. "I think I should just turn in, though. Wicked tired." She liked going to bed when Sarah did—liked falling asleep to the even sounds of her breathing. It was comforting.

"Me, too. Hey, did you get good footage tonight?"

"Definitely," Rory said. She nudged Sarah with one elbow on her way into the bedroom. "You're a good public speaker, y'know."

"Yeah? Really?"

"Yeah," Rory said as she slipped into her pajamas. It felt nice to be able to give Sarah compliments. There was so much she kept bottled inside when it came to her, but about this much, she could be truthful. "You're poised, articulate, easy to hear. You don't look like you have the jitters at all."

"Jeez. Flattery will get you everywhere."

Rory padded out of the bedroom, toothbrush in hand. "Oh?" she said, arching one eyebrow and pursing her lips slightly. "I'll be sure to remember that."

She flashed Sarah what she hoped was a mysterious smile before heading out the door toward the bathroom. Part of her was cringing in fear that Sarah would see through her flirting, but the rest of her was pleased at the reaction she'd elicited. Sarah had gotten all blinky. Slack-jawed, even.

I affect her, Rory thought. *I do. Maybe...just maybe this isn't completely hopeless after all.*

CHAPTER TWELVE

February 17

"This is hopeless," Sarah called, turning away from the mirror on the back of their door. She tossed the tie she'd borrowed from Matt onto her desk. "I can't do it. Totally beyond me."

"You can't tie a tie?" Rory shouted back from the bedroom, where she was getting dressed. "What kind of lesbian are you?"

"Clearly a subpar one." Sarah inspected herself in the mirror. She was wearing black slacks, a light blue French oxford shirt, and a black jacket that she had borrowed from one of the guys across the hall. Matt's rainbow tie would have been the perfect addition to an otherwise banal outfit, but despite having watched her father tie a Windsor many times, she couldn't even get close. "I'll just bring it along and have Matt do it."

"The hell you will!"

When the bedroom door banged open, Sarah felt her jaw drop. Rory was striding toward her purposefully, one hand outstretched. She was dressed in a black strapless gown, and she had curled two thick locks of hair so that they framed her face. *Oh my God. She's stunning.*

"Where is it? I'll tie it for you. I'd teach you, but we're already running late."

Sarah pointed to the desk, not sure she was capable of speaking. *Incredible. She looks…incredible.* Rory liked baggy clothes—sweats and cargo pants and loose-fitting jeans. The dress she had on tonight, though, clung to her body, accentuating her curves.

Sarah knew she was staring, but couldn't seem to stop. She let her gaze roam where her hands wanted to, lingering on Rory's breasts before moving slowly across her ribs and down toward the tantalizing swell of her hips.

Lush. That was the word for her figure. Desire ignited deep in Sarah's gut as Rory moved close to her.

"Stand still," Rory said, threading the tie underneath Sarah's collar and leaning in to work on the knot. "If you fidget, I'll fuck it up and then we'll be even later."

Sarah clenched her hands at her sides against an overwhelming impulse to rest them on Rory's waist. She tried to take a long, slow breath. *Normal. Have to act normal.*

"You look...really nice," she finally managed. *And you smell good, too.*

Rory expertly twisted the fabric, then leaned in close to adjust the knot. Her hair brushed against Sarah's cheek. "Why so surprised?" she asked dryly. "Didn't think I could clean up?"

"W-what?" Sarah spluttered. "I implied no such thing!"

"There. Done." She took a step back. "And yes, your tone of voice indicated mild shock."

As space opened up between them, Sarah found it easier to breathe. *Normal. Banter. C'mon.* She made a face and bent down to pull on her shoes. "Whatever. You're just trying to get my goat."

"Mission accomplished, huh?"

When Sarah glared, Rory winked at her and slid her feet into a pair of heels. She click-clacked over to the door and swung it open. Despite her recent resolution, Sarah was mesmerized by the way the black fabric hugged Rory's ass.

She blinked and focused on the floor, fighting off a twinge of panic. At this rate, it was going to be a long, long night.

"Chop chop, stud," Rory said from the doorway. "Matt's pre-parties are notorious for running out of booze before the main event begins. And I, for one, am not up for recapping my high school years at the big dance unless I'm at least tipsy."

❖

Rory allowed Sarah to open Matt's door for her and was immediately assaulted by the smell of beer and the sound of Madonna asking anyone and everyone to justify her love. The room was packed, and as she picked her way toward the coolers in the corner, Rory noticed that she was turning quite a few heads.

Including Sarah's. The expression on her face had been priceless. Rory couldn't help but feel smug. The sure and certain knowledge that Sarah was attracted to her was a rush. *New Year's wasn't a fluke after all.* And if dressing up like a real girl was what it took for Sarah to notice her, then dammit, she'd wear dresses more often.

"Rory!" Matt enveloped her in a hug, then took a step back to hold her at arm's length. He was wearing a white suit, and his hair was a brilliant blue. "That dress is fabulous. You're total heartbreak material tonight."

"Let's hope you're not the only one who thinks so," she said, trying to be enigmatic. "How about fixing us up with some beverages?"

"Us?" Matt looked around. "Us who?"

"Oh," Rory said as she turned. "I must have lost Sarah in the crowd."

Matt pointed toward the far corner. Chelsea had backed Sarah into it and was kissing her for all she was worth. Rory felt her stomach sink into her feet, even as she was mesmerized. *Is that what we'd look like if we were making out?*

"I think Chelsea found her."

"And is trying to swallow her tongue," Rory finished. She resolutely looked away and snapped her fingers. "Let's go, host, give a single girl a drink."

"You're getting the punch, m'lady. Beer is too coarse and unrefined for the likes of you."

"I do believe I'm flattered," Rory said, doing her best to affect a Southern accent.

Matt offered her a campy bow as he handed over a brimming cup, and was about to say something else when shouting erupted across the room.

"Aw, dude! Party foul!"

Matt's head whipped around and he grabbed for the roll of paper towels on top of the dresser. "Damn klutzes. Back in a sec."

Rory was faced with a choice. She could either stand around missing Sarah or find a way to hang out with her, despite Chelsea. A few months ago, she would have waited patiently for Matt's return. But Sarah had almost kissed her between now and then, and Rory was fairly certain that she'd wanted to again, earlier tonight. That had to mean something.

Suddenly determined, Rory filled two additional cups with punch and migrated slowly through the jam of people, nodding at those she knew and smiling at all the compliments on her attire. As she approached Sarah, though, her smile faltered. Something about Sarah's body language looked off. She seemed stiff, as though Chelsea's attention was unwanted.

As much as Rory wanted to feel grateful for that, she was also concerned. *Something must be wrong.* The feeling intensified when Sarah caught sight of her and immediately looked relieved.

"Rory! Hey, what's up?"

"I brought you each a drink." Rory set the cups down on the windowsill and managed to grin. "Figured you'd be thirsty after all…that."

"Oh, that was sweet of you," Chelsea said, taking the proffered punch. "Thanks."

She sipped delicately. Sarah, however, downed her entire cup in three long swallows. Rory raised her eyebrows. *What the hell is going on?* Sarah had been happy enough just five minutes ago. What had happened in the meantime?

"Need me to get you another one, roomie?"

"I'll come with you." Sarah leaned down to kiss Chelsea on the cheek. "See you in a minute, 'kay?"

"You all right?" Rory asked as they crossed the room.

"Yeah, sure." Sarah jammed her hands in the pockets of her slacks and hunched her shoulders. "I just needed a breather."

"Literally?"

Rory expected a friendly retort, but Sarah just nodded. She was slipping into one of her pensive moods, and Rory had no idea what to do. She wanted to ask what was going on, but had a feeling that Sarah would shut down if she did. So instead, she handed over two more cups.

"You look tense," she said. "Why don't you drink one of these now and take the other back?"

Sarah cracked a half-smile. "Are you trying to get me drunk?"

"Damn, you saw right through me," Rory said, hoping for a laugh. "Does that mean I can't take advantage of you now?"

She had meant it as a joke, but Sarah's grin disappeared completely. *Shit*, Rory thought, watching her take a long swallow from the cup in her right hand. She seemed even more uneasy than she had been a few minutes ago. *I'm off my game tonight.*

Sarah looked over toward the corner, then back again. For some reason, she wouldn't meet Rory's gaze. "I should get back, I guess," she said.

"Yeah, okay." Rory contented herself with patting Sarah gently on one shoulder. "Relax and enjoy the night, will you?"

"Of course." Sarah favored Rory with a small smile before turning toward Chelsea. "Thanks."

"And don't let her win at tonsil hockey!" Rory called.

She was gratified to get the finger in response. *That's more like it.* It was hard to watch Sarah walk away, so instead, she poured another cup full of punch. A few seconds later, Matt slid past her to grab a beer from one of the coolers and slouched despondently against the wall.

"Why, why did I have to make that damn punch bright red? I'll never get the stain out of my carpet. Never."

Rory rolled her eyes. "Chill. You are the king of dye. You'll figure it out." She raised her cup and clinked it with his bottle. "Quit worrying and have a good time. For fuck's sake, I sound like a broken record."

❖

Sarah handed her ticket to the volunteer standing outside the door, and followed Chelsea into the dance. Having helped to set up the hall earlier in the day, she knew what she would find. A large disco ball hung from the ceiling and rainbow streamers crisscrossed the room. The lights above the dance floor alternated red, green, and blue.

"I'm going to go request some songs," Chelsea said, fiddling with Sarah's collar. "To set the mood for...later." She winked, then turned her face up for a kiss before moving toward the DJ.

Sarah watched her go. When the strobe kicked in, Chelsea's light blue dress shimmered tantalizingly. *She's beautiful, and sexy, and really into you. What the hell is your problem?* Ever since Chelsea had pulled her into the corner at Matt's party, kissed her passionately, and then whispered that she'd reserved them a room at a nearby hotel for after the dance, Sarah had felt queasy. *This is ridiculous. Something is seriously wrong with me.*

"Hey, dark and broody!" Rory approached her from the dance floor, holding several strands of rainbow beads. "Or should I call you 'dark and stormy'?" She grinned as she threw one gaudy necklace over Sarah's head. "Come dance with me, or I'll tell everyone in this room that you own a pair of pink underwear."

Sarah couldn't help but laugh. "That kind of threat makes you irresistible."

"Damn right."

Sarah followed Rory into the center of the room and did her best not to flail around too much. She was impressed. Rory had moves. She could do this swirling thing with her hips that was really quite sensual. And now that Sarah thought about it, she was pretty sure that Rory wasn't wearing a bra.

She lost track of the rhythm when she realized where her thoughts had wandered off to. How could she be thinking about Rory that way, when she was going to make love to her girlfriend later that night?

"I don't think being slightly tipsy helps me much with my technique," she said, trying to laugh off her awkwardness.

"Seriously? I *only* dance under the influence. If I were sober, I'd be a wallflower."

Sarah raised her eyebrows. This was new information. "Oh yeah? Are there any other strange behaviors I should expect from drunken Rory?"

Rory chose that moment to grab Sarah's hand, raise it high and twirl herself underneath. When she emerged from the spin, Sarah automatically rested her other palm on Rory's waist. *Soft.*

"Chattiness. And flirtiness." Rory cocked her head slightly. "Are we really going to try to waltz to J.Lo?"

"Of course not. We're going to polka."

Rory giggled and moved a little closer. *Well,* thought Sarah as their bodies touched, *this must be what she means by "flirtiness."* But before she could figure out what to do next, Rory was pulling back and she was being embraced from behind.

"Hey, baby." Chelsea slid around to nestle against Sarah's chest. She looked over her shoulder at Rory. "Mind if I cut in?"

"'Course not. Go to it." Rory waved at Sarah and spun on one heel. If she heard Sarah's "see you," she gave no indication.

"Miss me?" Chelsea asked, threading her arms around Sarah's neck.

"Definitely," Sarah said, trying to ignore the surge of dread that spiraled in her gut.

"How about we dance a few songs and then get out of here?" Chelsea murmured. Her tongue traced the shell of Sarah's ear. When Sarah shivered, Chelsea sucked on her earlobe. "You like that, hmm?"

Sarah ruthlessly tamped down her rising panic. *Stop thinking. Just go with it.*

"Yeah," she said, pulling Chelsea closer. "Feels good."

❖

"Let's have some champagne," Chelsea said. She was lounging on their king-sized bed while Sarah hung their coats in the closet.

"Okay." Sarah picked up the bottle that was resting in the ice bucket and carefully worked it open.

"I love watching you," Chelsea said. "You are so crazy hot."

Sarah looked over and smiled, trying hard not to betray any of her inner turmoil. "Thank you for all of this. It's really romantic."

"Well, I wanted this to be special—the first time we're *really* together."

Sarah poured the champagne slowly. It frothed, wanting to bubble over the flute rims. Love was supposed to be like that, wasn't it? A sort of joyful, barely contained madness—a riot of emotion and sensation that would fill her up until she felt as though she might overflow.

She handed over Chelsea's glass before promptly draining her own.

"Oh, baby. Are you nervous?"

"A little." Sarah wanted to tell her that she couldn't go through with this. That it just didn't feel right. That she needed more time. But Chelsea had set up this entire scenario, and the pressure of it all—the huge bed, the celebratory drink, the fancy clothes—weighed in against honesty.

Chelsea patted the space beside her. "Come here. You don't need to be, you know. It's not like either of us is new at this. And you look so damn good tonight. I'm so turned on already."

When Sarah obliged by climbing onto the bed, Chelsea pulled her down for a long, wet kiss. Sarah tried to relax into it—to get so caught up in the slow thrust of Chelsea's tongue against hers that she had no brainpower left for wondering what this would feel like with Rory. That was working pretty well until Chelsea began to unbutton her shirt. Sarah's stomach flip-flopped even as she got wet.

She stilled Chelsea's fingers automatically. But when Chelsea's features dissolved into an expression of hurt and confusion, Sarah realized that she had to pretend. "I want you naked," she said, toying with the hem of Chelsea's dress. "Now."

Chelsea's eyes got wide and her breathing sped up. "God, I love when you get assertive." She raised her hips, and Sarah skimmed the dress up her torso and over her head. Beneath, Chelsea wore only a tiny blue thong.

"You're beautiful," Sarah whispered. That, at least, was not a lie. Chelsea's rosy nipples begged to be sucked, and the delicate muscles of her taut stomach trembled beneath Sarah's right hand.

"Want you so bad—"

Chelsea's words ended in a cry as Sarah bent down to lick a slow circle around first one nipple, then the other. As she sped up the motion of her tongue, Sarah worked Chelsea's thong down her legs. When Chelsea kicked off the tiny scrap of material, Sarah slid one thigh between hers and pressed up firmly. Chelsea groaned.

Sarah felt as though she were acting out a love scene on a movie set. She followed her own inner script, raising her head to kiss Chelsea firmly, as she rolled her hips. It was a strange sensation—as though she were at once inside her body and hovering above it.

"Oh, please touch me," Chelsea begged, her breaths stuttering in her throat. "I'm so hot for you, Sarah."

Sarah saw herself slip her right hand between their bodies. She felt herself push one finger into Chelsea while bringing her thumb down gently but firmly on her clit. Chelsea's soft cry seemed to come from miles away.

And then Sarah's thumb was making tiny circles, and her finger was thrusting slowly in and out, and Chelsea's body was as tight and arched as a bowstring. "Come for me," Sarah heard herself say. And Chelsea did, bucking and shuddering beneath her.

Sarah watched herself watch Chelsea in the throes of passion. Aesthetically, the scene was perfect, but it didn't move her. She felt nothing—nothing except relief.

She left Chelsea's body as carefully as she had opened the bottle of champagne.

"So good," Chelsea murmured, her eyelids fluttering. "Mmm, you wiped me out, baby."

"Just rest for a bit," Sarah whispered. She turned onto her side and began to lightly rub Chelsea's stomach. *That's it. Sleep. Sleep, now.*

The rhythm of Chelsea's breathing changed almost immediately, slowing and deepening. Sarah waited for several minutes, just to be certain, before easing off the bed. She poured another flute of champagne and drank it slowly while looking out the window at the lights of Kingston. As the buzz kicked in, she leaned forward to rest her forehead against the cool glass.

When she finally let herself think of Rory, the tears came. They leaked out of the corners of her eyes, tracked down her cheeks, and clung stubbornly to her chin before plunging into the thick carpet. Sarah held her body perfectly still and let them take their course.

Can't do this anymore, she realized numbly. In place of the panic, there was only a dull fatigue.

When her eyes were dry again, she wrote Chelsea a brief note on the hotel letterhead. She slipped into her shoes and jacket, then quietly opened the door and stepped out into the brightly lit hallway.

❖

Rory glanced at her watch. Three a.m. Her eyes were burning in exhaustion, but she just couldn't go to bed when Sarah wasn't there. *Looks like I'm pulling an all-nighter,* she thought grimly, pressing A to start another game of Halo. Fortunately, massacring aliens almost completely distracted her from thoughts of Sarah and Chelsea making love. Almost.

And then the door opened.

Rory spun around, forgetting to hit the pause button. Sarah stood in the doorway blinking at her. She looked confused and sad, and her eyes were red and swollen. *Has she been crying?*

"Hey," Rory said. For a moment, she considered trying to say something funny, but Sarah looked far too raw for humor. It was time to be genuine. "Everything okay? I didn't expect you home till morning."

Sarah kicked off her shoes and shrugged out of her jacket. As she was slinging it over the back of her desk chair, she said, "I'm going to break up with her."

Rory couldn't move. She'd been wanting to hear those words out of Sarah's mouth for the past two months, but in this moment, she felt no triumph. Sarah was clearly suffering. She wanted to make it all better, and had no idea how.

"What happened?" was all she could think to ask.

Sarah sat down and rested her elbows on her knees. When she met Rory's gaze, her face was troubled. "I care about her, you know? I really do. She's a good person, and she's fun, and she's beautiful."

Rory nodded, but Sarah didn't speak again for a long time. She seemed to be struggling to find the right words. "But?" Rory prompted gently.

"But I can't be with her, because I'm not in love with her. And she wants things from me that I can't..." Sarah trailed off, shaking her head. "I dunno. I think I'm pretty messed up. She'll be way better off with someone who will really appreciate her."

Rory wanted to press for more details, but she didn't think that was wise. If Sarah wanted her to know exactly what had happened between the dance and this moment, she would elaborate. "I don't think you're messed up," she said. "And it sounds to me like you're not happy with her."

"You're right." Sarah rubbed at her neck. "I want to be, but I'm not."

Rory fiddled with a loose thread on the inseam of her sweats. *Could I make you happy, Sarah? Could you fall in love with me?* She glanced up to find Sarah gazing out the darkened window. She looked exhausted and forlorn, and Rory wanted to enfold her in a long hug. But she stayed where she was.

"When are you going to do it?"

"Tomorrow. I left her a note asking her to call me when she got up because I wanted to talk to her over breakfast."

Rory nodded. She racked her brains for some words of comfort, but nothing came to mind. What did you say when the woman you wanted was tearing herself apart because she didn't want her girlfriend?

"I should have ended it months ago," Sarah murmured. She turned back toward Rory. "Do you think I'm a terrible person?"

"What?" Rory had to clutch her beanbag chair to keep from getting to her feet. "Of course not. I think you're…well, frankly, I think you're the most remarkable person I've ever met." She bit her lip, wondering if she'd gone too far, but Sarah only laughed hollowly.

"You're being too nice to me."

"What have you done that's so awful?" Rory demanded.

"I'm not in love with Chelsea," Sarah said. Her voice was growing louder. "But I think she might be in love with *me*. I should have ended it a long time ago, when I knew I'd never feel that way about her. I've been leading her on!"

She got up, then, and began to pace. "You know what? I should never have gotten involved with her in the first place. Maybe I'm just not cut out for relationships. Maybe I don't deserve one. Or maybe Dar *broke* me and now I'm incapable."

Rory couldn't maintain the distance between them any longer. She rose to her feet, stood in front of Sarah, and put both hands on her shoulders. Sarah was shaking. The muscles beneath Rory's palms quivered slightly.

"You listen to me," Rory said fiercely. "You're not broken. You're not incapable. You're not undeserving. You started dating Chelsea because you liked her and were attracted to her. Now you're realizing that isn't enough for you." Rory tightened her grip when Sarah tried to look away. "That sucks, for sure. Breaking up fucking *sucks*. But I know you, Sarah Storm, and I know you're not malicious."

Sarah just stared at her for several seconds, and Rory stared back, her jaw set. *You have to believe me. You have to.*

Miraculously, a smile played around the corners of Sarah's mouth. "I'm not allowed to argue, am I?" she asked wryly.

"Hell no." Rory squeezed once, then forced herself to step away like a normal roommate would. "I don't know about you," she said as she turned off the television, "but I'm totally wiped. Bedtime?"

"Yeah."

Rory grabbed her toothbrush and toothpaste and was heading out the door when Sarah's hand on her arm stopped her in her tracks.

"Thank you," Sarah said quietly. "For listening to me and for, y'know, not letting me self-flagellate too much."

Impulsively, Rory hugged her. It was the right thing to do, after all, and so what if she let her fingers play lightly in the short hairs on the back of Sarah's neck before pulling away?

"You're going to be okay," Rory said firmly. "Tomorrow, the next day, and every day after that." She fought back the sudden urge to cup Sarah's face, and lightly punched her upper arm instead. "I promise."

CHAPTER THIRTEEN

Sarah pulled up the collar of her coat and bent her head into the chill morning wind. Grains of snow blew down off the tree branches, dusting her head and stinging her cheeks.

The problem, she reflected as she trudged on toward Roger Williams, was that there wasn't a "good" way to break up with someone. Over the phone was tacky, e-mail even tackier. Leaving a text message was cowardly. Voicemail was insulting. But if you decided to do it face-to-face, where were you supposed to go?

Now that she thought about it, choosing a dining hall was pretty lame. And despite the fact that she'd woken up hours ago, thinking about this very scenario, she still had no idea what to say. Her stomach roiled. *Will she ever forgive me? God, I don't want to hurt her.*

Sarah paused in front of the double doors and kicked at a loose ball of ice on the sidewalk. There was still time to bow out—to go back to her room and write that e-mail, or even take out her phone right now and send a text.

I owe her so much more than that, Sarah told herself firmly. *She deserves some kind of explanation. If I even have one.*

She took a deep breath of frigid air, welcoming the sharp stab of pain in her lungs, and threw open the doors. As soon as she stepped inside, Chelsea hugged her fiercely.

"Are you okay, baby? What happened last night?"

Sarah's heart lurched in her chest, her arms going automatically around Chelsea's waist. *Oh God. Can I really do this?*

"I am *so* ashamed that I fell asleep on you," Chelsea said as she combed her fingers through Sarah's hair, brushing off the snowflakes. "Didn't wake up until the morning, and you were gone…"

"I'm sorry I left," Sarah said. "I—I couldn't sleep."

"Oh no," Chelsea said, looking suddenly anxious. "Was I snoring?"

Sarah managed to crack a smile. "No, nothing like that." She gestured toward a table in the corner. "Want to sit down?"

"Aren't you hungry?"

"Oh yeah." Sarah followed Chelsea obediently through the cafeteria line. Her stomach was pitching and rolling worse than ever, so she settled on a banana and a cup of much-needed coffee. As they made their way toward a small table in the far corner of the hall, Sarah wished the floor would just open up and swallow her. *I don't want to do this. But I have to, dammit. I have to.* Keeping up this charade wasn't fair—to either of them.

"So what happened? Why did you have to leave?" Chelsea leaned forward and lowered her voice. "I woke up wanting to go down on you."

Sarah swallowed hard. Her body reacted to Chelsea's words, even as her brain shied away from the idea. Why couldn't she be one of those people who enjoyed casual sex? Why couldn't she stop overanalyzing? *Hell…why can't I just be in love with her?*

Chelsea was regarding her expectantly, waiting for an answer. Sarah licked dry lips. This was it. She had to do it. Right. Now.

"Chelsea," she said, her voice cracking on the second syllable. "I don't really know how to…the thing is…" She trailed off, looking away for a moment, then back again. "Please believe me, I don't want to hurt you," she finally blurted. "But I can't do this anymore."

"What?"

Shock and pain infused that one, tremulous word. Sarah felt her heart constrict in sympathy and empathy. *Goddammit. I'm making her feel the way Dar made me feel.*

"You're so beautiful," she said, desperate to prove to Chelsea that this really, truly wasn't about *her*. "And you're sexy and fun… smart and talented…God, Chelsea, you're amazing." Chelsea's eyes were brimming over with tears, and Sarah clutched at her napkin as though it were a lifeline, or an anchor. "Please, you have to believe me."

"Then why are you—" Chelsea stumbled over the words. "You're breaking up with me?"

"I want to be in love with you," Sarah said, staring hard into Chelsea's bright blue eyes, willing her to hear the truth. "I should be. But I'm…I'm not."

Chelsea's mouth trembled, and two tears streaked down her face like falling stars. She took a deep, shuddering breath. "I knew it."

Sarah blinked in confusion. "Knew it? I—"

"It's Rory, isn't it?" Chelsea's voice was harsh. "You're in love with Rory."

"What?" Sarah sat back hard in her chair, feeling dizzy. She opened her mouth and then closed it again, searching desperately for the right words. "That's…I mean…Rory's not even queer!"

Chelsea arched one perfect eyebrow, her lips twisted in a sneer. "Doubtful. I've seen the way she looks at you. And even if you're right—so what? You think you're the first lesbian to fall for a straight girl?"

Sarah shook her head, wondering if she looked as shell-shocked as she felt. In love? With Rory? How could that possibly be? Yes, she was attracted to her. Yes, she had been jealous of Jeff. Yes, she loved spending time with Rory—more, she admitted, than she enjoyed anyone else's company. *But wouldn't I know if I were in love with her?*

"I don't know what to say."

"You're not denying it," Chelsea said coldly. "That says a lot."

Sarah sucked in a breath, fully intending to explain that there was no possible way that she could be in love with Rory…and found that she couldn't speak the words. She sat very still, looking into Chelsea's bright, angry eyes, and said nothing. The silence was a wedge, driving them apart.

"I think I have my answer," Chelsea whispered. She got to her feet, yanked her coat off the back of her chair, and walked away without a backward glance.

Sarah reached for her coffee. The cup shook as she lifted it to her mouth. She stared at the chair that Chelsea had just vacated, trying to force her brain to make sense of what had just happened. Why hadn't she denied it? Could Chelsea possibly be right? Sarah began replaying every significant encounter she'd had with Rory since New Year's, searching for the truth. But the more she tried to analyze her feelings and motivations, the harder her head began to throb.

"This is useless," she muttered as she pushed her chair back. Brooding wouldn't accomplish anything. Frankly, it didn't matter if she was in love with Rory or not, because Rory certainly wasn't in love with her.

As she headed for the door, Sarah realized that she was dreading the return to her room. She could never tell Rory what Chelsea had said, of course. And now, it was going to be even harder than before to act "normally." Whatever that meant.

But when Sarah tried to open their door, she found it locked. *Thank God.* Once inside, she paused just long enough to throw a few textbooks in her backpack. She could spend the afternoon doing some FRI business and the evening in the library. It would feel good to accomplish something today—to make up, in some karmic way, for the relationship she had just destroyed.

Deep in her left jeans pocket, her phone suddenly vibrated. She fished it out, squinting at the message on the screen: *am editing film in studio. thinking about you. how'd it go?*

The text made Sarah's pulse stutter. *Thinking about you.* It felt good to know that Rory was thinking about her. Really good. Too good.

"Okay, clearly I have feelings for her," Sarah confessed to the empty room. Unable to help herself, she reread the words, examining them for a deeper significance. The message was friendly. No romantic overtones, no teasing innuendos—just warm and caring. One friend to another. That was all.

An aching, hollow feeling opened up in the center of her chest. *Of course she's not in love with me.* She was still crushing on Jeff. Had been for years. Their almost-kiss had been all Sarah's doing, and thankfully, Rory had had the grace to just laugh it off. To move on.

Chelsea had been wrong about her. *But she wasn't wrong about me.*

"Oh, give it a rest. You're making yourself crazy." She quickly tapped out a reply to Rory, then shoved the cell back into her pocket and left the room.

Stay focused, she thought as she walked toward the stairwell. Midterms were starting next week, the candlelight vigil would come a week after that, and the election was less than two months away. She couldn't afford any distractions. Not now.

❖

Sarah was just wrapping up a phone call with a nice elderly woman in Brockton who had listened very patiently to her explanation of the issues at stake in the upcoming referendum, when Nancy entered the office. Sarah waved.

"Hi," Nancy said once Sarah had hung up. "I didn't expect to see you here this evening."

"Evening?" Sarah turned toward the window. Sure enough, it was dark outside. "Jeez. What time is it?"

"Almost six. How long have you been at it?"

Sarah shrugged. "A while, I guess. I came in early this afternoon to make a few calls." She smiled faintly. "I must have hit my stride."

Nancy laughed. "I think you're the only person I know who has ever lost track of time while phone canvassing. How did it go?"

"Not too bad." Sarah stood up, stretched, and turned off her computer monitor. "The way this is breaking down by age demographic is really interesting to me." She gestured toward her phone. "Take Mrs. Delaney, there, who sounds exactly like my grandmother. She was willing to hear me out, but I'm pretty sure she's going to vote yes. Most students that I talk to, on the other hand, are all about voting no."

"The polls are showing exactly that trend," Nancy said, nodding. "It's a good sign. If we lose in May, I think it's safe to say that loss won't be permanent."

"If we lose..." Sarah trailed off. Thinking about that made her stomach hurt again. It was a very real possibility, of course. The Rhode Island Attorney General's move to recognize gay marriages performed in Massachusetts had caused a significant backlash. "What are the latest numbers?"

"Fifty-six to forty-four, in favor of the amendment." Nancy idly played with one of her earrings, flicking it back and forth. A nervous habit. "It's going to be close."

"Yeah," Sarah said. "Makes me want to get back on the phone."

"Please take a break," Nancy urged. "You've been going above and beyond, Sarah. Really." She looked Sarah up and down. "And you seem tired. Is everything okay?"

For a second, Sarah considered telling Nancy about the breakup with Chelsea and her confusion over her feelings for Rory. It would be so nice to just confess everything to someone not involved—someone older, who could give her a sympathetic ear and maybe even some wise advice.

But Nancy didn't need to hear any of that. She had far too much on her plate, and she probably wanted to get started on whatever project had brought her to the office on a Saturday night. *She's not your mother*, Sarah thought bitterly. *Just say you're fine, and be done with it.*

"Oh, I'm doing all right," she said. "A little tired, yeah. Two midterms next week." She slipped on her coat and shouldered her backpack. "Speaking of which, I'm going to hit the library."

"Good luck," Nancy said. "Hang in there."

Sarah nodded and braced herself for the chill of the February night. As she trudged back toward campus, she slipped both hands into her coat pockets. Her fingers brushed against the cool metal of her phone, and she had the sudden urge to check it for any more messages from Rory.

Don't be pathetic. Gritting her teeth against the impulse, Sarah turned toward the library. It didn't matter whether Rory had texted her or not. She was going to spend the rest of the evening studying, not obsessing over how she'd managed to develop a crush on her roommate after all, or wallowing in her guilt over Chelsea. If she could just manage to act like everything was fine, maybe it would be.

Maybe.

❖

"I have news," Rory announced. She set her tray down across from Matt's with a thump. The chocolate milk in her cup sloshed dangerously close to the brim, threatening to spill over onto her mashed potatoes.

"Oh?" Matt arched one blue eyebrow. "Spill it, gossip girl."

"Sarah broke up with Chelsea this morning."

"What?" Matt froze, his forkful of mushy green beans poised halfway between the table and his mouth. "Are you serious?"

"Yeah." Rory reached around the back of her chair and grabbed the cell phone in her right jacket pocket. Still no message. It had been a whole five…no…almost seven hours, since Sarah's last text. *Dammit. Where are you? Why won't you talk to me?* She wanted to be understanding and patient. After all, Sarah had had a rough day. Maybe she was just one of those people who needed time alone to process. But what if she was angry for some reason? Or what if she'd been in some kind of accident? Or what if—

Matt's screeching put the brakes on her anxious introspection. "Oh my God, why? What happened? Is Chelsea okay? Is *Sarah* okay?"

"I don't know why, exactly," Rory said as she cut up her breaded chicken. "Sarah didn't go into details last night. All she said was that she couldn't be with Chelsea because she wasn't in love with her." Rory set her knife down on the tray and stabbed at a piece of meat with her fork. "Last I saw Sarah, she was heading out the door to talk to Chelsea. She texted me after to say that it had been tough but that she was all right. Whatever that means."

"Jesus." Matt took a sip from his soda and leaned back in his chair. "Never saw that coming."

"Me, neither." For about the thousandth time that day, Rory wondered what had happened after Sarah and Chelsea left the dance.

"I'm glad you told me," Matt said. "I'll stop by Chelsea's room later to check on her."

Rory nodded. She had no doubt that Chelsea was in need of some comfort, and Matt could be a very good cuddler when necessary. "I just wish Sarah would tell me where she is, so I could do the same."

Matt froze again, frowning at her. Then he put down his fork, rested his arms on the table, and leaned forward. "What's going on with you, exactly?"

"Huh?" said Rory, nonplussed by the abrupt change of subject. "What are you talking about?"

"You. And Sarah. You and Sarah."

"Me and Sarah what?" Rory was starting to feel more than a little panicked. She rubbed suddenly sweaty palms on the legs of her jeans.

"You guys were on the verge of making out at my party," Matt said. He held up one hand when Rory began to splutter. "I haven't brought it up because it was really, really obvious that you didn't want me to. But I have eyes, and I have ears, and you know what, Ror? It looks and sounds to me like you have one hell of a crush on your roommate."

Rory couldn't believe what she was hearing. *Holy shit,* she thought, over the insistent alarm bells in her brain. *He's calling me out.* She swallowed hard, but her mouth remained dry.

Matt was watching her intently, but after a long moment of silence, he smiled. It was an expression she'd never seen before— gentle, and almost sad. He reached across the table to grip one of her hands tightly.

"The first time is always scary as hell," he said quietly. "But it helps to actually say the words. Believe me."

Rory couldn't seem to suck in a deep enough breath. Her eyes stung and her head was spinning and she wanted to burst into tears. But she really couldn't. Not here. *Fuck. Fuck fuck fuck. He's not going to let me off the hook.*

Matt squeezed her hand and she squeezed back. His eyes silently encouraged her. Was this how Sarah had felt back at Yale, in that eternal instant before first confessing her attraction to another woman? Who had it been for Sarah? A friend, like Matt? A mentor? Her soon-to-be girlfriend?

She could picture that Sarah easily—her eyes slightly downcast, shoulders hunched, fingers clenching and unclenching as she battled her insecurities. She had been beautiful, Rory was certain. Strong and scared and hopeful and anxious and resolute.

Her mind's image of past-Sarah shifted into the memory of how she'd looked this morning, on her way out the door. Tired and sad, determined but guilty. Emotionally bruised. Rory would have given anything to take some of that burden off her shoulders. The fact that she couldn't was still haunting her.

I love you, she thought. Yes, she was desperately attracted to Sarah. And yes, they shared many interests. But this feeling—it wasn't really about any of that. It was about something else. Something deeper, more essential. *I love you. I do.*

It wasn't difficult to accept that. Loving Sarah felt natural and right. Easy. The tricky part, she was coming to understand, was telling someone else. Once the words were out there, she couldn't take them back. Once the words were out there, people would think differently of her. But what else could she do? Hide in silence forever, paralyzed by the fear that someone would discover her secret? *If I do that, I'll be miserable.*

Rory sat up straight and looked Matt in the eye, determined not to suffocate under the weight of her anxieties. "I'm falling for Sarah," she said, relieved that her voice remained steady. She even managed a crooked smile. "Which means I'm at least bi. Hell... maybe I'm a lesbian."

Matt squeezed her hand again. "You don't have to pick, sweetie. Not now, not ever. Not unless you want to. Don't let anyone tell you different."

"Okay." Rory was feeling a little shaky, all of a sudden. She took a long drink of milk and then gently withdrew her fingers from Matt's to brush at the corners of her eyes. "Whew. Scary…no shit. Jeez. What a fucking day, huh?"

"I'm proud of you," Matt said. "I hope you're proud of you, too."

Rory rolled her eyes. "Thanks, Mr. Rogers," she quipped, relieved to be able to fall back on her defensive humor routine. "Where's your sweater vest?"

Matt ignored her jibe. "So hey, do you need any rainbow pins? Stickers? Flags? I can totally be your supplier."

"Okay, whoa," Rory said, tensing up again. "I'm glad I told you. I'm really glad. You were right. It does feel good. It's a relief. But no one else can know right now, okay?"

"Sure, fine, if that's what you want."

"That's what I *need*," Rory said. "Think about it, dude. I should wait at least a few weeks before coming out to Sarah. I don't think she can handle any more weirdness today."

"I see your point," Matt said. He mimed zipping and buttoning his lips, and went back to shoveling green beans into his mouth.

Rory halfheartedly pushed some potatoes around on her plate, but she had lost her appetite. Come to think of it, she was exhausted. *I came out today,* she thought. *I came out.* It was exhilarating and scary and humbling, all at once. Suddenly, she felt the urge to do something very normal, like watch a movie or mow down aliens with machine guns.

"I think the adrenaline killed my appetite," she told Matt. "I'm going to head back to my room."

"Want company?"

Rory shook her head as she pushed back her chair and picked up her barely-touched tray. "Nah. I'm good. Go find Chelsea." She tamped down a rush of irrational guilt. "Talk to you later. And… thanks."

"Anytime, sister," he said, blowing her a kiss as she walked away.

Sister. She thought about the word as she pulled her hat down over her ears and walked out into the night. She had never particularly relished that label before. Both in school and at home, she'd always been compared unfavorably to Michelle. "You need to focus on getting better grades in math, like your sister did," her father had often said. And every teacher in both middle and high school had known her as "Rory, Michelle's sister."

But now, "sister" didn't mean standing in someone's shadow or failing to fulfill someone's expectations. It meant that she fit in.

Family, she thought, smiling despite the bitter cold. *I'm family now.*

Chapter Fourteen

Two weeks later

Rory let her head rest against the passenger side window and watched the highway—tinted red by the late afternoon sunlight—slide by. Her eyelids wanted to drift closed, and she fought against the wave of drowsiness. All she had to do was make it through the vigil tonight and then she could get a few days' rest over the weekend. It didn't matter that the following week was spring break—neither she nor Sarah was leaving campus. *Way too much to do.*

She shifted slightly in her seat, trying to get comfortable. Next to her, Sarah was focusing on the road, while behind them, Matt, Travis, and John were uncharacteristically quiet. *We all need a real vacation,* Rory thought. *Maybe next year we should go to Cancun or something.* She could see it now: Sarah playing beach volleyball, sand clinging to her chiseled legs and sweat coating her tight stomach—

"Saa-rah," Matt whined. "We're all bored to tears. Put on some music, will you?"

"Sure, okay," she said. "Rory, would you mind?"

Rory blinked and crossed her legs, trying to subtly ease the ache that her daydream had inspired. She leaned forward to rifle through Sarah's portable CD case. When she found a Bon Jovi disc, she put it in right away. *Almost as good as G&R.*

Within seconds, the boys were happily belting out "Living on a Prayer." Rory smiled but didn't join in. She sneaked a quick glance at Sarah before returning her gaze to the road. Things had been strange between them—stilted, somehow—since Sarah's breakup with Chelsea. Rory couldn't tell whether the weirdness was her doing or Sarah's or both, but she hated it. She felt as though she were back in the very beginning of their friendship, when Sarah had been nice and polite, but completely closed off. And they hadn't really hung out at all over the past two weeks—not that there had been time to.

Rory sighed. *Maybe that's all it is. Maybe we're both just too stressed.* It was by far the easiest explanation to stomach, especially since Matt had repeatedly insisted that he hadn't breathed a word about Rory's epiphany to anyone. Rory wanted so badly to tell Sarah everything. The impulse burned inside her, and she had caught herself on the precipice of a confession more than once. Although she had once been fairly confident that Sarah returned her feelings, now…she wasn't. And it scared her. That in itself was unsettling. Unrequited love had never frightened her before. *I'm an expert.* But whenever she considered the possibility that Sarah didn't want her and might never…

She shivered and swallowed hard as the now-familiar fear constricted her chest. *Quit it. Stop driving yourself crazy.* "So hey," she said, trying to draw Sarah into conversation. "Think we'll make tomorrow's papers?"

Sarah shrugged. "Depends on how well Brown and Providence College advertised." She grinned faintly. "I just hope they brought enough candles."

"It's too bad Kate Clinton couldn't make it," Rory pressed, wanting to keep Sarah talking.

"Yeah," Sarah said. "She would have lightened it up some." She glanced briefly at Rory. "Did you watch some of her stuff on YouTube?"

"Hilarious," Rory said. "Though I still think that Margaret Cho routine about the Asian chicken salad is the best I've seen."

When Sarah laughed, Rory started doing an impersonation.

That made her laugh even harder, and they almost missed their exit. A few minutes later, Rory opened her door and stepped out onto Brown's campus feeling much more lighthearted than she had earlier...only to watch Sarah's smile fade as soon as she took a good look around.

Was it because they were at Brown? Did it remind her of Yale? Or was it because Chelsea, who had just climbed out of Nancy's van, was all over some sophomore kid who was unlucky enough to be her rebound girl? Rory kicked at a rock in frustration and only managed to stub her toe on the curb. *I want to make you happy, and I have no idea how.*

"Okay, everyone," Sarah said, calling the group to order. "Be back here at five fifteen to get your candles. Nancy, Kelly, and I are going into the Union to meet with the other organizers." She lowered her voice and turned to Rory. "What's your filming plan? Are you going to hang out with the others or come in with us?" She leaned a little closer, and Rory clenched her hands into fists against the overwhelming impulse to slide one finger into a belt loop of Sarah's jeans and tug. "Just to warn you—the meeting will probably be boring."

Boring or not, the choice was a no-brainer. "I'm sticking with you," Rory said.

Sarah smiled. "Sounds good."

And just like that, Rory reflected as she popped the trunk to grab her equipment, hope sprang eternal.

❖

"See you soon," Sarah said as Rory broke away from the procession and hurried toward the steps of the capitol building. From there, she would be able to capture the full effect of their approach. Sarah turned slightly, glancing behind her at the long train of supporters who had turned out to protest the proposed amendment. There were well over a hundred people present—maybe even closer to two hundred. When they gathered at the base of the stairs and lit their candles, they'd look even more impressive.

Pride at the success of the event rushed through Sarah. This had been *her* idea, and although the majority of the planning had ultimately fallen to FRI's Providence branch, the University of Rhode Island had managed to bring the largest student contingent. That felt good.

"This is an impressive turnout," said Lee, the executive director of GLAD, who was walking to Nancy's right. She pointed to several vans that had parked near the steps. "And look, the media's here. What an excellent way for us to get some much-needed attention."

Behind her, Matt started a rhyming chant about voting no that was taken up by most of the line. Sarah joined in enthusiastically, exhilarated by the sound of so many voices in unison. Right here, right now, she was a part of something extraordinary. It was like being part of a sports team again, only better.

The sensation of belonging was a relief. She had felt so alone for the past few weeks. Guilt for hurting Chelsea had mingled with the hopelessness of her feelings for Rory. She had wanted to talk to someone, anyone…but Rory was out of the question, and it wasn't safe to spill her guts to Matt. What she had really wanted was to be able to call her mother—to lay everything at her mom's feet the way she had when she was in high school. To be comforted and reassured. To know that she was okay, and that things were going to get better.

But that door was closed to her. *Should I try to open it?* Sarah wondered. Maybe enough time had passed. *Maybe she doesn't feel ashamed of me anymore.* But if that were true, then wouldn't she have reached out? For the thousandth time, Sarah wished that she had been brave enough to tell her parents about Dar before they had discovered the truth. Maybe if she had taken control of her coming-out process, it would have gone more smoothly. *By keeping Dar a secret, did I help* convince *them that our relationship was…wrong, somehow?*

"Hey," Nancy said, jostling her lightly with her elbow. "You okay?"

Sarah blinked, realizing that she had sunk so deep into introspection that she'd stopped chanting along with the others.

She tried to give Nancy a reassuring smile. "Yeah, sorry. Lost in thought."

"None of that, now," Nancy chided. "We need your voice."

Sarah took a deep breath and joined back in, shaking off her anxiety. *What's done is done,* she told herself as they crossed one last road and spilled onto the sidewalk in front of the capitol building. She couldn't change how she had come out to her family, but she could make a decision to live bravely from now on.

❖

Rory would have joined in the applause after Lee's speech if she hadn't needed both her hands to adjust the camera. Lee had spoken eloquently about the legal importance of the marriage question and had urged everyone present—and those who might see a clip on TV, Rory supposed—to continue spreading the word about why voting no was so critical. Her speech had followed one from Michael Bronski, a Dartmouth professor who had talked briefly about the history of LBGT rights and how marriage fit in. Rory had been at once fascinated by the topic and chagrined by her ignorance. *These are my people now,* she thought as Nancy took the microphone from Lee. *I should buy one of Bronski's books.*

She zoomed out slightly in order to remind her audience just how many people were present. Nancy stood on the stairs with her back to the gleaming capitol building. Beneath her was a sea of flickering light.

"Thank you, Michael and Lee," she said. "And thanks to all of you for showing your support by coming out on a chilly night." A small cheer rose up from the crowd and she smiled. "We've just heard two perspectives on the proposed amendment from recognized experts. Now, I'd like to open up the microphone to anyone who would like to say a few words about why the Vote No campaign is important to them." Nancy surveyed the audience, which had gone quiet. "Don't be shy," she said. "You're all among family."

Even so, you'd have to be crazy to get up there in front of everyone and just say something off the top of your head, Rory thought, leaning forward to double-check that her battery was holding up in the cold. She glanced over to her right, where two of the local news stations were also filming, and sighed. Their equipment was significantly cooler than hers. *I have camera envy.*

And then a ripple went through the crowd as someone stepped out, taking Nancy up on her offer. Rory's jaw dropped. *Sarah?* Hurriedly, she focused in as much as she could. Sarah didn't look nervous at all. In fact, she was smiling slightly. How she could manage to be that self-possessed in front of all those strangers was beyond Rory's comprehension. *God, you look so good.*

"Oh good, Sarah," Nancy was saying. "This is Sarah Storm, a junior at URI and the student intern for Fair Rhode Island's Kingston office."

"Yeah, Sarah!" shouted Matt, and Rory had to bite down hard on her lower lip to stifle her laughter.

"Hey, everyone," Sarah said easily. She even gave Matt a little wave. The breeze gently ruffled her short black hair, and the candlelight made her eyes sparkle, and even though Rory knew it was medically impossible for her heart to be doing somersaults, that's sure what it felt like.

"I learned a lot from our two speakers today about why voting no is important in general—for our legal system and for equal rights. As for why it's important to me…" She paused briefly, and Rory saw then that she was nervous after all—just hiding it well.

"The closet bothers me," she said, her voice growing stronger. "Most of us have probably been in it at some time or another, and it's not inherently bad. Sometimes it's necessary for survival, right?" The audience murmured its assent. Rory shivered at the restrained emotion in Sarah's voice, realizing that as she was speaking, Sarah was reliving her own closeted days. *It's in her nature to be genuine. Keeping a secret like that must have felt so wrong.*

"But that's the worst part about it," Sarah continued. "When you're in the closet, that's all you're doing—surviving. You're not living. You're just getting by, day to day, and you can't stop and enjoy or savor anything because you're always afraid. That's why it's so important to me that gay marriage be possible throughout the

United States. When our relationships become legally acceptable—supported by society—there won't be any more closets." She ducked her head, grinning a little sheepishly. "Or at least…that's my idealistic hope."

She handed the microphone back to Nancy and returned to her place in the crowd to loud applause, cheers, and whistles. Rory's breaths were shallow and her vision was blurry, but she managed to follow Sarah's progress with the camera. *My God,* she thought, automatically working the controls as someone from Brown got up to speak next. *It's like she was talking to me.*

For the past few weeks, she hadn't been living. Not really. *I've just been getting by.* Her fear that Sarah would find out about her attraction had put a strain on their relationship. *Well, no more,* Rory vowed. *I'm going to tell her. I'm going to figure out a plan—write a little speech if I have to—and tell her the truth.*

Sarah deserved honesty from her, yes. But more importantly…*I deserve it for myself.*

CHAPTER FIFTEEN

March 23

Rory couldn't stop whistling. It was unseasonably warm—forty degrees today—and after a cold snap in which the temperatures hadn't reached above the teens, it felt positively balmy outside.

But the temperature was only icing on the cake. Today was Sarah's birthday, and unbeknownst to her, Rory had organized a celebration. She couldn't wait to see the expression on Sarah's face when she walked into Kingston Pizza and saw all of her friends wearing corny party hats.

Rory took the steps up to FRI's office two at a time. She paused briefly to extract a noisemaker from her pocket before shouldering open the door and blowing on it as loudly as possible. Sarah looked up from her desk, clearly startled. But then she saw Rory and burst out laughing. Rory grinned around the plastic tip of the toy. *Best sound ever.*

"Happy birthday, roomie! C'mon, I'm taking you out for cheesesteaks."

Sarah's smile became wistful. "Oh man, that sounds amazing. But I really should—"

"You should really go out to dinner on your birthday," Nancy said, poking her head out of her office. "In fact, I insist."

That big smile was back, and it was making Rory feel like it was difficult to catch her breath. *I love her face. So expressive.*

"Well," Sarah said. "In that case, let me grab my coat."

Nancy and Rory shared a look while Sarah's back was turned. *Meet you there,* Nancy mouthed. And then Sarah was standing next to Rory, and Rory slipped one arm around her waist, ignoring the warning bells. *Today's the big day. Don't be a coward, Song.*

"You didn't have to do this," Sarah said as they walked out the door and turned left.

"You're absolutely right," Rory said. "I didn't have to. Maybe I should just go home instead, huh?" She teasingly veered toward campus, but Sarah pulled her back on track.

"Too late now. You promised me a cheesesteak."

"So I did." She nudged Sarah playfully with her elbow, just because she could. "So, birthday girl. How's your day been so far?"

Sarah launched into a description of the interesting discussion she'd been a part of in her political science class, but Rory found it difficult to concentrate on what she was saying. Instead, she soaked it all up—her shoulder occasionally brushing Sarah's as they walked together in the—relatively—warm night: Sarah's voice growing louder the more enthused she became; Sarah's gentle tug on her arm, urging her back from the edge of the street while they waited at a crosswalk.

Their vibe had been much more relaxed ever since the night of the vigil. On the way home that night, Rory had resolved to come out to Sarah, for better or for worse, on her birthday. Maybe it had been a silly idea to wait for a special occasion, but it felt like the right thing to do. Of course, there was a risk that she was about to destabilize everything later tonight, but it was a risk she had to take. She was well aware that by admitting her newfound understanding of her own sexuality, she would also be confessing her attraction to Sarah. That prospect was scary as hell, but the alternative was stagnation. Sometimes over the past few weeks, Rory had caught Sarah looking at her with the same expression she'd had on her face that night at Matt's party. *Longing.* If she was right—and God, how she hoped she was—Sarah wanted her right back. Of course, even if Sarah did reciprocate, she'd never make a move so long as she considered Rory to be straight. *Good thing Matt jumped at the chance to help me plot a seduction.*

Rory struggled to suppress a knowing grin when they reached the front door of Kingston Pizza. *Surprise time, baby.* Sarah lingered near the front of the restaurant, but Rory urged her farther inside.

"Shouldn't we wait to be seated?" Sarah said, pointing to the sign in front of the hostess's station.

"Already got a place," Rory said tersely. "C'mon." She took Sarah's arm and dragged her around several tables, then down a short corridor. When they emerged into the back room a moment later, they were greeted by a loud cheer.

"Happy birthday, Sarah!"

Rory stood aside and watched Sarah's jaw hit the floor. Close to twenty people were gathered, most of them URI students affiliated in some way with the GLBT student center. A few FRI volunteers and employees had also been able to join them.

"How did you…but…" Sarah was having trouble speaking coherently. It was cute. Rory watched her focus on Nancy, who was seated in a corner with Kelly. "Nancy, how did you get here before we did?"

"This great invention called a car," Nancy said, winking. "Maybe you've heard of it?"

Sarah laughed. She looked dazed and happy, and Rory felt a surge of pride. *I did it. I've given her a good birthday.*

"You guys are amazing," Sarah said, finally managing to be coherent. "This is just too much. I don't even know what to do to thank you!"

"You should start by sitting down and ordering a beer," called Matt, "now that you're twenty-one."

"And don't thank us," Travis said. "Thank Rory. She organized the whole thing."

Sarah turned to Rory then and hugged her fiercely. Rory smiled into Sarah's shoulder, reveling in the sensation of being held. *So good. You feel so damn good to me.*

"Thank you," Sarah said, whispering against Rory's left ear. Her breath was warm and moist, and Rory couldn't help but shiver. "You are the best. Thank you."

"Happy birthday," Rory murmured back. She wanted to say more—so much more—but now wasn't the time. *Later. When I give her the gift.* Reluctantly, she pulled away. "Now c'mon, sit down and get them to card you."

After that particular ritual had been observed, Sarah moved slowly around the room, chatting with each of her friends while proudly sipping a frosty mug of Miller Lite. Matt pulled his chair closer to Rory's and bent his head toward hers.

"You done good, cowgirl," he drawled. "Ready for tonight?"

Rory nodded, keeping one eye on Sarah. "Yeah. Nervous, though."

"She's into you," Matt said confidently. "No doubt. That hug just now? Clearly not platonic. Hell, she practically starting sucking on your earlobe!"

Rory's pulse jumped as she thought about what that would feel like. "Jesus," she muttered. "That'd be nice." She looked over to see Matt grinning wickedly at her, and slapped him lightly on the arm. "You're really getting a kick out of this, aren't you?"

Matt ignored the question. "What did you end up getting her as a present?"

Rory reached into her coat pocket and pulled out a small black box. Matt's eyebrows shot into his neon green hairline when Rory opened it. A silver claddagh pendant lay on the faux velvet interior.

"Wow," Matt said. "You are really serious, aren't you? About her."

"Yeah." Rory closed the box with a click and secreted it away again. She felt a sudden spike of anxiety about Matt's reaction. "Do you think it's too much?"

"No," he said. "I don't. In fact, I think it's brave of you to show Sarah your hopeless romantic side."

"She knows it exists," Rory said, remembering back to one of their earliest conversations. "I told her, back in the fall."

"Showing is different from telling."

But before Rory could ask him to elaborate, Sarah returned to her seat. Her eyes were bright and she was still smiling. "God, this is fun," she said, slinging one arm around Rory's shoulders. "Have I said thank you yet?"

Rory leaned back into Sarah's touch, resisting the urge to close her eyes and bask like a cat in the sunshine. "You may have mentioned your gratitude a few times," she said. "But keep it coming."

Sarah laughed and took a long sip from her beer. "Thank you. A thousand times, thank you."

Rory was about to make a witty rejoinder when their waitress showed up with the food. Unfortunately, the arrival of Sarah's cheesesteak meant that she needed to withdraw her arm from around Rory's neck. Rory masked her disappointment by reaching for a slice of pizza.

"Is there anything else I can get you?" the waitress asked.

Sarah looked at her nearly empty glass and grinned. "Actually, yeah. Could I get another beer?"

❖

Sarah couldn't believe that she had just walked into her own room. A disco ball hung from the ceiling, twinkling Christmas lights had been draped haphazardly over the bookcases, and music blared from Rory's computer speakers. In one corner, Matt was standing behind a card table, mixing drinks. *Unreal. She's turned our room into a nightclub.*

Halfway across the room, Rory was watching for her reaction. "This is amazing!" Sarah shouted over the noise. "*You* are amazing."

Rory's answering smile was happy and triumphant, and it inspired in Sarah a sudden, sharp desire to cross the space between them, press Rory up against the wall, and kiss her harder than she'd ever kissed anyone before. Sarah clutched at the drink in her hand for purchase and looked away, afraid that she was an open book.

These compulsions had been getting stronger and more difficult to resist over the past few weeks. At first, most of her daydreams had been PG-13. But gradually they had changed, until instead of kissing Rory, she was undressing her. Now every time she walked into their shared bedroom, Sarah was assaulted by the image of Rory naked on her bed, biting her bottom lip in pleasure as Sarah's hand found its way between her legs.

Sometimes, the fantasies went even further. Sometimes, instead of stroking Rory with light, gentle touches, Sarah drove into her with two fingers, hard and fast, watching in satisfaction as Rory's head snapped back and her mouth opened silently. Sometimes, she imagined pressing Rory into the mattress with her free hand as she took her, over and over. Never, ever in a million years did she want to hurt Rory, but sometimes…

I want to fuck her.

The impulse frightened her a little. It was a new urge, one she didn't fully understand. Not to mention the fact that real Rory, unlike fantasy Rory, was *straight.* Sarah sighed and took a sip from her ridiculously strong rum and Coke. Why did hope have to spring eternal? Every time she thought she was getting over her completely inappropriate feelings, Rory did or said something—like that hug, earlier tonight—that made Sarah wonder if maybe, just maybe…

"Hey, brood machine," Rory said, reaching up to squeeze Sarah's shoulder. "Quit looking like someone killed your dog and start enjoying this elaborate party that I so painstakingly organized for you."

"Sorry—I'm sorry," Sarah said, laughing. Plus, Rory's hand hadn't moved. She was rubbing her thumb back and forth along the tendon between Sarah's shoulder and neck, and it felt amazing. "I'm completely in awe. First dinner and now this…and I can't believe that so many people showed up, either."

Rory looked at her as though she'd just grown two heads. "Earth to Sarah. You have a lot of friends. Deal with it."

At that instant, one of said friends decided that it was time to deviate from Rory's dance party play list. The opening strains of "Cotton Eye Joe" were met with both cheers and groans. Matt let out the shrillest cheer of all, ordered Travis to tend the bar, and dragged Sarah into the center of the room. Rory, apparently not yet tipsy enough to join in the dancing, laughed at them as she leaned against Sarah's desk.

Sarah struggled briefly with a bout of self-consciousness until she realized just how silly Matt looked as he flapped his arms and tried to approximate a jig. After that, she let loose. She even managed to coax Rory onto the makeshift dance floor after a while. They danced close together, hips bumping and thighs brushing. Once, Rory even reached for Sarah's arms, drew them around her body, and then turned so they were grinding together. Sarah's mouth went dry but she played along, fanning her fingers over Rory's stomach and leaning in to rest her cheek against Rory's head. Her hair smelled faintly of strawberries.

Sarah clung to that all-too-brief moment of intimacy, knowing that it was the best present she'd receive all day. Right here, right now, she could pretend that Rory actually shared her feelings. *God, she feels so good.*

When John appeared at Rory's elbow, Sarah took a step backward and let her arms fall to her sides, suddenly mindful of how they must look to everyone in the room. But Rory would have none of it. She reached back to grab Sarah's hands and fold them around her waist again as John asked whether they could stop the music and start playing Guitar Hero instead. Sarah was more than happy to oblige, and even dared to stroke her thumbs lightly over the warm fabric that hugged Rory's abdomen.

"Hmm." Rory craned her neck so she could meet Sarah's gaze. Her hair brushed Sarah's chin. "What do you think, birthday girl? Have you had enough of Club Storm? Should we turn this joint into an arcade?"

"I think I have no idea what Guitar Hero is," Sarah said. "So I defer to your superior wisdom."

"Oh my God, Sarah, it's, like, the coolest thing ever," gushed John. "You'll see!"

As he sprinted from the room to retrieve his copy of the game, Rory snuggled even deeper into Sarah's embrace. "You know that time at my parents' house, when you wanted me to air guitar during karaoke?"

"Yeah, and you wouldn't go for it," Sarah said, taking the opportunity to lightly poke Rory just below her rib cage. "Spoilsport."

Rory stuck out her tongue. In a parallel universe, parallel-Sarah spun parallel-Rory around in her arms and sucked that tantalizing tongue deep into her mouth. As it was, Sarah contented herself with letting her chin come to rest on Rory's shoulder while Rory explained in painstaking detail exactly how one played Guitar Hero.

When John returned, breathless, bearing two plastic guitars and the video game, Sarah was forced to let go of Rory so that she could hook everything up to her television. She meandered over to the "bar" and got another drink from Matt. If he thought it strange that she and Rory had been cuddling like long-term girlfriends, he didn't say so.

"Having fun?"

"Yes," Sarah said, suddenly reminded of when he had asked her the very same question on New Year's Eve. She had had to lie then. She didn't now. "So much fun."

"Cool. Rory's been pumped about it ever since she came up with the idea a few weeks ago."

"This is…" Sarah shook her head, struggling to find the words. "Amazing. Rory is amazing. I am so lucky to know her."

Matt opened his mouth to say something more, but Rory's voice cut him off. "Hey, Sarah, come check out the game," she called from where she was crouched near the television. "You're going to love this!"

Sarah raised her plastic cup in a toast to Matt before crossing the room. As she watched John and Travis manipulate the faux frets on their guitars, she was struck by a sense of rightness—of peace, even—unlike anything she'd felt before. *I belong here. With these people. I'm home.*

The phone rang. Sarah made a move to grab it, but Rory was faster. "I got it. Stay and watch. You're up next." But after a few seconds, Rory was at her side, pressing the phone into her palm. "For you—not sure who it is."

In retrospect, Sarah realized that she should have been

suspicious. Who, outside of those already present, would be calling her at ten thirty at night? But she was happy and content and unsuspecting, and when Rory handed her the receiver, she spoke cheerfully into the mouthpiece.

"Hello?"

First, silence. And then: "Sarah," her mother said.

The rush of adrenaline slammed through her body, forcing Sarah back until she could lean against something, anything. Every muscle in her body was suddenly trembling. *Oh my God. No. They found me.* Her vision was blurry and her heart was hammering against her rib cage, and for some reason, she couldn't seem to catch her breath. After eight months of no contact, she had thought they'd given up. But no—they had just been biding their time.

"Sarah," her mother said again, sounding close to tears. "Why are you doing this?"

❖

Rory had turned her attention back to the videogame once she had given the phone to Sarah. But when Sarah stumbled backward and thudded hard against the wall, Rory turned in alarm. Sarah's face was white and her entire body was shaking. As Rory watched, Sarah tried unsuccessfully to clench the trembling fingers of her free hand.

In that instant, Rory knew who had called. And she cursed herself for not asking—for not figuring it out, somehow. For not protecting Sarah from this moment, on today of all days.

"Mom," Sarah whispered.

The word was colored with fear. Rory felt paralyzed, rooted to the spot by her inability to help. She wanted to yank the phone from Sarah's hand and smash it on the floor. She wanted to hold Sarah tightly and whisper the truth into her free ear. *You're perfect and I love you.* She wanted to shout at Sarah's parents—to force them to see how just how deeply their rejection had wounded their daughter.

She couldn't do any of those things. What she could do was to give Sarah some privacy. *She wouldn't want her friends to see her like this.*

Rory moved forward to clasp Sarah's left hand. It was cold and clammy. She tugged lightly.

"Come on, baby," she said, the term of endearment slipping out effortlessly as she moved toward the bedroom door. "Come on in here."

"What do you mean?" Sarah said into the phone. Rory was glad to hear that her voice was louder, sharper. *Good girl. Don't let her bully you.*

She reached just inside the room to turn on the light, then gave Sarah's hand a reassuring squeeze. When her fingers brushed Sarah's wrist, the pulse stuttered frantically beneath her touch, as though it were trying to escape.

"I'll be back soon," she murmured before reluctantly disengaging and closing the door behind her.

Rory hurried over to Matt and briefly explained the situation. "We have to get everyone out of here," she concluded. "Is your room okay?" When he nodded and began packing up the supplies, Rory made her way around the room from group to group, explaining that Sarah had just received an important phone call and that the party needed to move elsewhere.

An eternity passed while everyone slowly filed out of the room. Rory did her best to act the part of the gracious hostess, but inside, she was dying of impatience. What was Sarah talking about with her mother? There hadn't been any yelling, yet, but was that a good or a bad sign? And what the hell did her parents want, anyway? *They've already taken enough.*

As soon as the room was empty, Rory yanked open the bedroom door. Sarah was standing exactly where she'd left her, but now her cheeks were red and her pupils dilated. The muscles in her neck bunched up as she ground her teeth. *Angry. That's good.*

"I'm telling you, I won't," she said—and if there was fire in her eyes, then her voice was laced with ice. "You made it perfectly clear that you don't want me. Well, I don't want you either. And I certainly don't need you. I'm doing just fine."

Rory suddenly ached to touch her. Slowly, carefully, she slid her arms around Sarah's waist from behind, mimicking the way she'd been held earlier. Sarah's stomach muscles were tight and tense under her hands, but she didn't pull away.

"I don't owe you anything," she said forcefully. Rory felt a shudder run through Sarah's entire body and pulled her even closer. "Don't call me again."

The phone beeped as Sarah turned it off. Her breaths came quickly, rasping in her throat as though she'd been sprinting. Rory kept her face pressed to the indentation between Sarah's shoulder blades, suddenly uncertain about what to do. *Do I ask her what they said? Do I just stand here? Do I try telling a joke?*

And then Sarah began to cry. It was barely noticeable at first— just a few sniffles, and one surreptitious swipe of her wrist across her eyes. But once Rory realized what was happening, she twisted Sarah around in her arms, caught her chin between two fingers, and looked up into dark, wet eyes.

The look that passed between them was charged with an unnamable emotion. Sarah jerked her head away, buried her face in the crook between Rory's neck and shoulder, and began to sob. Rory felt her chest tighten up, as though someone had reached in and squeezed her heart. Hard.

"That's it," she murmured, stroking up and down the length of Sarah's back with both hands. "You're okay, Sarah. You're just fine." Words flowed from her—the counterpart of Sarah's tears. "You're perfect, you know that? You are the best thing that's ever happened to me."

Rory held Sarah that way for a long time—long enough for her arms to get tired and the words to run out. But she kept on rubbing Sarah's back, and when she could think of nothing left to say, she began to hum. After a little while, Sarah pulled back. Her face was splotchy and her hair disheveled, but Rory thought she'd never seen anyone as handsome.

"Thank you," Sarah said, her voice low and rough. "I'm sorry."

"Don't you dare apologize," Rory said fiercely. She wanted

desperately to keep touching Sarah but held her ground, sensing that she might need some space. "What did you…what did they…"

Sarah sat down hard on her bunk and massaged the back of her neck with both hands. "They saw me on television. Working with FRI."

"Fuck," Rory gasped, one hand going to her mouth. "My commercial. Goddammit, Sarah, I didn't even think—I'm so sorr—"

"I'm glad they saw," Sarah said vehemently. "I wasn't hiding from them. I'm proud of FRI, and I'm proud of your commercial and dammit, I am *not* a fuckup!" She paused then to look up. "Am I?"

"No, baby, no. No." Rory sat down next to Sarah and started rubbing her back again. That forlorn note in Sarah's voice had made her heart catch again. "You're perfect to me."

"They told me to stop working for FRI," Sarah said dully. "And to come home."

"I won't let you," Rory said fiercely. "And they can't make you. You belong here."

"Yeah," Sarah said. "I know." Her eyelids were drooping now, and she swayed slightly, pressing more firmly against Rory. "God. Sleepy all of a sudden. I'm sorry."

It felt so wrong to pull away from Sarah, but Rory got up briefly to grab her pajamas from the top dresser drawer. "Put these on, okay? And slide into bed. I'll be back in just one second."

Rory watched Sarah stare blankly at the soft flannel cloth in her hand before rousing herself with a shake of her head. With no preamble or pretense at modesty, she stripped off her shirt. Suddenly blushing, Rory left the bedroom to lock their door and turn off the common room light. She could brush her teeth tomorrow. All that mattered right now was that Sarah felt warm and safe and comforted—that she sleep off the shock.

That little black box was still burning a hole in her pocket, but now was not the time for confessions. Now was the time for comfort and reassurance. When the moment was right, she'd tell Sarah everything. For now, she needed to be the anchor, not the whirlwind.

When she reentered the room, Sarah was lying in bed. Her eyes were closed. The delicate skin around them looked red and raw. Rory changed quickly, turned off the light, and then leaned over Sarah to brush a chaste kiss across her forehead.

"You just rest, for as long as you can. I'll wake you up in time for class, okay?"

When Sarah didn't answer, Rory wondered if she'd fallen asleep. But as she pulled away to climb the ladder, Sarah's hand closed around her wrist.

"Stay," she said, damp eyes glittering in the near dark. "Please?"

Rory's breath caught in her throat as Sarah held the covers open for her. She slid in on her side, and Sarah turned so they could spoon. Rory tenderly wrapped her left arm around Sarah's waist, unable to believe what was happening. She wanted to kiss the back of Sarah's neck, but didn't dare.

"Thanks," Sarah mumbled.

"No problem," Rory whispered back. She could feel Sarah's heartbeat against her palm. It was still far too fast. Sarah wasn't actually calm yet, despite her fatigue. So Rory listened to her instincts: she sucked in a deep breath and began to sing, making her voice soft and low. She sang the first thing that popped into her head—a song she'd learned in elementary school, about a ferryman on the Erie Canal and his trusty mule named Sal. It wasn't technically a lullaby, but the melody was slow and soothing.

As she sang, she was gratified to feel Sarah slowly relax under her hand. And by the time she'd gone through the song twice, Sarah's breaths were deep and even. *Asleep.*

For a moment, Rory debated whether she should stay in Sarah's bed or move to her own. There was no contest, though. Not really. Curling up around Sarah's body felt more than good, it felt right.

"I love you," she whispered against Sarah's neck, just before sleep claimed her.

❖

Sarah woke to the unfamiliar sensation of warm breaths on the back of her neck and an arm around her waist. When she inhaled, she caught the scent of Rory's strawberry shampoo. She smiled, pressing back into Rory's embrace…and then suddenly her brain caught up with her body and her eyes flashed open as the events of last night replayed themselves in her memory.

Oh God. Mom.

There had been so much pain in her mother's voice—hurt and disappointment and shame. *All my life, I've made you proud,* Sarah thought. She had gotten the best grades, excelled at sailing…she had been a golden girl. *I never even had a curfew in high school.* And now she was the black sheep. How could her sexual orientation—just one part of who she was—blot out everything else in her mother's mind? *How is that fair?*

Beside her, Rory stirred. Sarah tensed for an entirely different reason, wondering how Rory would react to waking up next to her. Would she feel self-conscious about falling asleep in Sarah's bed? *Did I do the wrong thing when I asked her to stay?*

Rory opened her eyes and blinked. She frowned in confusion, then sucked in a sharp breath. "Hey. Um." She blushed. It was adorable. "Sorry about…this." She gestured with one hand at the two of them lying next to each other. "I should have gone to my bed once you were—"

Sarah shook her head. "I asked you to stay. I'm so grateful that you did." She tried out a smile. "You are the best, you know. I'm sorry for being so needy last night."

"You don't have to be sorry," Rory said quietly. "How are you doing?"

Sarah scrubbed one palm over her face and through her tousled hair. "Okay, I guess. My mom…she really threw me by calling."

Rory frowned. "I should have known it was her. God, I wish I had just asked!"

Sarah awkwardly rested one hand on Rory's shoulder in an effort to comfort her. "It's really, really not your fault. That was always going to happen someday." She blew out a sigh. "I'm glad it's over with. For the moment, anyway."

"So…you're not going to do what she asked?"

"You mean quit FRI and go back home?" Sarah laughed harshly. "No way. If anything, I want to work even harder now. Maybe when the amendment fails, my parents will finally get it into their thick skulls that there's nothing *wrong with me.*"

Rory closed her eyes and exhaled. "Okay. Good. Yeah."

"Were you really afraid I'd go?" Sarah asked. The relief on Rory's face was obvious. It brought warmth to the cold hollow that her mother's words had opened in her chest.

Rory shrugged and swung her feet over the bed. When she stood up, Sarah had to clench her teeth to keep from expressing her disappointment. *You already asked her to stay once. Don't drive her off!*

"I was just worried about my Bio grade," Rory quipped, turning around with the familiar, mocking grin on her face. "If you go, who will make sure I pass the final?"

Sarah rolled her eyes and let the comment pass, but she could tell that Rory hadn't said what was really on her mind. *Do you need me?* she wondered. *As much as I need you?*

Chapter Sixteen

Mid-April

W hen her alarm went off at six a.m., Rory shut it off immediately and sat up in her bunk, fully awake. Normally, she liked to take her time in the morning—to doze for a while, luxuriating in the warm cocoon of her covers. But today was Election Day, and she needed to get some footage of the polls opening. In an hour. *Up and at 'em,* she thought as she climbed down the ladder.

Sarah was still asleep. As she had done for the past two weeks, Rory crouched down, leaned in, and cupped her cheek lightly to wake her. "Sarah," she said. "Time to get up, babe. C'mon."

Sarah stirred and opened bleary eyes. When she smiled, Rory smiled back. It felt so good to know that just by being there first thing in the morning, she could make Sarah happy. "Today's the big day," she said, still touching Sarah's face with gentle fingertips. "You excited?"

At that, Sarah's eyes focused and she sat up straight. "Yeah. Jeez. God, I hope…"

She left the sentence unfinished. Rory nodded before getting to her feet and grabbing her robe from the hook on the back of the closet door. The vote was going to be close—only a few percentage points, if recent polls were any indication. "Me, too."

"Go take your shower," Sarah mumbled, waving her hand toward the door. "I'll be there soon."

Rory couldn't resist the opening. "Promise?" When Sarah swatted at her playfully, Rory jumped away, laughing. She hurried to the bathroom, ducked into one of the stalls, and brushed her teeth as the water heated up.

This was going to be a watershed day, one way or another. And not just politically. The past two weeks had been a strange kind of limbo where Sarah was concerned, and Rory had a feeling that something was going to happen soon to snap them out of their stasis. Ever since Sarah's birthday, they'd been closer than ever—studying together, eating every meal together, meeting up briefly between classes. Nothing decidedly romantic had happened, yet, but Matt had told Rory that people were starting to speculate about the two of them.

After her talk with her parents, Sarah had needed comfort. Nurturing. Rory had watched her like a hawk for days afterward—bringing her food, trying to distract her whenever she seemed sad, making sure she got as much rest as she could. After a little while, Sarah had seemed much more like her old self, but even if Rory had wanted to make a confession then, there simply hadn't been time. Last-minute preparations for the election had made both of their lives frenetic.

Just one more day, Rory thought as the steaming water sluiced over her back. One more day of filming and then she could stop running around like a headless chicken, lock herself in her room, and spend the next two days making final cuts. And maybe, just maybe, this weird stalemate with Sarah would end, too.

The door to the bathroom opened and closed again. Rory grinned. "I'm in the third stall down," she called teasingly.

"If I come in there," Sarah said, "there's no way we're making it to the polls by seven."

Rory shivered despite the clouds of steam rising from the water. What would Sarah do? Would she throw the flimsy curtain aside, stalk into the stall, and press Rory hard against the tile wall? Would her tongue fuck Rory's mouth while her fingers reached down to find Rory wet, throbbing, oh-so-ready? Or would she thrust one leg between Rory's and tease her nipples while driving her thigh—

"No witty retort? Who are you and what have you done with my roommate?"

Rory cursed her overactive imagination as she shut the water off and reached for her towel. "It's too early for comebacks," she groused.

"It's too early, period. Will you make some coffee?"

"Your wish, my command," Rory said, sliding back into her robe. Sarah laughed, of course, because she thought it was a joke.

But it wasn't—not really.

❖

Spring had truly arrived, Sarah realized as she and Rory walked toward Boss Arena. The crocuses were coming up, and the trees were budding. The earth smelled like itself now—rich and loamy and green instead of the crisp, sterile ice-scent of winter. Occasionally, birdsong filtered down from the treetops.

Sarah felt hopeful. Sure, the election was going to be close. But in the end, how could a majority of Rhode Islanders vote for an amendment that was in direct contradiction with equal rights? Especially given the shining example of Massachusetts. She smiled, envisioning the celebratory atmosphere in the FRI office late tonight when the results had been totaled.

"It's kind of strange to be voting in the hockey arena," Rory said, adjusting the position of her camera bag on her shoulder. "I mean, wouldn't it be crazy if they still had the ice on the floor, and you had to slip and slide into your booth?"

Sarah had to giggle. That mental image was just too much. "You're a weirdo."

"Takes one to know one," Rory fired back. "Think about it— Election Day Ice Capades!"

That kept Sarah laughing until they reached the front doors of the arena. She hung back and watched as Rory spoke to the election officials about where she'd be able to set up her camera. Rory was wearing olive cargo pants and a black hooded Nirvana sweatshirt. She kept having to push her hair back in the breeze, and Sarah was fascinated by the graceful movements of her hands.

Those hands. They had touched her so often in the past few weeks—always gently, always in comfort. Whenever Sarah thought about how she had let her guard down in front of Rory on her birthday, she got more than a little scared. Rory had seen her when she was pure *need*—vulnerable and hurting. But unlike Dar, Rory hadn't been scared off. She hadn't turned her back.

I loved her before. But it's even stronger, now. Sarah looked over to where Rory was assembling her tripod. Every morning when Rory woke her up, Sarah struggled not to kiss her. Every time Rory handed her a mug of chai, Sarah forced her fingers not to brush Rory's knuckles. Every time Rory hugged her, Sarah fought off the impulse to press her lips to the side of Rory's neck. Loving Rory and not being able to express her feelings was a constant struggle. Suppressing the impulse was tiring.

"Hey, go get in line," Rory called, pointing at the short line of people in front of the arena's massive double doors. "I'll start filming once you're there."

"What a demanding director, jeez," Sarah said, huffing a sigh. When Rory stuck out her tongue, she couldn't resist another jab. "Sorry, I don't French long distance."

That did it. Rory cracked up. "French long distance? That's the lamest comeback I've ever heard."

"You thought it was funny, though," Sarah pointed out. She would make every corny joke in the book and then some, if it meant that she got to be responsible for Rory's laughter.

"Get. Over. There," Rory insisted. "It's almost seven, and I want footage of the poll's opening moments."

This time, Sarah obeyed. She rocked back on her heels and looked from her watch to the doors. She couldn't wait to get into her booth, find the marriage question on the ballet, uncap her black marker, and fill in the middle half of the arrow pointed at "REJECT."

"All right, everyone," called one of the officials. "We're opening the doors. Please follow the signs to the registration area."

Sarah paused to grin at the camera and give Rory the thumbs-up. And then she ducked inside the arena, intent on doing her part to make history.

❖

"Hey, guys," Sarah said to a group of students on their way out of Roger Williams. "Have you voted yet today?" Without waiting for an answer, she began distributing small, grainy maps of campus that displayed Boss Arena as a large star. "Anybody ever been to see a hockey game?"

"Uh, I'm on the team," said one of the guys, looking mildly annoyed.

"Oh!" Sarah gave him her most winning grin. "Cool. Well, that's the polling place. So if you head over there by nine o'clock, you'll be able to cast your vote." She looked at her watch and raised her eyebrows. "It's almost 8:30, so you'll want to hurry."

"What's the big deal?" asked one of the girls. "It's not a presidential election."

Sarah grinned. A comment like that was the perfect lead-in to the speech she'd perfected months ago about the amendment. "There's a really important question on the ballot," she explained, "about whether Rhode Island's state constitution should be amended such that marriage is defined as between one man and one woman, and such that no legal states like marriage would be valid for unmarried people."

A few of them looked confused, so she hurried to clarify. "Basically, the amendment would make it so that gays and lesbians can't marry, and so that civil unions—for gay or straight people— wouldn't be allowed."

"Oh, okay," the girl said. "Thanks."

"Sure," Sarah said. She watched them leave, mentally crossing her fingers that they would cast their votes against the amendment, and looked back down at her watch. It didn't really make sense to stay here any longer, since the polls closed in less than half an hour.

She began to pack up the supplies from the table where she'd been sitting—stacks of maps, FRI brochures, and colorful signs urging everyone to Vote No all went into a box. Rory had stopped by earlier for about an hour to get some footage before moving on to some of the other locations where FRI employees and volunteers were trying to mobilize the student body. Sarah missed her, of course, and the knowledge that she'd get to see Rory again soon made her clean up quickly.

This is it, she thought as she carried the box outside into the cool night. The nearly full moon blinked fitfully at her as feathery clouds scudded across the sky. *In a matter of hours, we'll know.* Nancy had invited all employees and volunteers to the FRI office to watch the compiling of the results. Suddenly impatient to know what the exit polls were projecting, Sarah dug her cell out of her pocket and hit speed-dial.

"Hey," Rory said, a moment later. She had to speak loudly to make herself heard over other voices and the sound of a television in the background. "Exit polls are showing us just slightly ahead at the moment."

"Sweet!" Sarah grinned broadly. "I'll be there in about ten minutes."

"Better hurry," Rory said. "The pizza just got here and everyone's starved."

"I'm hurrying." Sarah ended the call and quickened her steps. She was hungry, too. It had been one of the busiest days of her life, and she hadn't eaten a substantial meal all day.

When Sarah finally shoved the FRI office door open, a cheer went up. She set her box down on the floor and smiled. "You love me, you really love me."

"You're the last one back," Nancy said.

"I saved you some pizza," Rory said, gesturing to the table. She was squeezed into the far corner of the room next to her tripod. A small TV perched on Sarah's desk. The floors and chairs were packed with people. Everyone even remotely affiliated with the Kingston FRI office had apparently decided that this was the place to watch the election results. Even Chelsea, who still hadn't spoken more than a few words at a time to Sarah since their breakup, was there.

Sarah grabbed her pizza and found an empty few feet of wall to lean against next to Rory. "Am I okay here?" she asked. "Not blocking anything?"

"You're good," Rory said, adjusting her camera with one hand and holding a slice of pizza in the other.

"So," Sarah said, "just how busy are you going to be for the next few days?" It was a Tuesday, and Rory had to turn in her completed film in class on Friday. Silently, Sarah vowed to do everything in her power to make it easy for Rory to work. Including staying out of her way, if that was what she needed most.

Rory made a face. "Let's just put it this way: no sleep till Brooklyn. And I'm already so wiped."

Sarah winced. "You're going to let me help you out, right? However I can?"

"I will absolutely play on your sympathy," Rory said, sparing her a quick grin. "You can be my official Jolt supplier, and—"

"Quiet!" Matt screeched, pointing to the television, where the news anchor was describing the updated exit poll results. When she announced that the election was now too close to call, Sarah frowned. A few people groaned.

Rory whispered, "Dammit."

"Chins up, people," Nancy reminded them all. "These aren't the real results yet. We always knew it'd be close."

Sarah had been about to take a bite of her second slice of pizza, but her rising anxiety quashed her appetite. In an effort to distract herself, she turned to watch Rory fiddling with the camera. "So... once you've turned a copy of the movie in to your prof, can I see it?"

"You surely *may*," Rory said. "In Independence Auditorium,

even, a week from tomorrow. The film department always has a film festival at the end of the academic year for final projects, senior theses, et cetera."

Sarah raised her eyebrows. "That's really cool. Can I sneak popcorn inside?"

Rory patted her on the shoulder. "Good luck with that, babe."

They hushed up as the commercials ended, but Sarah was only half paying attention to what was happening onscreen. *Babe.* She loved when Rory called her that. Or "baby." Those particular terms of endearment had always seemed strange to her—juvenile, somehow. Until now. They were Rory's words, and she loved them.

Besotted. That's what I am. Completely besotted.

"We're now getting the first reports from several polling places throughout southern Rhode Island," the news anchor said. "Thus far, our results show that a slim majority of Rhode Islanders favor the proposed amendment to the constitution that would define marriage as between one man and one woman. The numbers are currently fifty-one percent for, forty-nine percent against."

"What?" said Sarah, unable to believe what she had just heard. *Is this for real?* "But—"

"Don't worry," Rory said, resting one hand on her forearm. "That's just a small slice of the pie." She squeezed lightly. "This isn't over yet."

"It drives me crazy when they simplify the issue like that," Kelly said. "What about the whole second half of the amendment?"

"It's the most complicated part," Nancy pointed out.

"*And* the part that cuts into heterosexual rights as well as homosexual ones," Sarah said bitterly. Her stomach was roiling. *We really might lose,* she realized. Intellectually, she had known that it was a possibility. But now, with the numbers and pie charts staring coldly at her from the television, she finally felt the truth of it all. *We might lose. After all of this hard work, all the effort...*

"Hey," Rory said, nudging her. "You okay? Talk to me."

"Yeah." Sarah dumped her plate into a garbage can and pressed two fingers to her temples. "I guess I just...I didn't..."

"It's one thing to know that the race is tight," Rory said quietly. "It's another thing to see it playing out that way."

Sarah met Rory's gaze, incredulous. *How did she know exactly what I was thinking?* "Yeah," she said, hearing the roughness in her voice. "Exactly." *And I'm scared.*

Updates were coming in frequently, now, and the room fairly vibrated with tension. At one point, the numbers evened out again. But only ten minutes later, the vote had tipped back in favor of the amendment.

Ten o'clock came and went—then eleven. Sarah's eyes were burning with exhaustion. She pressed the heels of her hands against them before returning her focus to the television. *Please,* she thought, directing her silent plea to all of the polling places that had not yet reported in. *Please, just...please.*

"We now have the final results of today's election," the anchor finally said.

Sarah sucked in a deep breath, staring intently at the screen. *Please.* When one of Rory's hands found hers, she latched on gratefully. Their sweating palms slipped together—a perfect fit. She squeezed Rory's hand gently as the anchor read off the winners in various state- and county-wide races. And then—

"In one of the closest referendums in state history, fifty-two percent of Rhode Islanders voted today that the constitution should be amended to include a clause that defines marriage as between one man and one woman, and makes the creation of civil unions or similar institutions invalid."

Rory squeezed Sarah's hand so hard that she thought her bones might shift. Sarah welcomed the pain. It echoed the growing ache between her breasts. *No.* It was all she could think. *No, dammit. No no no.*

"What the fuck?" Matt said into the shocked silence. "Who the hell votes *against* civil rights?"

Pushing off the wall and away from Rory, Sarah moved forward to squint in disbelief at the television. "But we worked so hard," she said. Her head felt fuzzy and her fingers numb, and how, *how* could this happen? "So damn hard."

Everyone started talking at once, then, until Nancy turned off the television and cleared her throat. "Sarah's right, everyone," she said. "We worked hard. We should be *proud*. I know that the results didn't go the way we wanted them too, but just you wait. It won't be long before this and every other law discriminating on the basis of sexual orientation will be overturned."

She smiled, but the expression didn't reach her eyes. Sarah wondered what it was costing her of all people to put on a brave face in the immediate aftermath of this defeat.

"We lost a battle, not the war," Nancy continued. "When I wake up tomorrow, I'm going to do the same thing I always do—devote my day to equal rights. I'm going to fight the war every single second."

She looked around the room, meeting the eyes of her employees, her friends, her volunteers. "Liberty and justice for all. I believe in that, and I know you do, too. I believe that the United States has a good system—imperfect, but good. I believe that we are doing exactly the right thing—exposing and working to change the parts of that system that are weak. I'm proud of us. And I'm so grateful to all of you, for what you've accomplished over the past several months."

"Hear, hear!"

Someone started the applause, and within seconds, every person in the room was on their feet. Sarah knew exactly what she was clapping for—for Nancy's leadership, for her colleagues' courage and dedication, for herself. Nancy was right, of course. This was only the end of a chapter in Rhode Island's battle for equality. So much of the book had yet to be written. *I won't give up either,* she promised, blinking against the tears of frustration that threatened to spill over.

When the applause ended, Sarah retreated to the wall, leaned back against it, and closed her eyes. She had a dull headache, and the familiar tightness that so often haunted her shoulders was back. *Why?* she asked again, thinking of those who had voted for the amendment. People like her parents. What good, sound reason did they have? *Why?*

Fighting to breathe and not to sob, Sarah remained motionless until Rory's hand covered her shoulder. "Hey," Rory said. Her voice sounded as tired as Sarah felt, and hollow. "Come on. Let's go home."

"Okay," Sarah said dully.

"Do you want to say good-bye to Nancy first?" asked Rory, pointing in her direction.

Sarah shook her head. If she talked to Nancy, she would burst into tears. She knew it. "Not right now," she managed. "I just…I just want to sleep." *And wake up in a kinder, fairer world.*

"Yeah. Me, too."

They walked back to campus slowly. The night smelled as good as the morning had—clean and fresh, like springtime—but Sarah could find no joy in the promise of renewal. Beneath her exhaustion and disappointment, anger simmered, waiting its turn to boil over.

"Do you feel…empty, kinda?" asked Rory as they entered Hutchinson and headed for the stairs. "It's like—like a pumpkin on Halloween. Like someone scooped out all my insides."

"I feel like I want to punch somebody," Sarah grated, surprising even herself with the vehemence of her words. She wanted to take them back, but now that her rage had been uncorked, it continued to spill over.

"I mean…what the *hell* is wrong with people? I am not a freak! I'm not asking for special treatment!" She followed Rory into the room and stood just inside the door, her entire body trembling. "My parents are *wrong* to treat me the way they do. I know it! But now, thanks to this goddamn amendment, they'll feel justified!"

She slapped her palm hard on the wooden surface, perversely glad of the sting that vibrated through her hand and into her wrist. "I'm not trying to be some fucking *rebel* or social anarchist or…or, I don't even know what! I'm just trying to be me." Sarah took a deep, shuddering breath and stared hard into Rory's wide eyes. "This is who I am! What's so wrong with me, and Matt, and Chelsea and Nancy and John and Travis and God knows how many others…why the *fuck* should we have to live with being treated like trash?"

She slumped to the floor, then, her back sliding against the door.

Leaning her head on her knees, she took a deep, hitching breath. Her head was on fire and her throat felt raw from yelling and she was tired, so very tired. *Poor Rory,* a still-lucid corner of her brain thought. *I must be scaring her half to death.*

"And me," Rory said softly.

Sarah raised her head, blinking. "And you?"

Rory nodded, coming closer. "You were listing names. Matt and Chelsea and Nancy and John and Travis…and me." She swallowed audibly. "I've been wanting to tell you for months now, ever since I realized. I'm—I'm queer."

❖

Rory waited several seconds for some kind of response, but when Sarah just continued to stare up at her, she shrugged self-consciously. "Uh, surprise," she said with a sickly smile, trying to make light of her revelation. *You idiot! Why did you have to spill it now, when she's completely overwhelmed already?*

She jerked her head toward the bedroom. "I'm, ah, going to get some sleep. Busy day tomorrow and all. So. Um, good night." Realizing that she was babbling, she hurried to get out of Sarah's sight.

Can this day get any worse? she thought as she stripped off her clothes. The thought of going back over the footage she had just shot—the footage of everyone's stunned and dismayed reactions to the election—was about as appealing as the cafeteria's green bean mush. *At least I got the guts to come out today,* she considered glumly, *even though my timing sucks.* Even so, Rory couldn't help but feel that the enormity of tonight's defeat rendered her small, personal victory practically meaningless.

Naked, she reached into the dresser for her pajamas. She wanted to fall into bed, burrow under the covers, and wake up when it was time for summer vacation. But at the sound of a low, choking noise behind her, Rory spun to see Sarah standing a few feet away. Her fists were clenched at her sides and her short, sharp breaths whistled through her teeth.

"Rory," she said in a voice that sounded pained. When she took a step forward into the pool of light cast by the standing lamp, Rory saw her expression. Need. Sarah's face was taut with need, and her shining eyes felt like spotlights. A rush of adrenaline left Rory feeling dizzy.

"I can't…dammit, if you can't pretend anymore, then neither can I."

Finally. It was the only coherent thought she could manage, before she was hopelessly overwhelmed by the most intense kiss of her life. Sarah's lips were forceful, insistent, constantly moving in an effort to be closer. Her tongue plunged repeatedly into Rory's mouth, stealing precious oxygen. One of Sarah's hands cradled the back of Rory's head and the other squeezed the soft skin just above her hipbone while their teeth clashed and their bodies molded together and *God, oh God, Sarah*, this was it—the passion she had been waiting for all her life.

Sarah pulled back, panting. Her eyes were dark and wild, and Rory felt a thrill that she could affect Sarah—*Sarah*, of all people—so strongly. In one fluid motion, Sarah took off her shirt. When she removed her bra as well, Rory sat down hard on Sarah's bunk. Her breasts were small and firm, in perfect proportion to her lean arms and torso. She looked like some kind of Greek god—regal and androgynous.

"You are so fucking beautiful," Rory whispered hoarsely.

Sarah shook her head once. "No, you."

For one insane moment, Rory wondered whether this seduction scene was going to pause while she and Sarah argued the point like third graders. But then Sarah was urging her to lie down on the mattress, and *then* Sarah was looming over her, sliding one leg between Rory's and leaning down to kiss her hard again. The sensation of Sarah's breasts brushing against her own made Rory moan around Sarah's tongue.

Sarah's hands cupped Rory's face and she kissed her even harder. Rory clutched at Sarah's shoulders as she was consumed, urging Sarah closer. The muscles of Sarah's back contracted under

Rory's hands and she dug in hard with her fingertips. She was dizzy with lack of breath but couldn't bear to pull even an inch away.

When Sarah jerked up her head, gasping for air, she stared at Rory for a long moment. The intensity of Sarah's gaze burned her soul. For one exhilarating instant, she felt like she was back on her swing set, rising up toward the pale November moon.

"I need to touch you," Sarah whispered.

Rory pulled her head back down. "I need you to," she said against Sarah's mouth.

Sarah exhaled hard and immediately skimmed her fingers down across Rory's collarbone. When her hand closed gently around one breast, Rory shuddered. When her thumb slid across Rory's nipple, every muscle in Rory's body tensed at the surge of pleasure. And when Sarah pressed down, moving her thumb in tiny circles, Rory's back arched involuntarily.

"Oh God. Yes."

Rory fought to keep watching Sarah, but when Sarah's mouth closed over her other nipple, the sensation was too intense. Her eyes slammed shut and she groaned, deep in her throat. Sarah swirled her tongue as she sucked, and it was so *damn* good that Rory almost missed the feeling of Sarah's palm sliding down over her ribs to rest in the dip between her leg and abdomen.

Her hips lifted of their own accord. The ache between her thighs was suddenly unbearable. She needed Sarah to be inside of her, the way she'd never needed anyone before. *Oh please. Please.*

Sarah lifted her head from Rory's breast. "Look at me," she murmured.

Rory forced her eyes open. Sarah's gaze was tender and hungry at the same time, and Rory reached one trembling hand out to cup the side of her face. "Watch me touch you."

"Yes," Rory whispered.

Sarah bit her lower lip as she shifted her fingers. Rory trembled violently and clutched hard at the blanket when Sarah brushed her clit. The touch was fleeting and only sharpened her need. But when she bucked her hips, trying to maintain contact, Sarah brought her other hand down to press firmly on Rory's abdomen. She shook her head, a faint grin playing around the corners of her mouth.

Rory didn't think it was possible to get any more aroused, but Sarah's gentle restraint was driving her crazy. She could feel herself becoming impossibly wet. "Sarah," she said hoarsely. "God, plea—"

She cried out when Sarah returned to her clit, circling it lightly. Rory felt her self-control slipping away as Sarah's fingers moved deliberately against her. She whimpered in need, and every muscle in her body was taut with desire. When Sarah changed the motion of her fingers, slipping up and over instead of around, Rory groaned and spread her legs even wider.

"I want to be inside you," Sarah said. She looked fierce and uncertain all at once, and Rory loved her for it.

"Yes," Rory whispered again. Her lips were dry and her nerves were on fire, but she needed Sarah to know the truth. "I've never…I mean…" *Be in me. A part of me.* "I want it to be you, Sarah."

But Sarah didn't lean down to kiss her. She didn't push one finger into Rory's body, easing the desperate and unfamiliar ache. She didn't murmur something romantic or soothing or erotic.

She froze. And then she pulled away. Rory's body screamed in protest at the loss of contact. Even in the dim light, she could see the change come over Sarah. She watched helplessly as the hunger on her face gave way to fear.

"Sarah?" She propped herself up on both elbows, blinking furiously. "What is it, baby?"

Sarah stood up and backed toward the door. "Rory," she said, holding out one hand even as she continued to move backward. "I—I'm sorry."

"What?" A surge of dread overwhelmed any self-consciousness that Rory might have felt. *I'm losing her.* She sat up on the bed, determined not to let Sarah out of her sight. "Why the hell are you sorry? What are you talking about? What just happened?"

"I can't do this to you. I won't."

"Do this? Do what?" Rory could hear her voice becoming

shrill, but the panic made it hard to think. "Kiss me? Touch me? Make love to me?" Rory took a deep, shuddering breath. "I want all of that from you. You know I do."

Sarah was shaking her head vehemently as she pulled up her jeans. "No. You can't."

"Why the fuck not? Because I just came out?" Rory stood up, stark naked, determined to prove to Sarah just how wrong she was. "I've been wanting you ever since fall semester, you idiot."

"No! I am not going to ruin your life!" Sarah shouted, halting Rory in her tracks. "I've met your family. What the hell do you think this will do to them?"

Rory just stared, momentarily stunned. That's what all of this was about? Her family? But of course it was—when Sarah's parents had discovered that she was gay, they'd rejected her. *And she thinks mine will do the same. Fuck.*

"It's not like that," she said, trying to make her voice calm. Soft. "They're not going to—"

"You can't say that! You don't know." Sarah had pulled on her bra and a long-sleeved shirt. Rory was getting increasingly desperate. Sarah was clearly on the verge of leaving.

How can I stop her? How can I make her understand? "You don't get it," she said, her words tripping over themselves as she tried to find a way to make Sarah comprehend the truth. "Yeah, they'll be surprised, and not exactly *happy* about it, but they're not going to kick me out or cut me off. I swear it."

"That's what you think," Sarah said. She was bracing herself against the doorframe and her breaths were shallow and quick. "But are you sure? Of course you're not."

"Are you telling me that you know my family better than I do?" Rory was getting angry now—angry on top of frightened. She glared at Sarah, even as the slice of her brain that could still think rationally pointed out that Sarah probably needed calm reassurance, not a verbal sparring partner.

"I'm saying that I love you!"

Rory's mouth dropped open and her pulse spiked and she sat

back down, totally in shock. *She loves me. My God. Sarah. Loves me. How did that—*

"I love you and I care about you and I need you to be happy!" Sarah continued, clearly on the edge of tears. "So stay the hell away from me. You hear that? Stay *away.*"

And then she was gone. A second later, Rory heard the door slam behind her. She stared blankly at the wall for several seconds before cradling her head in her hands.

"Fuck. Fuck fuck *fuck!*" Suddenly enraged, she kicked viciously at the bottom drawer, only to curse again as pain shot through the top of her foot. "Goddammit!"

This had *really* not been a good day—first, the lost election, and now Sarah's panicked retreat. Rory's body still throbbed with desire, and her toes were probably swelling, and she had a sinking feeling that Sarah wasn't just going to return in a few minutes and admit that she had overreacted.

Fuck. Everything is so messed up. Finally, she got to her feet and pulled on her pajamas. She eyed the ladder for a second, before flopping down onto Sarah's bed. If she came home tonight, Rory would be sure to know. And if she didn't…the sheets and pillow smelled like her. They were a poor substitute for the feeling of Sarah's body pressing hers into the mattress, but they were better than nothing.

Rory inhaled deeply and focused on calming her racing heartbeat. Everything would be better in the morning, of course. Sarah would come home and she'd actually start listening and they'd kiss and make up and she'd finish what she had started. And there would be a recount of the ballots, which would reveal that the anti-amendment faction had won, after all.

And moncy would start growing on trees. And there would be peace on earth, goodwill toward men.

Right.

Chapter Seventeen

Sarah was driving too fast and the radio was far too loud. Her ears were throbbing in sync with the bass line, and her eyes were watering with the effort required to safely navigate S-curves at twenty miles above the speed limit. But try as she might, there was no way to escape the vivid memory of how badly she had just hurt Rory.

To her left, the ocean appeared briefly. The wind was up, and whitecaps shimmered in the intermittent moonlight. For one wild, irrational moment, Sarah wanted to yank her steering wheel hard enough to send her car flying down into the surf. It would be so easy. Probably painless. Her parents wouldn't be too sad, seeing as they'd already cut her out of their lives. Rory would take it hard at first, but eventually, she'd move back to Jeff. *Where she belongs.*

Her fingers tightened on the wheel, but she continued along the sinuous path of the road as it wound closer and closer to Wakefield. For whatever reason, she was incapable of yielding to her death drive. Hope just kept on springing eternal, refusing to let her off the hook. Even now—even after she'd lost it with Rory and all of her hard work for FRI looked as though it had been for nothing—she just couldn't lie down and give up.

But I want to. It'd be...easier.

Her lips still burned from Rory's kisses. She pressed one finger against them, remembering how good, how *right* it had felt to give in to her desire. When she inhaled, Rory's scent made her stomach clench. *I touched her. She let me. She wanted me to.*

"No," Sarah said out loud, returning her right hand to the wheel and pressing harder on the gas pedal. Rory didn't know what she wanted. She was confused. She was only beginning the coming-out process. She had admitted that herself. What if she was just curious, or wanting to experiment? And even if Rory did feel the way she claimed to, how could Sarah allow herself to be the one to rip Rory's family apart?

Suddenly realizing where she was, Sarah hit the brakes hard. Her car jerked to a stop in front of Corrie's driveway. The Vote No sign was still standing next to the mailbox. Sarah winced as a hot rush of anger and sadness welled up to press behind her eyes. *Dammit.*

Just as she had so many months ago, she sat motionless behind the wheel for several minutes before getting out of the car. This time, Corrie had no idea that she was coming. Sarah hadn't even brought a toothbrush. She was counting heavily on Corrie and Quinn's benevolence, because there was no way that she could stay in her dorm room for the last few weeks of the semester. She didn't trust herself to do the right thing anymore—not when it had become clear that her self-control was in tatters around Rory. *I'll go back and get my stuff sometime while she's in class.*

Squaring her shoulders, she gritted her teeth and rang the doorbell. Corrie opened the door after a few seconds. Her hair was back in a ponytail, and her left hand was curled around Frog's collar to keep him from lunging forward.

"Storm, hey," she said, frowning in surprise. "What's up? Is everything all right?"

Sarah shook her head. "No. Not really." She sucked in a deep breath. "I don't want to ask you this, because you both have already given me more than I can ever repay. But—"

"Come inside," Corrie said, cutting her off. "For as long as you need."

Relief began to melt the cold pit that had formed deep in Sarah's stomach. She smiled wanly and followed Corrie into the foyer, patting Frog as she went. They ended up in the den, where Quinn was sitting on the love seat, balancing a book on her knees.

The television was on in the background, tuned to one of the local news channels. The anchorwoman was talking about the election.

Quinn looked up with a warm smile for Corrie, which changed into an expression of concern when she saw Sarah. "Sarah? What happened?"

Sarah shook her head, tears clogging her throat at their generosity. "Can I save it for tomorrow?" she managed.

"Of course." Quinn set her book aside, got to her feet, and gave Sarah a long hug. "It's good to see you."

"You look exhausted," Corrie said. "Go get some rest, okay?"

"Okay. And thank you. So much." Sarah gave them both a little wave and then headed up the stairs. She paused in the bathroom off the hallway to splash some water on her face and then went into the guest room. It was exactly as she remembered it.

She took off her clothes, hung them over the back of a chair, and burrowed under the blankets. She wished it were warm enough outside to open the window and fall asleep to the sounds of the tide, like she had during the summer.

Sarah closed her eyes and tried to relax, willing the tension to fade from her shoulders and back. She tried mentally reciting the periodic table of elements. She tried revisiting happy memories. But no matter what trick she used, her mind returned to the image of Rory, naked, watching through hazy eyes as Sarah stroked her toward ecstasy.

Sarah rolled onto her stomach and buried her face in the pillow. What was Rory doing now? Had she fallen asleep? Or was she still awake, too—playing video games or surfing the Web? The pit in Sarah's gut returned full force, aching with the intensity of how much she missed her.

Turning her head to one side, she sighed heavily and tried to get comfortable. She focused on the light background noise filtering up from downstairs, but that didn't help, either. The sounds of the news were nothing like the muffled bursts of Rory's video games. And Corrie and Quinn's voices were nothing like the soft sounds of Rory's even breaths.

Can't live with her, can't live without her. Sarah flipped onto her back again and stared up at the shadowed ceiling. *What am I supposed to do?*

❖

Sarah woke to the smell of waffles. She was disoriented for a moment, until yesterday's events came crashing back into her immediate memory. *The vote. Rory.* She stared at the ceiling, wishing that it were possible to go back to those precious seconds just before full consciousness, when everything hadn't been completely screwed up.

Sighing, she looked over at the nightstand, checking her watch. Nine o'clock. *So much for making it to Chemistry.*

She rolled out of bed, slipped into her clothes, and headed downstairs. There was no use in lying around. Today was going to be a wash as far as classes went, but there was plenty of other stuff to do. Including returning to the FRI office to do some debriefing on the election. *Great. That should be cheery.*

"'Morning," Corrie called from the kitchen. "What do you want on your waffle? Syrup? Strawberries? Whipped cream?"

Sarah walked in and took a seat at one of the stools surrounding the island. She smiled at the sight of Corrie spooning batter into a large Belgian waffle maker. "Strawberries and whipped cream sound great. Thanks."

"A woman after my own heart," Corrie said. "Quinn's a traditionalist. She only does syrup."

"Where is she?"

"She had to go in early." Corrie closed the lid and the batter sizzled. When Rogue brushed up against Sarah's foot, Sarah reached down to stroke the cat's silky coat.

"Have you been on the water yet this year?"

"Hell, yeah." Corrie looked out toward the ocean. "I started going out in March." She turned her gaze back to Sarah and quirked a grin. "Let's sail together sometime. If you think you still remember how to crew, that is."

Sarah rolled her eyes. "Just for that, you have to let me skipper."

Corrie laughed. "Fair enough." She opened the lid. "Breakfast's ready."

A few minutes later, Sarah pushed back her plate and rested her elbows on the counter. "I know you want to know why I'm here," she said.

Corrie looked up from the newspaper and shrugged. "Only if you want to tell me. You can stay as long as you need, no questions asked. You know that."

"Thank you," Sarah said, her throat tight. She cleared it before beginning the story of how she had fallen for her roommate and ruined everything. When she finished, Corrie blew out her breath on a long sigh.

"Okay, let me get this straight. You're into Rory, but when you discover that Rory is into you…you run for it." Corrie tilted her head to one side. "Does that make sense to you? Because it doesn't to me."

Sarah frowned. "But…but I told you. What about her family? Being with me will make things so hard for her."

"Are you sure about that?"

"No," Sarah admitted. She hunched her shoulders. Why was she on the defensive here? *Corrie's supposed to be on my side.* "But it sort of feels like the situation with Dar all over again. If she hides from her parents, she'll always be afraid of our relationship. And if she tells them, they could convince her that her feelings aren't real or that…that being with me is a mistake." Goose bumps rose on her arms at the thought. *I couldn't stand it if that happened.*

"Or maybe they wouldn't think of this as a big deal," Corrie said. "My parents rolled with my sexual orientation from the beginning. They were surprised but never disgusted." She reached one hand across the island to squeeze Sarah's shoulder. "The point is—you never know. And if Rory's telling you that her family isn't going to consider her coming out to be the Apocalypse…well, you have to believe her."

Sarah opened her mouth, intent on arguing the point, but paused when Corrie suddenly got up and started to pace the kitchen floor. She did this, Sarah realized, whenever she was deep in thought.

"But what if *that's* the problem," Corrie continued. "What if you don't believe her?" She looked at Sarah intently. "Do you trust her?"

"Of course," Sarah said. She had trusted Rory with her secrets all year long.

But Corrie shook her head. "I'm not sure you do—not really. Not the way one lover has to trust the other."

"What do you mean?"

"Look," Corrie said, bracing her arms on the counter. She was wearing a short-sleeved shirt, and her triceps jumped out in definition. "You've had a rough year. First, your parents disown you. Then, your girlfriend breaks up with you. Are you worried about what Rory's family will think? Sure, of course. But I think the real reason you ran out last night might be because you're afraid that she's going to leave you, too. You said it yourself, just a minute ago."

Sarah blinked hard in surprise. Was it really that simple? She had thought that by leaving, she was acting on Rory's behalf. But what if Corrie was right? What if her own insecurities, and not some selfless impulse, were blocking her from accepting Rory's love and passion?

"Huh," she said, trying to crack a smile. "When did you get so wise?"

"It's all Quinn's influence," Corrie said, smiling.

Sarah reached back to massage her tense neck with one hand. "So…let's say you're right. What am I supposed to do about it?"

Corrie sat back down on the stool, speared a leftover strawberry with her fork, and popped it into her mouth. "I guess you have to figure out how to not be so afraid," she said.

"Yeah." Sarah felt her gut tighten. How was she supposed to get rid of her abandonment issues, just like that? "Got any ideas?"

"I wish I did," Corrie said. "But how about a deal? If you

promise to work on beating the fear, I promise to make you breakfast every morning until you do."

For the first time since she'd walked out of her dorm room, Sarah's smile was genuine. She stuck out her hand and shook Corrie's firmly. "Deal."

❖

The next day, Sarah walked slowly up the stairs to the FRI office and paused at the door. Yesterday, when she knew that Rory would be in Biology, she had stopped by her room to gather the essentials. Now, it was time to do a similar job at the office, seeing as Friday was the last day of FRI's lease. If everything had gone well, the prospect of packing up the office would probably have felt like part of the victory celebration. Instead, it felt like salt in the wound of defeat.

"Hey, Sarah," Nancy said when she opened the door. She sounded tired. "Rory just stopped by about half an hour ago, looking for you."

Sarah froze in the doorway, her heart suddenly pounding. She didn't know whether she was relieved or disappointed. Probably both. Rory had been on her mind constantly, from the instant she woke up until the moment she fell asleep. *I love her. I want her. I need her. But no matter what Corrie says, I will not cause her life to fall apart.*

"Oh, okay," she said, trying to sound casual. "Thanks for letting me know." She closed the door behind her and picked her way through the boxes on the floor. "How's it coming?"

"Slowly but surely," Nancy said, dropping a stack of posters into the recycling bin. "Thanks for dropping by."

"I'm free for the rest of the day," Sarah said. "I can help out for as long as you need."

After Nancy explained the basics of what to save and what to pitch, Sarah sat down at her desk for the last time and began going through her drawers. She felt a pang of nostalgia for the days when the outcome of the referendum had still been up in the air—when the vote could have gone either way. When she had been optimistic.

"So," Nancy said, "what are your plans for the summer?"

"I'm going to teach sailing in Wakefield," Sarah said. "It should be fun." She mustered up a laugh. "Totally different from canvassing."

Nancy nodded. "I can imagine."

"If you'd ever like to get out on the water, just give me a call," Sarah said. She tossed all of the pens and markers in her top drawer into a box. "How about you? What will you do now?"

"I'll go back to work in GLAD's main office in Boston," Nancy said. "Keep on fighting the good fight."

"Yeah." Sarah pulled open her second drawer to find copies of the first flier she'd ever printed for FRI, way back in November. "You know," she said, "I can't even tell you how much I've learned here. I'm even thinking about doing a poli sci major now."

"Instead of chemistry?"

"In addition to." When Nancy whistled, Sarah grinned. "I know it sounds crazy."

They worked for a while in silence, before Nancy paused again. "Oh—Rory invited me to her film's screening next week. I just checked my calendar and unfortunately, I can't make it. I'll be at a conference on the West Coast. Will you let her know, and tell her how much I wish I could be there?"

"Uh, sure," Sarah said.

"She did such a great job with that commercial," Nancy continued, oblivious to Sarah's discomfort. "I'm no expert on film, but it seems to me that she has real talent."

"She's amazing," Sarah agreed, looking down at the contents of her third drawer without really seeing anything. *Amazing and kind and generous and passionate. She doesn't deserve me and my baggage. She deserves to be happy. To be with someone who can make her happy. Like Jeff.*

Sarah shook her head and got back to work, dumping the drawer's contents into a trash bag. She wished that it were just as easy to dispose of unwanted emotions—to compartmentalize them, seal them off, and throw them away forever. Maybe, if she avoided her long enough, Rory would be able to do just that.

❖

Rory had never been to the engineering building before. She was more than a little embarrassed that here she was, a junior, carrying a map around campus like a frosh. But making Sarah see reason was far more important than her pride.

It was midafternoon on Friday, and by all rights, she should have been in bed. She hadn't slept more than two hours at a time since Wednesday morning, but the film was finally done—she had just turned it in an hour ago. On the one hand, the last-minute, frenetic editing had distracted her from thinking too hard about how much she missed Sarah. On the other hand, her busyness had prevented her from going after Sarah and forcing her to see reason. She had tried calling Sarah's cell a few times, but unsurprisingly, there had been no answer.

She knew exactly where Sarah was living, of course—her friend Corrie's place, in Wakefield. That was a no-brainer. She had thought more than once about borrowing Matt's car and showing up at Corrie's front door. The only thing that had stopped her was the certain knowledge that she didn't know how to convince Sarah to come back. She needed help.

Which was why she was on her way to the godforsaken engineering building. Corrie, she'd once heard Sarah mention, was a mechanical engineering graduate student. It hadn't been difficult to find a list of the engineering doctoral candidates online. Once she had Corrie's last name, it had been even easier to track down her office number.

Rory paused on a corner and looked to her left and right, then back down at the map. Sure enough, that was it—straight ahead. Kirk Engineering Lab. She crossed the street, walked through the double doors, and found the bank of elevators in the atrium. A few minutes later, she was standing in front of Corrie's office. The door was cracked. Rory took a deep breath, let it out, and knocked. *Here goes nothing.*

"Come in," a voice said. A feminine-sounding voice. Good sign.

Rory pushed open the door. The office was longer than it was wide. The desks to the left and right were occupied by men. At the desk directly opposite the door, however, sat a lithe blonde woman in cargo pants and a tank top. She had really nice arms, Rory realized as she stepped inside. And nice breasts. Pretty much nice everything.

"I'm looking for Corrie Marsten," she said.

"That would be me," the hot blonde said. "What can I do for you?"

"I'm Rory."

"Ah." Corrie looked surprised for an instant, before the expression morphed into a smile. She rose fluidly to her feet. "Well then. How about we go for a walk?"

They turned right out of the office. Corrie led her down a stairwell and out onto a small balcony. Rory guessed that it was a popular place for people to take smoke breaks.

"Can't say that I was expecting you," Corrie said, leaning her chiseled arms on the half-wall and looking down at the people walking below. "But it's good to meet you. Sarah's talked about you frequently over the past few days."

"All good things, I hope," Rory said sarcastically.

"Well, yeah. She's crazy about you, you know."

Rory narrowed her eyes. "She left and won't return my calls because she's crazy about me? In what universe does that make sense?"

Corrie sighed. "I think she's trying to protect—"

"I don't need her protection," Rory said fiercely. "She won't listen to me. My family would never do what hers did. Not ever! I'm certain of it."

There was a long moment during which Corrie regarded her

speculatively. "I wasn't going to say 'you,'" she said. "I was going to say 'herself.' Although, yes—when we talked, she was very concerned about how your family will react if you come out to them."

"How is she trying to protect herself? From what?" Rory clutched at the wall as though it was the only thing holding her up. As grateful as she was to be having this conversation with Corrie, she was also still furious that Sarah had walked out on her. *I want to understand. I need to. Help me.*

"Look," Corrie said, "Sarah's had the year from hell. First, her parents cut her off. Then her girlfriend dumps her on her ass with no warning. Are you picking up on the theme, here?"

"Yeah," Rory snapped. Her temper flared at Corrie's attempt to play counselor. "I get it, okay? The people she trusts leave her hanging. What's your point?"

Corrie just looked at her. Rory glared back...until the puzzle piece finally clicked into place.

"Oh," she said, wondering how the hell she'd never thought of this before. "She thinks I'm going to leave her, too." Was it really that simple? Sarah's misguided, backassward attempt at nobility stemmed from her fear of abandonment?

"She's trying to get over that particular issue," Corrie said. "And she feels awful for running out on you. For what it's worth."

Rory nodded. She rubbed at her eyes, feeling the exhaustion crash over her like an ocean wave. But she couldn't afford to be exhausted. She had a scared, lonely woman to reassure. *It'd be a helluvalot easier to reassure her if she'd talk to me, dammit.*

"This is going to sound like a strange request," she said to Corrie, "but do you have a piece of paper? And something to write with?"

❖

The thick envelope burned Sarah's fingers. She couldn't stop glancing down at it—at the familiar blue and white seal and the flowing motto beneath—as she walked toward the engineering building. *Lux et veritas.* Light and truth. She didn't have to open the envelope to know that she had been readmitted to Yale. Part of her didn't *want* to open it, because getting reaccepted threw another wrinkle into her already hopelessly messed up life.

Oh, stop being melodramatic. This is good news. A way out of a sticky situation. You can go back and forget this year ever happened.

But was that what she really wanted? Academically, going back to Yale made sense—it was the more prestigious institution, after all. And yet, when she thought about returning to New Haven, she didn't feel excited or eager or proud. She felt…hollow.

She rode the elevator up to Corrie's office and knocked tentatively on the door. *I hope she's not too busy.* Sarah knew that she should have held off on talking to Corrie until they were at home, but checking her mail had thrown her for such a loop that she just couldn't wait.

"Come in."

When Sarah did, Corrie laughed. "Wow," she said, leaning back in her chair. "Rory was here about an hour ago. What am I, Dr. Phil?"

"She was? Really? What'd she say? How did she look? Is she—"

When Corrie held up one hand, Sarah shut her mouth. She fidgeted where she stood, unable to stand still. Her heart was pounding and her palms were sweating and more than anything in the world, she wanted to know what had driven Rory to seek Corrie out.

Corrie reached into her pocket and extracted a small, black box. She held it up. "She wanted me to give this to you. There's a note inside."

Fingers trembling, Sarah took the box and cracked it open. She took out the neatly folded piece of paper and sucked in a sharp breath at what lay beneath it: a silver claddagh pendant on a chain. *Whoa.* She set the box down carefully and unfolded the note, smiling when she saw Rory's scrawling script.

I meant to give this to you on your birthday. I was going to tell you that I was falling for you. But then your parents called and there just wasn't a good time, and now I'm afraid it's too late.

Sarah's eyes burned. *Falling for me.* Her birthday had been almost two months ago. Rory had kept her feelings to herself for a long time, and when she finally dared to confess...*I let her down. She was brave and honest and I refused to believe her. I was selfish. Afraid.*

Sarah blinked hard, cleared her throat, and focused on the last line of the message: *I miss you. I love you. Have faith in me.*

"For what it's worth," Corrie said, "I like her. She's pissed as hell at you, but she's not giving up."

Sarah pocketed the note and shut the box with a click. "She should be angry," she said, her voice thick. "I really don't deserve her."

"Oh, shut up," Corrie said, rolling her eyes. "That's such a bullshit line. Everybody's fucked up in their own personal way, Storm. Love isn't about deserving."

Sarah stood with her head bowed, unsure of what to say. Was that true? Could she trust that Rory loved her for exactly who she was? That she wasn't tolerating her flaws, or turning a blind eye to them—but that they just didn't matter? *I want to believe that. I really do.*

She took a deep breath and met Corrie's gaze again. "In other news," she said, tossing the envelope onto the desk, "look what I got in the mail today."

Corrie picked it up, raising her eyebrows. "You haven't opened it."

"Be my guest."

Corrie handed it back to her with a slight grin. "No way. That's a federal offense. You do it."

"Fine." This was why she had come here, after all. Corrie wouldn't let her be a coward. Snatching back the envelope, she ripped it open and extracted the letter. "Dear Sarah Storm," she read aloud. "We are pleased to offer you admission…" She replaced the letter on Corrie's desk. Her stomach was doing the twist. "Just like I thought. Now what do I do?"

"You know," Corrie said, standing up and stretching. "I'm flattered as all hell that you keep coming to me for advice. But if you want me to tell you whether to stay or go, then forget it. You're the only one who can make that choice."

Sarah flushed, ashamed at being called out. She had wanted to use Corrie, she realized, to keep herself from being accountable. "Sorry," she mumbled. "Guess I'm not doing too great at dealing with that fear thing, huh?"

Corrie rested one hand on her shoulder. "Don't be so hard on yourself," she said. And then she grinned. "But don't be chicken shit, either. Now get out of here and go do something productive. I'll see you at home tonight."

"All right," Sarah said. "Yeah. Thanks."

But when she dutifully parked herself in the library to go over her poli sci notes, she couldn't stop wondering what Rory was doing at that moment. She had turned in her film that morning, Sarah knew. Was she sleeping? Playing video games? Writing an English paper? Messing around on Facebook?

Is she thinking about me? Is she still angry?

❖

Sarah parked outside of Independence Auditorium but didn't open her door. She reached deep into her right jeans pocket and withdrew the small black box containing Rory's claddagh pendant. Over the past few days, she had reread the note a hundred times. *I miss you. I love you. Have faith in me.*

Sarah let the chain slide between her fingers, but didn't put it on. She pooled the necklace back into the box and returned it to her pocket. Tonight was Rory's big night. In just a few minutes, her documentary, which she had titled *Free Rhode Island,* would be shown as a part of the film department's spring festival.

She glanced down at her watch and got out of the car. Most people would be in the auditorium by now. It would be easy to unobtrusively claim a chair near the back. And sure enough, she ended up in an aisle seat in the third to last row. Rory would be sitting somewhere in the front, she knew, along with all of the other film students whose movies had played throughout the day. Not for the first time, she wondered why *Free Rhode Island* had been given the last—and premier—slot. Was it coincidence, or a reward for brilliant work?

"It's going to be wicked hard to see, all the way back here," Matt said from just behind her. Sarah felt her pulse jump and she twisted around in her chair to look him in the eyes. "We've got an extra seat in the fourth row, center." He held out his hand. "C'mon."

She hadn't spoken with Matt in a week, figuring that he must be furious with her for how she had treated Rory. But he didn't look angry at all. In fact, he was smiling kindly at her under his shock of metallic gold hair.

Sarah wanted to take him up on his offer, but she was afraid. Obviously, he was sitting with everyone from the GLBT student center. How many of them had heard what had happened? What if *they* were mad at her?

"Thanks, Matt," she said. "But I think I'd better stay here."

"No way, stud," he said, and his use of Rory's teasing moniker made Sarah's heart thump painfully. "Come on. Sit with your family."

Sarah's eyes filled with tears and she blinked furiously. *I will not lose it. Not here. Not now.* Matt's demand was irresistible. It was exactly what she wanted. "Yeah," she said, willing her voice not to shake. "Okay."

From her new position, Sarah could see the back of Rory's head clearly, several rows in front of them. When she sat down, Sarah realized that she had ended up between Matt and Chelsea. There was an awkward moment of silence for several seconds, and Sarah could practically feel Matt racking his brains for some funny story that would diffuse the tension. But that wasn't his responsibility. *It's mine.*

She turned to Chelsea. "So hey, does Afterhours have any more performances before the semester ends?"

Chelsea looked surprised but recovered quickly, launching into an animated discussion of her *a cappella* group's schedule over the next week. Sarah nodded, already planning to ask what her summer plans were next, when the house lights came down. A surge of excitement coursed under her skin. *I've been looking forward to seeing this since Rory started filming in November.*

The film began to roll—first a few credits and then the title screen. Sarah was disappointed. She had wanted to see Rory standing up in front of everyone, acknowledged for her work. Her gaze wasn't on the screen, but on Rory. Being this close to her was comforting and maddening, all at once. *I miss you. I don't know what to do. Loving you scares me half to death, but I can't make it go away.*

She returned her gaze to the screen when Matt elbowed her in the ribs. There *she* was, back in the fall during her first week of interning for FRI. Sarah watched herself look up from her new desk to grin at Rory, who had been making funny faces behind the camera. She watched herself working at her computer, photocopying fliers, talking with Nancy. She watched herself handing out those same fliers to students, engaging them in conversations about the upcoming referendum. She watched herself holding a sign and a candle outside the capitol building, canvassing in the cafeteria, chalking the sidewalk outside Memorial Union.

The dramatic irony made some parts difficult to watch—like Lee's inspirational speech, and Sarah's own hopeful declaration in January about the election's outcome. But revisiting all of her FRI memories wasn't nearly as painful as Sarah had anticipated. *I have a lot to be proud of,* she realized for the first time. *I helped build community. I helped give people a mission. I changed and opened minds.*

And that's when she understood that this wasn't just a film about GLAD or FRI or Rhode Island or the fight for equal rights. Rory had spent hours upon hours shooting—at the FRI office, at every event, and around the university. While editing, she could have chosen to focus on someone else, like Nancy. Or she could have made a more conceptual movie, one that wasn't attached to any one individual's journey. Instead, *Free Rhode Island* was a film about *her*—about Sarah Storm—created by the woman who knew and loved her best. It was a love letter and a photo album and a mix CD, all tossed together.

It was a glimpse of what Rory saw in her. Rory saw a strong woman, someone unafraid to fight for her beliefs. Rory saw a compassionate woman, a good listener, firm leader, and inspirational speaker. Rory saw a dedicated woman, creative and hardworking.

Rory saw the good in her. She brought out the best in her. And in that moment, as Sarah stared at herself on screen, she realized that Rory wasn't confused at all.

She really is *in love with me. She really means it.*

Sarah had no idea what the rest of the audience was seeing, but she *knew*, with the kind of absolute certainty that made the hairs on the back of her neck stand up, that Rory had been thinking about her during every single moment of filming, editing, revising. This was her floating bottle, and Sarah was the only one who could open it and read the message inside.

I love you. I want you. I need you. Out of everyone in the world, I choose you, Sarah. Just you.

The last scene of the film was Nancy's final speech on election night. Rory had focused her camera not on Nancy, but on Sarah. As Nancy spoke about how important it was to be proud of their progress and continue strong in the fight for equal rights, Sarah watched her own expression change, from despair to determination. She remembered her resolve in that moment never to give up. And then the screen faded to black.

Without checking to see whether anyone else was standing, Sarah rose to her feet and clapped as hard as she could when Rory and her peers dutifully appeared onstage. She had no idea whether Rory could see her in the glare, but just in case, she looked directly at her the entire time. Rory had made her proud—not just of FRI, but of herself. It didn't matter that her parents were disappointed in her—not really. What mattered was that she not be disappointed in herself.

"Well," Matt said as the lights came up. "That was all kinds of awesome."

"Yeah," Travis said from a few seats down. "I mean, wow."

"If that doesn't win an award..." Chelsea said.

Sarah nodded, but didn't contribute to the praise. She felt full, somehow—supersaturated with emotion. It was so clear what she had to do, now. Rory had laid all her cards on the table, and she had to do the same. *No holding back.* The thought should have frightened her, but didn't. Not anymore.

She caught a glimpse of Rory at the foot of the stage, talking with her film professor and someone else—a distinguished-looking, middle-aged guy—before Matt distracted her by tugging on her sleeve. "I have it on good authority that the after party is at Kingston Pizza," he said. "I'm going to head over there soon. Anybody else?"

"Sure." Sarah felt a little dazed. The need to see and talk to Rory was overwhelming, and she had lost her in the crowd of people now trying to leave the auditorium. "We can take my car."

But when they walked through the doors of the pizzeria, Rory was nowhere to be found. The other members of her class were there, but when Sarah questioned them, they couldn't tell her anything concrete.

"I thought she was coming," one said. "She left with us. But..." He gestured expansively and almost spilled his beer on Sarah's black T-shirt.

"Thanks." Sarah returned to Matt's side. "They don't know where she is. I'm going to try the room."

He nodded. "Good luck." For a moment, he looked as though he wanted to say more, but then he patted her arm and moved off toward a knot of people near the bar.

Sarah hurried back across campus to Hutchinson. She jogged up the stairs and down the hall, mindless in anticipation. *She'll be there. She has to be there.* But the door was locked, and when Sarah used her key to get in, the room was dark and deserted. She stood in the center of the common room, feeling lost.

Where would she go? If she didn't want to be with her friends to celebrate her accomplishment, why wouldn't she have come back here? And then suddenly, Sarah remembered a mild November night, and the conversation they'd had in that tiny park on top of the hill.

Do you come here a lot?

Once in a while. Mostly when something's bugging me.

Sarah closed her eyes, imagining that she could feel the pull of Rory's beautiful, burning soul as her body glided through the warm spring night.

"Wait for me," she whispered.

She fumbled in her pocket for that little black box, then fastened the pendant around her neck for the first time. The silver chain felt cool against her neck, and the light pressure of the claddagh symbol against her collarbone was comforting. She smiled. And then she hurried out the door, down the stairs, and out of the building, turning away from campus and toward the town.

Chapter Eighteen

Rory leaned back a little and inhaled deeply, welcoming the flying sensation. The night was warm and clear. Stars pricked the sky like pins in a black velvet cushion. She smiled a little, feeling strangely at peace. Sarah had been at the screening. If the film hadn't proven to her just how deeply Rory cared, then she would never be convinced. Rory was still afraid, of course, but for now, the fear hovered on the edges of her consciousness, banished by a sense of accomplishment.

After the screening, her professor had introduced her to a friend of his—a New York–based director who just so happened to be in production over the summer. He had asked Rory whether she would be willing to work on his set, and she had jumped at the chance. She still couldn't believe her luck—to have that kind of experience before she graduated was just…unreal.

Somewhere below her and to the west, her friends were celebrating with pizza and beer. Part of her wanted to go and join them—to soak up their congratulations and answer their questions. To bask in her moment of glory—to feel like a Very Important Person. But most of her needed to be here, soaking up the wind and the starlight, basking in the quiet knowledge that she had done the best she could.

She closed her eyes and pumped her legs harder. Crickets chirped in the grass and a lily-scented breeze blew her hair back from her face, and someone's footsteps crunched rhythmically along the gravel path—

Footsteps. Rory's eyes flew open to see Sarah standing several yards away, watching her. She was dressed in a black T-shirt and jeans. A silver chain around her neck gleamed in the dim light. A painful jolt of hope shot through Rory's body. *My necklace. She's wearing it.*

"Hey," Sarah said. Her voice was soft and hesitant, and she shifted her weight back and forth, clearly nervous. "I just wanted to tell you...I mean, your film is...it's amazing, Rory. Everyone was saying so, not just me. Chelsea thinks you'll get an award, and you totally deserve one..." She paused for a second, running one hand through her hair. She looked vulnerable and handsome and anxious. "They all loved it. But I don't think they really *got* it. Not like—not like I did."

Rory had thought through this moment frequently, over the past week. Sometimes, when she had felt absolutely miserable, visualizing what would happen when Sarah finally started speaking to her again was the only way she had been able to keep from falling apart. Sometimes she had imagined shouting at Sarah—sometimes kissing her. She had never expected to feel calm and poised when the moment arrived, but somehow, she did.

"I made it for you," she said, gradually slowing the momentum of the swing.

Sarah nodded. "I know."

"I fell in love with you while shooting it." Rory watched Sarah closely, wanting so badly to believe that *Free Rhode Island* had truly affected her in the way that she had hoped. But she had to be sure. She had to be clear. "I fell in love with you all over again while I was editing."

Sarah swallowed hard, the motion visible even at a distance. "Really?" Her voice was low and hoarse.

"Yeah." The swing had slowed almost completely, now. Rory let the toes of her boots scuff lightly against the grass as she watched Sarah take a few steps forward. *Believe me. Have faith in me.*

"I'm sorry for leaving," Sarah said. "I know that apologizing isn't enough, but I want you to know that I really am sorry. And that I missed you."

"Why did you do it?" Rory asked, wanting to understand. She could come up with theories about Sarah's behavior until her head exploded, but she needed to know the truth.

Sarah ducked her head and rocked on the balls of her feet. When she looked back up, her eyes were shining. "I was afraid," she said quietly. "When you told me that you had never—that I was going to be your first..." Her voice cracked and she cleared her throat. "I realized just how big this was. Us, I mean. How much I wanted you. How much I needed you. And it scared me."

"Why?" Rory asked again, sliding her sweating palms up and down the chains of the swing. *Keep talking, baby. Help me understand. I need to.*

"I couldn't believe what you were saying," Sarah said. "I loved Dar more than she loved me, and I loved Chelsea less. I think...I was scared that it would be the same way with you. Imbalanced. And that when you realized it, you'd leave."

"And? Are you still afraid of that?"

Sarah smiled tentatively before shaking her head. "No. Not anymore. Not after seeing your movie."

Rory nodded. The strange calm that had suffused her earlier had all but disappeared. She wanted to jump off the swing, hug Sarah tightly, and kiss her with all the ferocity that had been pent up inside of her since Election Day. And now, she was sure that Sarah wanted the exact same thing. *Grand passion.* The knowledge was heady. But...

"What about my family? Are you still worried about what they'll do?"

Sarah's smile faded. "Yes. I don't want them to hurt you."

"They can't, baby," Rory said, leaning forward to emphasize her point. "Not if I'm with you. They can't touch me if I'm with you."

"But—"

Rory stood up. "You can't make this choice for me. That's not your right."

Sarah sucked in a deep breath. "I know."

Rory took a step toward her. "You have to trust me."

"I do."

Sarah stayed where she was, but her gaze roamed Rory's body, making her feel warm deep inside. *She loves me. She wants me.*

"I need you to love me with everything you've got," she said, taking yet another step. She was almost close enough to touch Sarah now.

Sarah's eyes shone even brighter. "I can't do anything less," she said, her voice thick.

Rory smiled—really smiled—for the first time since Sarah had left. "Then we're going to be just fine," she said. And with one last step, she bridged the distance between them, threw her arms around Sarah's neck, and pulled her head down for a long, hungry, loving kiss.

❖

Sarah drew Rory into the room, pushed the door closed, and pressed her back against it before leaning in to thrust her tongue deep inside Rory's mouth. She groaned as Rory's hips jolted against hers, and shifted so she could slide one thigh between Rory's legs. When she pressed in and up, it was Rory's turn to moan.

When Sarah finally pulled back, she was gasping. She let her forehead rest against Rory's and tried to catch her breath. "I love you. Even more than I want you."

This time, Rory started the kiss. It was gentle at first. She sucked on Sarah's lower lip, flicking lightly at it with her tongue. But within a few seconds, Rory was grasping the back of Sarah's head to pull her close, and their teeth were scraping and their tongues were dueling and the need to feel Rory's skin against hers rose in Sarah like a flash flood.

"I have to feel you," she panted, trailing her fingers under the hem of Rory's shirt "Please."

"Take it off, then," Rory challenged. When Sarah skimmed her knuckles along Rory's sides as she did, she was rewarded by a sharp intake of breath.

Sarah stepped back to set the discarded shirt over the back of

Rory's desk chair. When she turned around she paused, her mouth going dry at the sight of Rory wearing only a dark blue satin bra and slacks. Desire seared her brain like lightning, white-hot and crackling.

"See something you like?" Rory teased.

Sarah nodded, trembling. Her body cried out for her to do something, anything—to take Rory against the door, to pick her up and carry her into the bedroom, to pull her to the floor, slip one hand down her pants, and finger her until she came. Frozen in place, she fought against the competing urges, refusing to give in. *I'll scare her.*

But Rory frowned and came to her. "You're holding back on me," she said, her tone accusatory. She pressed a quick, hard kiss to Sarah's lips. "Stop it. I want you. I want you, Sarah, the same way you want me. What do I have to do to prove it to you?" She reached for Sarah's hands and brought them to her breasts. "Touch me, dammit. Please."

Sarah stroked Rory lightly, watching her face. When her eyes fluttered in pleasure, she made her fingers firmer. She pinched Rory's nipples lightly through the fabric, then harder when Rory whispered her name. The satin felt amazing, but she needed skin. She stepped closer to Rory, reaching around to undo her bra. It fell to the floor, unveiling the gentle swells of Rory's breasts. Her nipples were exquisite—large and dark.

Sarah's breaths were coming short and fast, and she felt a little dizzy. Rory's voice echoed in her ears. *You have to trust me. I want you, Sarah, the same way you want me.* She closed her eyes, inhaled deeply, and sacrificed her fear. When she opened them, Rory was looking up at her, concerned.

"What—"

"Sit down," Sarah ordered, barely recognizing her own voice. Rory sat in her chair immediately, eyes wide. They grew wider when Sarah dropped to her knees and sucked one nipple deep into her mouth.

"So good—"

Sarah skimmed her teeth across Rory's nipple, bringing one

hand up to roll the other between her thumb and index finger. After a minute, she alternated her hand and mouth. Rory was making small, breathy sounds of encouragement that ratcheted up Sarah's arousal. She was wet and throbbing, but she needed to make Rory come more than...anything.

With her mouth still at Rory's nipple, Sarah slid her right hand down Rory's body. Rory trembled violently when Sarah's fingers skated over her clitoris through the material of the slacks. When Sarah pressed down firmly and made slow circles, Rory's hips jerked forward.

Sarah released Rory's nipple with a pop. "I'm going to taste you now," she murmured, undoing the button and pulling down the zipper on Rory's slacks.

"Yes," Rory whispered as she lifted her hips. Within seconds, she was naked, and Sarah was pushing her legs apart.

"So beautiful," Sarah said reverently, transfixed by the sight of Rory's sex. Short, dark hair framed her swollen clit, and beads of moisture clung to her labia. *Exquisite.* Sarah lowered her head and sent her breath cascading over Rory.

"Please," Rory said, tilting her hips.

Unable to resist any longer, Sarah licked Rory from her opening to her clit. She tasted incredible—warm and salty and rich.

"Fuck!"

Rory's thighs were trembling. Sarah smiled, her heart thumping hard in pride that she was bringing Rory pleasure. She teased delicately at her clit with the tip of her tongue—first swirling around it, then pressing in firmly, then backing off to feather gentle licks across the sensitive tip. And then, finally, she closed her lips around it and hollowed her cheeks.

"Sarah!"

She sucked even harder, thrilling to the sound of her name cried out in passion. But when Rory's muscles began to tighten under her hands, Sarah pulled away.

"Not yet, love," she said over Rory's protests. "Not yet."

"You're going to kill me," gasped Rory, leaning back in the chair and gripping the handles hard.

Sarah stood up as gracefully as she could manage. The maelstrom of desire still pulsed under her skin, stronger than ever. She extended one hand to Rory. "No," she said. "I'm going to make you come in my bed."

Rory blinked and took Sarah's hand. "Shit," she breathed, allowing herself to be led into the bedroom.

"Lie down," Sarah said, stripping off first her shirt, then her bra, then her pants. Every nerve in her body was telling her to finish what she'd started, but she paused before joining Rory on top of the blankets. "You know how much I love you, right?"

"As much as I love you," Rory said, holding her arms open. "Come here."

Sarah went willingly, kissing Rory fiercely as she squeezed one hand between their bodies. "I want to be inside you," she murmured against Rory's lips.

"Yes," Rory said, spreading her legs even wider. "Need to feel you in me."

Sarah pulled back far enough so that she could focus on Rory's eyes. She teased Rory's clit with her index finger before moving down to her opening. *So wet.* The sensation made Sarah throb even harder.

"I love you," she said, sliding just the tip of her finger inside.

"I love you," Rory echoed breathlessly. "So good, baby, please—"

Sarah watched Rory's expression as she slipped further in. No pain registered on her face, only pleasure at being filled. When she was all the way inside, she moved her finger gently and was rewarded by a low gasp.

"Good?" Rory nodded, and Sarah kissed her lightly on the lips. "You feel amazing, love. So warm. So tight. I can't believe I'm inside you."

Sarah pulled out slightly—just an inch—before gently pushing back in. Rory's eyes closed and her back arched, so Sarah did it again. And again. Each time, it was a miracle. *I love you. God, how I love you. More than I've ever loved anyone.*

When Rory's eyes suddenly flashed open, Sarah paused, afraid that she had hurt her. But Rory reached for her wrist and pulled in, urging Sarah to continue moving.

"Don't stop," she said. "Fuck me, Sarah. Fuck me."

Oh my God. Sarah's entire body clenched, reacting to Rory's explicit command. Her words pushed Sarah over the edge of caution, and into passion. Pulling almost all the way out, she pushed her finger in again, hard.

"Yeah," Rory said hoarsely. "That's it. Fuck me like that."

Sarah obeyed, moving her finger faster and faster, wanting to tell Rory just how beautiful and sexy she was but unable to catch her breath. Her heart hammered against her ribs and she watched through narrow eyes as Rory moved against her, willing herself to remember this moment forever.

"It's so good," Rory chanted. "Don't stop, don't stop, oh please—"

Still working her finger in and out of Rory, Sarah moved down the bed. She bent her head and sucked Rory's clit into her mouth, swirling her tongue rapidly at the same time. *Come for me.*

Rory screamed. Her hips surged and her muscles contracted around Sarah's finger as she came, long and hard. Sarah didn't stop until the last of the tension eased from Rory's body. Only then did she lift her mouth from Rory's throbbing clit and gently withdraw from her body. She pillowed her head on Rory's thigh, breathing deeply and loving that she caught Rory's scent every time she inhaled. *I don't ever want to leave this spot,* she thought, closing her eyes and letting her heartbeat return to normal. *Not ever.*

After a little while, Rory's fingers began to comb through her hair. "Come up here," Rory murmured. "I want to see your face."

Sarah obliged, collapsing next to Rory and sliding one arm over her stomach. Rory turned to kiss her, and Sarah could tell that she was tasting herself on someone else's mouth for the first time. "Okay?"

Rory gave her that look—the one that said she was clearly insane. "Okay? *Okay?*" She shook her head. "No. It was awful. Never do that again. Ever." When Sarah muffled a laugh against her neck, Rory pulled away so she could look her in the eyes. "Listen up, you insecure nutcase. That was the most intense, incredible experience of my life, thank you very much."

Sarah grinned brightly and kissed Rory's nose. She hadn't felt this carefree...ever. "You're welcome very much," she said. "Please let me know if I can do it again sometime."

"Oh baby," Rory said, punctuating her words with kisses. "You can do that any. Time. You. Want." And then she reached down to tickle Sarah's ribs. Sarah shrieked and tried to roll away, but in a surprising show of strength, Rory slid on top of her and held her down. "Not so fast, stud."

Sarah was laughing helplessly and squirming. Against Rory's naked body. Suddenly, she didn't feel so ticklish after all.

"What?" said Rory, feeling the sudden change in mood.

"You're beautiful," Sarah said, in awe. "You feel amazing."

"And you are the hottest girl I've ever seen."

"Whatever," Sarah said. "Isn't Chelsea considered the hottest girl on campus?"

Rory growled again. "Don't remind me. I have a jealous streak, okay? Thinking about her touching you made me crazy for months."

Sarah raised her head to kiss Rory gently. "She didn't."

"Huh?"

Sarah cupped Rory's face in her palms and kissed her again. "She never made love to me. I just...I never really wanted her to. I always felt weird about it."

Rory blinked down at her. "Seriously?"

"Seriously."

Rory's expression shifted from surprised to concerned. "Do you want *me* to?"

Sarah heard the uncertainty in her voice and brought her head down for a long, passionate kiss. "Does that answer your question?" she said, once they both surfaced to breathe. "Yes, Rory. Yes. I want you to touch me. I need you to."

The smile that curved Rory's lips was crooked. "I might be awful at it."

"Doubtful." Sarah reached for Rory's right hand, determined to ease her anxiety. "You turn me on so much," she said softly, easing Rory's fingers between her legs. "Feel."

She hissed in a breath when Rory brushed her clit. "See?" she said, forcing herself to keep her eyes open so that she could watch Rory's reaction.

"God," Rory whispered, teasing Sarah's opening. "You're so wet."

"For you."

And then, without any warning, Rory pressed one finger all the way inside. Sarah grunted in pleasure and her back arched involuntarily. When her vision refocused, she looked up to see Rory gazing at her intently.

"Feels so good," Sarah said.

"I love you." Rory pulled almost all the way out before pushing back in again, mimicking how Sarah had touched her. When Sarah moaned her pleasure, Rory leaned down to kiss her, hard.

"Your thumb," Sarah gasped against Rory's lips. "Use your thumb on my clit."

Rory nodded, shifting the angle of her hand. Sarah cried out softly as her finger slid even deeper inside. And then Rory's thumb was spiraling around Sarah's clitoris, and Rory's tongue was dipping inside her mouth to slide along her teeth, and Rory's finger was curling up inside her body, and all Sarah could do was to clutch at Rory's waist and hold on.

She could feel her climax approaching like a gust of wind on the water. "Harder," she said into Rory's mouth, and Rory's thumb moved more insistently. Yes, that was it—*yes, yes, yes, Rory, just like that*—and then it hit her, lifting her up, wringing out her muscles, driving her hard into Rory's possessive embrace.

After a while, the room stopped spinning. Sarah blinked, opening heavy eyes to the sight of Rory staring down at her in wonder. Exhausted, she nuzzled at Rory's shoulder.

"Came so hard for you," she murmured.

"Yeah. God. And you said my name, over and over." Rory sounded like she couldn't believe what she had heard. "That was the most beautiful thing I've ever seen."

"I know you are, but what am I?" Sarah said, grinning faintly even as her eyes closed again. She couldn't seem to keep them open.

"Oh, you wanna fight about this, huh?" Rory kissed her lips with a loud smack. "Do ya?"

Sarah inhaled deeply and burrowed even closer to Rory. She felt warm and safe and content. "Fight in the morning," she said. "Sleep now. Haven't slept well for days."

"Me, neither," Rory said, fighting to push down the covers and wrestle Sarah under them without having to break their embrace. "Don't you ever leave again, okay?" Her arms tightened. "I need you. I need you to stay with me."

"Don't worry." Sarah fought against the wave of exhaustion that was pulling her under, knowing that Rory needed her reassurance. "Not going to leave you. I'm home now."

When she felt Rory relax, Sarah smiled and kissed the nearest patch of skin she could reach. And then, secure in the knowledge that she was loved as she loved, she slept.

❖

Rory woke slowly, relishing the sensation of being held. Sarah's arm was tight around her waist, and her deep breaths puffed against Rory's shoulder. Rory smiled. She had never felt so relaxed. She closed her eyes again, fully intending to go back to sleep…but then she felt the muscles in Sarah's forearm twitch against her stomach, and realized that Sarah's breathing was much faster than it should have been. *Uh-oh.*

"I can practically hear you thinking," she said, turning so that she could see Sarah's face. She leaned forward to kiss her lightly on the lips. "What's going on in that stormy brain of yours, hmm?"

Sarah smiled against Rory's mouth. Her eyes were a brilliant blue today—darker than usual. "I love you," she said.

Relieved, Rory snuggled closer. As long as that was still true, they'd be okay. "Glad to hear it," she mumbled. "But something's bugging you. I can tell. Out with it."

Sarah kissed her forehead and began to gently massage her back with one hand. Rory shifted, sliding her thigh between Sarah's legs…and her eyes flashed open again when she felt wetness against her skin. "Holy shit."

Sarah's smile turned sheepish. "Sorry. I usually wake up a little horny, and with you here…" She trailed off, arching her eyebrows.

"Mmm. I see." Rory pressed up experimentally and grinned when Sarah gasped. "First of all, don't you dare be sorry. Second of all, I fully intend to take advantage of your weakened state, and to enjoy myself while I do, but I won't move a muscle until you tell me why you were all tense a minute ago."

"You drive a hard bargain," Sarah said. She leaned in for another kiss. "So…here's the thing. I got back into Yale. Just found out a few days ago."

"Oh." Rory suddenly found it hard to swallow. *It's okay,* she told herself through the panic. *We can do long distance. New Haven isn't that far away, and—*

"So, here's the other thing. I'm not going."

Rory pulled back, shocked. And determined to change Sarah's mind. "What the fuck? You *have* to go! It's Yale, for fuck's sake!"

But Sarah shook her head. "Nope. I'm not. I don't want to, and you can't make me."

"What are you, twelve?" Rory paused when she realized that she was almost shouting. She sighed, deciding to take a different tack. "Okay, look," she said. "Just give me one good reason why you should stay here."

"I can give you a few," Sarah said, leaning forward to kiss her nose. Rory struggled not to smile. It was hard. "For one thing, URI costs a lot less, so my debt won't be nearly as bad when I graduate."

Rory frowned. That was a good reason. Very rational and reasonable. "But—"

"For another thing," Sarah cut in, "I'm happier here than I was there."

"You are?" Rory didn't know much about Sarah's experience

at Yale, but she had always imagined it as an idyllic time. "You're not just saying that, right?"

"Remember how you told me last night that I have to trust you?" Sarah said. "Well...now you have to trust me."

"You're not staying because of me, right?" Rory blurted. *Oh God,* she thought, feeling her cheeks get hot. *What an arrogant thing to say.*

Sarah smiled, propped herself up on one elbow, and cupped Rory's cheek with her other hand. "Sort of, I guess," she said softly. "Or maybe it's more that...I'm staying because of me. Because of how I feel about you. Because you make me happy. I know I *could* go back, and that we'd be okay, but...I don't want to."

"I don't really want you to, either," Rory confessed.

"I know."

"Oh? You *know?*" Giddy with relief, Rory rolled them over so she could be on top. "Pretty sure of yourself, aren't you?"

When Sarah opened her mouth to reply, Rory kissed her deeply, sliding her tongue along Sarah's teeth. She pressed up again with her thigh, and was rewarded by a low groan. Rory pulled back, then, licking her lips. Sarah's eyes were hazy with need, and she apparently couldn't stop herself from arching against Rory's body. *So, so beautiful.*

"I just have one question for you now," Rory said, pausing to nip at Sarah's jawline.

"Oh?" Sarah asked, her breathing labored. "What's that?"

Rory slipped one hand between them and pushed just the tip of her finger inside Sarah. She felt so good—so tight and wet—that Rory had trouble catching her breath. Leaning forward, she put her mouth next to Sarah's ear, flicking the sensitive lobe with her tongue.

"Wanna be my roommate again next year?"

"Yes," Sarah gasped.

It was her last articulate syllable for a long time.

Epilogue

Two weeks later, Sarah stood on the sidewalk outside Hutchinson, her arms encircling Rory's waist. Next to them was a pile of boxes. Sarah checked her watch and hugged Rory tighter.

"What time did they say they'd be here, again?"

"Three." Rory turned in her arms and planted a kiss on her chin. "Will you stop worrying, please? They didn't flip out on the phone. They're not going to yell at you, or whisk me away to straight camp. Okay?"

Sarah blew out a sigh. "I know. Sorry." Her look turned speculative. "Maybe if you kiss me again, I'll feel better."

Rory rolled her eyes but obliged. "There. How's that?"

"Mmm," Sarah said. "Have I told you yet today how good you are at that?"

"Flatterer." But Rory kissed her again. And then once more for good measure. "I'm going to miss not seeing you all the time," she said, once Sarah was breathless and much more relaxed.

"It is going to be weird, isn't it?" Sarah said. "But at least we have a few days before you have to go to the big city."

"And I'll come to Wakefield every chance I get," Rory said. "You can take me sailing."

"Maybe I'll come to New York every chance *I* get," Sarah countered. "You can introduce me to all your movie star friends, and we can eat street dogs and hang out in the Village."

Rory laughed. "Sure you don't want to go to Ellis Island and up the Statue of Liberty while you're at it, tourist?"

Sarah pretended to push Rory away. "You making fun of me?"

"Always."

Just as Rory leaned in for another kiss, a red minivan pulled up next to them. Sarah recognized Mr. and Mrs. Song in the front seats. "Hey, look, there are your parents," she said, putting about two feet of air between herself and Rory. Despite her resolution to remain calm and collected, Sarah felt her stomach drop into her feet. *Don't be such a 'fraidy cat. If they start yelling at you, just keep cool. Rory is the most important thing. Just be what she needs.*

Rory stepped forward, smiling, when both car doors opened. "Hi, Mom and Dad," she said, giving each of them a hug.

Sarah was in awe of Rory's ability to act normally. Her palms began to sweat as the Songs approached. She nearly jumped a foot when Rory took her hand. *Oh jeez. PDA in front of the 'rents.*

"You remember Sarah, of course," Rory was saying.

Sarah watched their reactions closely—neither of them seemed thrilled to pieces to see her, but they weren't slamming her up against a wall or cursing her out, either. *Okay. That'll work. I'll take it.*

"Hi, Mr. and Mrs. Song," she said. "It's good to see you again."

"Hello, Sarah," Mr. Song said. "How did your spring semester finish up?"

But before she could answer, Rory was speaking for her. "Oh, she did great, Dad. Totally aced her bio and chem courses. She's got a 4.0, you know."

"Ah, excellent," Mr. Song said, nodding his approval.

"We should put you in touch with Thomas and Gwen," Mrs. Song said. "Rory's cousins who are in medical school. Remind me to give you their e-mail addresses, Sarah."

Sarah knew that her smile was far wider than the situation called for, but just that tiny demonstration of acceptance and support had made her day. "Okay," she said. "That'd be great. Thanks so much."

After they had made small talk for a few more minutes, Rory's dad opened the trunk and began piling Rory's things inside. Sarah immediately began to help.

"See?" Rory said, whispering as they lifted one of the heavier boxes toward the car. "No sweat."

Sarah smiled, still not completely at ease but definitely relieved. "They are being very cool about it."

"So," Rory said once all the boxes were loaded. "You'll follow us there, right, Sarah?"

"Yep. As long as it's still okay for me to stay with you for a couple of days." Sarah looked between Rory's mother and father, both of whom nodded. Rory's dad even smiled.

"You're always welcome in our home," he said.

"Thank you," Sarah said, hoping that her tone of voice conveyed just how much that sentiment meant to her. She turned to Rory. "See you soon. Have a safe drive."

"You too, baby." And then, to Sarah's complete shock and amazement, Rory curled both arms around her neck, rose slightly onto her toes, and kissed her. Thoroughly.

She could have jerked away. She could have not returned Rory's kiss. But instead, Sarah wrapped her arms around Rory's waist, pulled her as close as she possibly could, and gave back what she had been given. Unafraid.

About the Author

Nell Stark grew up predominately on the East Coast of the USA. She attended Dartmouth College in New Hampshire, where she met her partner, Lisa. She is now pursuing her doctorate in medieval English literature in Madison, Wisconsin. When she's not researching, teaching, or writing, she's either playing World of Warcraft or spending time outdoors. Nell is also a contributor to several erotica anthologies, including *Erotic Interludes* 3 and 4, *Wild Nights*, *After Midnight*, and the forthcoming *Romantic Interludes*.

Books Available From Bold Strokes Books

A Guarded Heart by Jennifer Fulton. The last place FBI Special Agent Pat Roussel expects to find herself is assigned to an illicit private security gig baby-sitting a celebrity. (Ebook) (978-1-60282-067-8)

Saving Grace by Jennifer Fulton. Champion swimmer Dawn Beaumont, injured in a car crash she caused, flees to Moon Island, where scientist Grace Ramsay welcomes her. (Ebook) (978-1-60282-066-1)

The Sacred Shore by Jennifer Fulton. Successful tech industry survivor Merris Randall does not believe in love at first sight until she meets Olivia Pearce. (Ebook) (978-1-60282-065-4)

Passion Bay by Jennifer Fulton. Two women from different ends of the earth meet in paradise. Author's expanded edition. (Ebook) (978-1-60282-064-7)

Never Wake by Gabrielle Goldsby. After a brutal attack, Emma Webster becomes a self-sentenced prisoner inside her condo—until the world outside her window goes silent. (Ebook) (978-1-60282-063-0)

The Caretaker's Daughter by Gabrielle Goldsby. Against the backdrop of a nineteenth-century English country estate, two women struggle to find love. (Ebook) (978-1-60282-062-3)

Simple Justice by John Morgan Wilson. When a pretty-boy cokehead is murdered, former LA reporter Benjamin Justice and his reluctant new partner, Alexandra Templeton, must unveil the real killer. (978-1-60282-057-9)

Remember Tomorrow by Gabrielle Goldsby. Cees Bannigan and Arieanna Simon find that a successful relationship rests in remembering the mistakes of the past. (978-1-60282-026-5)

Put Away Wet by Susan Smith. Jocelyn "Joey" Fellows has just been savagely dumped—when she posts an online personal ad, she discovers more than just the great sex she expected. (978-1-60282-025-8)

Homecoming by Nell Stark. Sarah Storm loses everything that matters—family, future dreams, and love—will her new "straight" roommate cause Sarah to take a chance at happiness? (978-1-60282-024-1)

The Three by Meghan O'Brien. A daring, provocative exploration of love and sexuality. Two lovers, Elin and Kael, struggle to survive in a postapocalyptic world. (Ebook) (978-1-60282-056-2)

Falling Star by Gill McKnight. Solley Rayner hopes a few weeks with her family will help heal her shattered dreams, but she hasn't counted on meeting a woman who stirs her heart. (978-1-60282-023-4)

Lethal Affairs by Kim Baldwin and Xenia Alexiou. Elite operative Domino is no stranger to peril, but her investigation of journalist Hayley Ward will test more than her skills. (978-1-60282-022-7)

A Place to Rest by Erin Dutton. Sawyer Drake doesn't know what she wants from life until she meets Jori Diamantina—only trouble is, Jori doesn't seem to share her desire. (978-1-60282-021-0)

Warrior's Valor by Gun Brooke. Dwyn Izsontro and Emeron D'Artansis must put aside personal animosity and unwelcome attractio to defeat an enemy of the Protector of the Realm. (978-1-60282-020-3)

Finding Home by Georgia Beers. Take two polar-opposite women with an attraction for one another they're trying desperately to ignore, throw in a far-too-observant dog, and then sit back and enjoy the romance. (978-1-60282-019-7)

Word of Honor by Radclyffe. All Secret Service Agent Cameron Roberts and First Daughter Blair Powell want is a small intimate wedding, but the paparazzi and a domestic terrorist have other plans. (978-1-60282-018-0)

Hotel Liaison by JLee Meyer. Two women searching through a secret past discover that their brief hotel liaison is only the beginning. Will they risk their careers—and their hearts—to follow through on their desires? (978-1-60282-017-3)

Love on Location by Lisa Girolami. Hollywood film producer Kate Nyland and artist Dawn Brock discover that love doesn't always follow the script. (978-1-60282-016-6)

Edge of Darkness by Jove Belle. Investigator Diana Collins charges at life with an irreverent comment and a right hook, but even those may not protect her heart from a charming villain. (978-1-60282-015-9)

Thirteen Hours by Meghan O'Brien. Workaholic Dana Watts's life takes a sudden turn when an unexpected interruption arrives in the form of the most beautiful breasts she has ever seen—stripper Laurel Stanley's. (978-1-60282-014-2)

In Deep Waters 2 by Radclyffe and Karin Kallmaker. All bets are off when two award-winning authors deal the cards of love and passion... and every hand is a winner. (978-1-60282-013-5)

Pink by Jennifer Harris. An irrepressible heroine frolics, frets, and navigates through the "what ifs" of her life: all the unexpected turns of fortune, fame, and karma. (978-1-60282-043-2)

Deal with the Devil by Ali Vali. New Orleans crime boss Cain Casey brings her fury down on the men who threatened her family, and blood and bullets fly. (978-1-60282-012-8)

Naked Heart by Jennifer Fulton. When a sexy ex-CIA agent sets out to seduce and entrap a powerful CEO, there's more to this plan than meets the eye...or the flogger. (978-1-60282-011-1)

Heart of the Matter by KI Thompson. TV newscaster Kate Foster is Professor Ellen Webster's dream girl, but Kate doesn't know Ellen exists...until an accident changes everything. (978-1-60282-010-4)

Heartland by Julie Cannon. When political strategist Rachel Stanton and dude ranch owner Shivley McCoy collide on an empty country road, fate intervenes. (978-1-60282-009-8)

Shadow of the Knife by Jane Fletcher. Militia Rookie Ellen Mittal has no idea just how complex and dangerous her life is about to become. A Celaeno series adventure romance. (978-1-60282-008-1)

To Protect and Serve by VK Powell. Lieutenant Alex Troy is caught in the paradox of her life—to hold steadfast to her professional oath or to protect the woman she loves. (978-1-60282-007-4)

Deeper by Ronica Black. Former homicide detective Erin McKenzie and her fiancée Elizabeth Adams couldn't be happier—until the not-so-distant past comes knocking at the door. (978-1-60282-006-7)

The Lonely Hearts Club by Radclyffe. Take three friends, add two ex-lovers and several new ones, and the result is a recipe for explosive rivalries and incendiary romance. (978-1-60282-005-0)

Venus Besieged by Andrews & Austin. Teague Richfield heads for Sedona and the sensual arms of psychic astrologer Callie Rivers for a much-needed romantic reunion. (978-1-60282-004-3)

Branded Ann by Merry Shannon. Pirate Branded Ann raids a merchant vessel to obtain a treasure map and gets more than she bargained for with the widow Violet. (978-1-60282-003-6)

American Goth by JD Glass. Trapped by an unsuspected inheritance and guided only by the guardian who holds the secret to her future, Samantha Cray fights to fulfill her destiny. (978-1-60282-002-9)

Learning Curve by Rachel Spangler. Ashton Clarke is perfectly content with her life until she meets the intriguing Professor Carrie Fletcher, who isn't looking for a relationship with anyone. (978-1-60282-001-2)

Place of Exile by Rose Beecham. Sheriff's detective Jude Devine struggles with ghosts of her past and an ex-lover who still haunts her dreams. (978-1-933110-98-1)

Fully Involved by Erin Dutton. A love that has smoldered for years ignites when two women and one little boy come together in the aftermath of tragedy. (978-1-933110-99-8)

Heart 2 Heart by Julie Cannon. Suffering from a devastating personal loss, Kyle Bain meets Lane Connor, and the chance for happiness suddenly seems possible. (978-1-60282-000-5)

Rising Storm by JLee Meyer. The sequel to *First Instinct* takes our heroines on a dangerous journey instead of the honeymoon they'd planned. (978-1-933110-86-8)

First Instinct by JLee Meyer. When high-stakes security fraud leads to murder, one woman flees for her life while another risks her heart to protect her. (1-933110-59-7)

Queens of Tristaine by Cate Culpepper. When a deadly plague stalks the Amazons of Tristaine, two warrior lovers must return to the place of their nightmares to find a cure. (978-1-933110-97-4)

The Crown of Valencia by Catherine Friend. Ex-lovers can really mess up your life…even, as Kate discovers, if they've traveled back to the eleventh century! (978-1-933110-96-7)

Mine by Georgia Beers. What happens when you've already given your heart and love finds you again? Courtney McAllister is about to find out. (978-1-933110-95-0)

House of Clouds by KI Thompson. A sweeping saga of an impassioned romance between a Northern spy and a Southern sympathizer, set amidst the upheaval of a nation under siege. (978-1-933110-94-3)

Forever Found by JLee Meyer. Can time, tragedy, and shattered trust destroy a love that seemed destined? When chance reunites two childhood friends separated by tragedy, the past resurfaces to determine the shape of their future. (1-933110-37-6)

Winds of Fortune by Radclyffe. Provincetown local Deo Camara agrees to rehab Dr. Bonita Burgoyne's historic home, but she never said anything about mending her heart. (978-1-933110-93-6)

Focus of Desire by Kim Baldwin. Isabel Sterling is surprised when she wins a photography contest, but no more than photographer Natasha Kashnikova. Their promo tour becomes a ticket to romance. (978-1-933110-92-9)

Blind Leap by Diane and Jacob Anderson-Minshall. A Golden Gate Bridge suicide becomes suspect when a filmmaker's camera shows a different story. Yoshi Yakamota and the Blind Eye Detective Agency uncover evidence that could be worth killing for. (978-1-933110-91-2)

Mistress of the Runes by Andrews & Austin. Passion ignites between two women with ties to ancient secrets, contemporary mysteries, and a shared quest for the meaning of life. (978-1-933110-89-9)

Wall of Silence, 2nd ed. by Gabrielle Goldsby. Life takes a dangerous turn when jaded police detective Foster Everett meets Riley Medeiros, a woman who isn't afraid to discover the truth no matter the cost. (978-1-933110-90-5)

Vulture's Kiss by Justine Saracen. Archeologist Valerie Foret, heir to a terrifying task, returns in a powerful desert adventure set in Egypt and Jerusalem. (978-1-933110-87-5)

Sheridan's Fate by Gun Brooke. A dynamic, erotic romance between physiotherapist Lark Mitchell and businesswoman Sheridan Ward set in the scorching hot days and humid, steamy nights of San Antonio. (978-1-933110-88-2)

Not Single Enough by Grace Lennox. A funny, sexy modern romance about two lonely women who bond over the unexpected and fall in love along the way. (978-1-933110-85-1)

Such a Pretty Face by Gabrielle Goldsby. A sexy, sometimes humorous, sometimes biting contemporary romance that gently exposes the damage to heart and soul when we fail to look beneath the surface for what truly matters. (978-1-933110-84-4)

Second Season by Ali Vali. A romance set in New Orleans amidst betrayal, Hurricane Katrina, and the new beginnings hardship and heartbreak sometimes make possible. (978-1-933110-83-7)

Hearts Aflame by Ronica Black. A poignant, erotic romance between a hard-driving businesswoman and a solitary vet. Packed with adventure and set in the harsh beauty of the Arizona countryside. (978-1-933110-82-0)

Running With the Wind by Nell Stark. Sailing instructor Corrie Marsten has signed off on love until she meets Quinn Davies—one woman she can't ignore. (978-1-933110-70-7)